Roux the Day

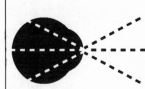

This Large Print Book carries the
Seal of Approval of N.A.V.H.

Peter King

Roux the Day

A Gourmet Detective Mystery

Thorndike Press • Waterville, Maine

Published in 2003 by arrangement with
St. Martin's Press, LLC.

Thorndike Press Large Print Mystery Series.

The tree indicium is a trademark of Thorndike Press.

The text of this Large Print edition is unabridged.
Other aspects of the book may vary from the original edition.

Set in 16 pt. Plantin by Al Chase.

Printed in the United States on permanent paper.

Library of Congress Cataloging-in-Publication Data

King, Peter (Christopher Peter), 1922–
    Roux the day : a gourmet detective mystery / Peter King.
      p. cm.
    ISBN 0-7862-4781-9 (lg. print : hc : alk. paper)
    1. Gourmet Detective (Fictitious character) — Fiction.
2. New Orleans (La.) — Fiction. 3. Cookery, Creole —
Fiction. 4. Cookery, Cajun — Fiction. 5. Gourmets —
Fiction. 6. Cookery — Fiction. 7. Large type books.
I. Title.
PS3561.I4822 R68 2003
  813'.54—dc21   2002032308

Roux the Day

chapter one

It was my first visit to New Orleans but I felt I knew it. Unforgettable images of black bands swaying through the street playing jazz music as they followed a funeral were largely responsible. The dazzling and colorful abandon of the Mardi Gras with its spectacular costumes, its nonstop music and its floats that had escaped from the world of fairy tale had to be held accountable, too. Delicately lacey wrought-iron balconies came into my slightly hazy memory, too, though these tended to have elegant ladies with shawls gazing down with casual disdain as they sipped mint juleps. This probably came from an earlier period although the balconies remained.

I had lunched in a veritable museum of classic New Orleans cuisine, Arnaud's. The restaurant spreads over an entire city block, twelve buildings all connected by hallways and stairs. It has a true sense of history; one wall in the main dining area was completely covered with photographs from 1918 onward. The only underground wine cellar in New Orleans is here, too. From the street, the leaded windows portray an earlier era, and inside are the potted palms in five-foot-high pots on pedestals, the dark wood panels, the twenty large ceiling fans and the fifteen crystal chandeliers. We had walked through this main dining room on our way to a small alcove that had undoubtedly seen its share of romantic trysts in its day.

I reminded myself sternly that I was here on business and firmly refused the offer of another Sazerac. But my host insisted and I was gracious enough to yield. He leaned forward, doubtless to press home his advantage while my mood was still mellow but not yet inebriated.

"You'll take the commission, of course. Franklin said you would — he also assured me that you were the best man for the job."

He had outlined the job between the main course and the dessert. It was superb timing. I was in a state of utter culinary satisfaction after a dozen plump oysters on the half shell followed by a delicious shrimp-and-crab étouffée.

I was mildly irked by his statement that Franklin had said I would take the commission. Franklin does not make decisions for me — well, he likes to do so but I don't always fall into line with his wishes, his dictates, really. The sop he had tossed out afterwards, saying that I was the best man for the job, was possibly true although it was just as likely that Henry O'Brien in Dublin and Jacques LaPoche in Montreal had been asked and turned it down.

"You will enjoy the event anyway — you must have been to a lot of these but as you will learn while you are here in our wonderful city, New Orleans knows how to put a different slant on many aspects of life."

Eric Van Linn was a robust (I avoid the word *fat* even for people I don't like), florid (I prefer it to *red-faced*) persuasive (it sounds better than *domineering*) individual. He was a well-known lawyer in New Orleans, I learned, and though I share the human race's feelings about the profession, I accepted when he phoned me in Los Angeles where I was attending a Food Fair. A client of mine wanted the fair assessed so that he could decide how heavily to invest in such an endeavor next year. The purpose of Van Linn's phone call was to invite me to stop over in New Orleans on my way back to London.

Why me? Well, I operate under the name

of The Gourmet Detective. I seek out lost recipes and rare spices, find substitutes for disappearing or suddenly expensive food ingredients. I advise on topics like the food to serve in a film set in the seventeenth century or at a suitable "theme" banquet for the fiftieth anniversary of a department store. The occasional job turns up, such as attending the Los Angeles Food Fair — not noticeably lucrative but easy to do and a good chance for me to pick up one or two prospective clients.

The phone call I had received in Los Angeles came in a richly rounded voice. Van Linn said that I had been recommended to him by a mutual acquaintance in London, Franklin Bardo, a lawyer with whom I had done a mercifully small amount of business. Would I, Van Linn asked, like to stop in New Orleans for a couple of days and fulfill a simple mission? It would take only a few hours and all expenses paid, of course.

The Big Easy happened to be one of the few major culinary cities in the civilized world I had not visited, and the suggestion had a certain lure. While talking on the phone, my elbow rested on a copy of the *Los Angeles Times* showing floods in London after days of torrential rain and predicting that worse was yet to come. I made a decision.

★ ★ ★

The decision was, naturally, not an immediate agreement. It was a decision only to stop in New Orleans and have the job explained. Van Linn said he preferred to do that in person rather than on the phone so that even if I declined to take the job, I would have a free stopover in New Orleans. He added in a persuasive courtroom tone that he could not contemplate a refusal on my part. So naturally, I said yes to the first part and "happy to hear about the job and consider it" to the second part.

Eric Van Linn proposed lunch at the prestigious Arnaud's Restaurant, which I certainly knew by reputation. So here we were after a superb meal and Van Linn was using all his legal training to cinch the deal.

"It's not a difficult task, as I told you," Van Linn continued. He leaned his bulk back in a big chair that the restaurant had had built with sufficient strength to support those diners who had eaten too much of their food. "This book auction is a major event and is always well-attended. You'll meet a lot of very nice people and have an agreeable day."

"Books are a bit out of my line. People call me The Gourmet Detective because I —"

"Yes, yes, you explained that — but this isn't a matter of merely buying a book. We could get anyone to do that. It's the contents of the book that we are concerned about. The book probably sounds authentic to ninety-nine out of a hundred. You're the hundredth — you're an expert who can verify that the recipes are exactly what they purport to be."

"There must be chefs by the dozen in New Orleans who can tell you if recipes in a cookbook are genuine," I protested.

Was there just the least hesitation in Van Linn's smoothly hearty manner? I thought I detected it but it might have been a suppressed hiccup from the hot sauce on his crawfish. "Chefs in New Orleans are the same as chefs everywhere — they are all limited in their outlook. Take them outside of Creole, Cajun and French cuisine and they are all adrift. For this task, we need a man with a wide international background, someone who knows all the cooking techniques, all the ingredients."

He seemed to want me to accept that, to believe him, to agree with him. Did I? I could not think of any reason why not. There was some feasibility in what he said and, anyway, what did I have to lose? Just a couple of days to give London a chance to sweep all that rain down the Thames and out to sea.

I suppose the only thought that held me back was that in the past, I had accepted many commissions to perform seemingly simple and straightforward tasks relating to food, restaurants, eating and related subjects. Most of the tasks had been just that — simple and straightforward — but a few had turned out to have embarrassing and even dangerous consequences. When mussels and marjoram turned into murder and mayhem, I wanted to seek the nearest exit — a course of action not viewed sympathetically by the employer. I always maintained that it was not cowardice but common sense.

"Tell me again about this book," I asked.

"Certainly. How about coffee?"

"I recall reading that New Orleans coffee contains chicory."

"Yes, terrible stuff."

"I've tasted it, it used to be very popular in England. It's not that bad, I think I'll have it for a change."

"Chicory's some kind of vegetable, isn't it?" Van Linn was not reconciled to the thought of anyone actually drinking a vegetable. What had been his comment on New Orleans chefs — in fact all chefs — that they

13

were limited in their outlook? Still, this was not the time to be picky.

"Yes, the roots of the vegetable you call 'endive' in the U.S.A. are the chicory used in coffee. Endives are eaten only in the form of the leaves. They use them in salad quite often."

Van Linn's pursed lips indicated that I had not converted him. "Terrible idea, putting a vegetable into coffee."

"Blame Napoleon," I said. "It was his fault."

"He's a bit of a hero in this part of the world," Van Linn reminded me.

"Yes, helped you fight against some occupying army or other, didn't he?"

"That's one way to put it." Van Linn's lips twitched. "There is a dessert named after him but I didn't know his interests extended as far as coffee."

"He set up trade barriers that severely limited imports into France. One of the commodities hardest-hit was coffee. The importers tried different additives to stretch out their restricted supplies — they found that chicory was accepted more readily than the others."

He waved the waiter over. "One espresso and one — er, chicory coffee."

When the waiter had left, Van Linn said,

"The book, yes . . . you will have heard of the Belvedere family?"

"Famous wherever food is discussed," I said promptly.

"Five generations of them have run the restaurant in New Orleans bearing their name. Five — that's more even than this place."

"Prominent in the history of New Orleans, originated several famous dishes," I contributed.

"True," said Van Linn. "Well, Arturo, the first in the dynasty, came to this country with his parents and his two sisters from Andorra. He was thirteen and had to go to work as did all of the family. Arturo worked twelve hours a day, six days a week as a cleaning boy in a restaurant. He was promoted to chopping potatoes then given more and more jobs till he was appointed a sous-chef. He saved money, other family members came from Andorra and chipped in to help him buy a small restaurant and that was the start of it all."

"How different," I commented, "from the hot, young, Generation X, fast-rising star, cutting-edge American type of chef that we hear so much of today and see too many of on TV."

"In the big cities mainly," said Van Linn.

"Yes — where the media are located. Does that suggest that culinary success is achieved with the aid of Madison Avenue hype rather than natural talent?"

"Hmph," Van Linn commented. It was probably a criticism of my interrupting his flow. "Anyway, each generation took over in turn and the reputation of the Belvedere family grew and grew."

The coffee arrived. Mine had that uniquely sharp aroma that chicory gives. Eric Van Linn inhaled his espresso with the snobbish look of satisfaction that his choice was superior.

"Which brings us to the book," he said. He sipped his espresso. I waited for my coffee to cool. "Arturo taught himself to read and write when he found he was climbing in the world. When he was advancing in age, he decided to write down his recipes — many of which he had developed himself. One of the recipes he wrote down was the one for oysters Belvedere."

"One of the most renowned dishes in the culinary repertoire," I added. I could see he didn't like my comments. It was not because of their content, but I supposed that years of courtroom oratory had caused him to have a lofty attitude about his own prowess. My knowledge of courtrooms did not extend further than Perry Mason and Horace Rumpole, and from this background I had come to think of "Objection, Your Honor" as punctuating every other sentence. This being fiction, I assumed the fact was that oration flowed largely unchecked.

Nevertheless, I had to make some input and intended to keep doing so. Van Linn acknowledged my words with the briefest of nods. "Just so. He passed the book on to his son and he passed it on — well, all the way down to Ernesto, the last Belvedere. Here's where the story takes on a sad note . . . Ernesto became senile. At first, it was considered as eccentricity and he was lucky in having an efficient and loyal staff who covered up for him. His wife, Matilde, refused to admit there was anything wrong with him. His behavior grew worse. He insulted customers, alienated suppliers by insisting their product was inferior, he failed to place orders, misplaced reservations . . .

"Well, the inevitable happened, business fell away and when Ernesto struck a diner for criticizing his food, the place closed. The accounts were in a shambles and it looked as if it were the end of a dynasty."

When he paused for another, longer sip of coffee, I tested mine. The chicory taste was not as strong as I would have liked but it was different from the average cup of coffee.

"You say, 'looked as if,' " I observed. "You mean it wasn't?"

Van Linn was pleased with the question. "Ernesto's son, Ambrose, was in college during the period that the restaurant was declining. He had no interest in the food industry. He has now graduated and has decided he wants to reopen the restaurant after all. He even envisions restoring it to its earlier glory."

"And all you want me to do is go to this auction and authenticate a book?"

"That, too, is correct."

"The book we are referring to is the recipe book that the Belvedere family has been using all these years," I persisted.

"Yes, it is."

"Now, tell me why the book is at an auction and not at the restaurant."

He sipped his coffee and looked at my cup in commiseration. "All of the Belvederes had added to the book that Arturo had started. The last time the book was seen, it was still in the restaurant. That was when Ernesto was first experiencing his mental problems. It was not really missed — apparently it's not the kind of cookbook that a chef has to refer to all the time."

"I can understand that," I told him. "This one obviously has historical value beyond its practical value. Still, it is common practice for a chef to have a book and write down all his favorite recipes and use it to refresh his memory. If the chef takes a day off or something like that, one of the sous-chefs can refer to it and that way ensure that the dish is cooked always in the same way."

Van Linn nodded. "In the case at hand, when the contents of the restaurant were being cleaned out, the absence of the book was realized. The staff were questioned closely and none of them knew anything about it. I was asked to question Ernesto in the nursing home he was committed to, as to its whereabouts, but by then he was too old and I could learn nothing."

"And now," I said, "it has surfaced at an auction."

"It's a charity auction, held once a year. It's a famous and popular event in New Orleans. Books come in from all sources — but where this book came from, nobody is sure. The books come, volunteers sift through them and pick out the more valuable ones. Individual books are sold, sometimes sets, sometimes small libraries or quantities of books all on one subject."

"A volunteer spotted this one and recognized its worth?" I asked.

"Exactly. If it has any worth."

"You mean, if it's not a forgery?"

"Certainly. People find lost manuscripts of Shakespeare, lost symphonies of Mozart . . . a few years ago, the diaries of Adolf Hitler were found and authenticated by several of the world's leading historical authorities before they were declared forged. Howard Hughes' will appeared and was naturally contested . . . The list is endless."

"I'm not an expert on books," I said. "I know I've pointed this out before but —"

"I know you're not. That's not why you are being hired. All you have to do is decide if the recipes in the book are genuine."

A light had just begun to shine in my brain. Chicory is believed in some quarters to have powers of augmenting mental activity. Maybe it worked?

"If the book is genuine," I said slowly, "it should contain the famous recipe for oysters Belvedere."

Van Linn pursed his lips, not altogether the effect of the espresso. "That's possible, I suppose."

"That alone might make it valuable."

I cogitated. "Your client is, I suppose, wanting to remain incognito?"

"For the time being," Van Linn said urbanely.

I cogitated some more. He finished his coffee and dabbed his lips elegantly with the lightly starched, snow-white napkin. He leaned back and observed me. There was nothing of the dealmaker wanting to press home his final offer. In fact, he sounded sincere as he said, "I should remind you that I have a prestigious law business here in New Orleans and I have no intention of doing anything to prejudice that. All that I have told you is true to the best of my knowledge and I have omitted nothing other than the name of my client — that being a common practice."

I drank the last of my chicory and gave it a few seconds to work on my neurals or whatever they are called. I put down the cup with the air of the Scarlet Pimpernel setting off to rescue one more unfortunate aristocrat from Madame La Guillotine.

"All right, I'll do it. Subject to financial terms being agreed, of course."

chapter two

I don't get many easy jobs like this, I was thinking as I walked along looking for a streetcar the next morning. It didn't have to be called Desire, that was too much to hope for and anyway, Tennessee Williams has had enough publicity. For a moment, I regretted that due to the unexpected nature of this assignment, I had not had the opportunity to reread John Kennedy Toole's *A Confederacy of Dunces*. It was, as I remembered, an evocative picture of New Orleans and its people.

Lunch the day before with Eric Van Linn had stretched out even further than the stingers. Born and raised in New Orleans, he was a bottomless source of information on the city and its denizens and he enjoyed telling tales both tall and terrifying. Still, all of them had the ring of "could be true" — and who could ask more than that?

This morning I was out early, enjoying the stark, deserted streets with a breeze off the Gulf of Mexico scattering crumpled sheets of newspaper and sending plastic cups rolling away merrily. I walked along Royal Street, the buildings washed in pastel colors in a sunlight that was eerie and opaque. The quiet was broken only by the squawl of a cat and the clattering of a shutter being pushed open, doubtless accompanied by a yawn. The smell of rain was in the air but Mother Nature had not yet made up her mind.

I walked more or less at random till I found a coffee shop that catered to the *precrowd* crowd. This time I had a regular brew that was noticeably superior to ninety percent of the coffee served in the country. I ate with it a beignet that a languid young woman told me was what everybody here ate. It was too sweet for a breakfast bun but the purveyors of such delights evidently think we need a massive input of sugar to start the day.

At the next table, a young man who kept dozing off and slipping from his seat had knocked back two brandies already and woke up long enough to order a third. A man in uniform, some kind of city employee, was the only other customer.

"Turn right at the signal — two blocks take you to the St. Charles streetcar stop," the waiter said in response to my question. Van Linn's offer of remuneration included "reasonable" expenses and I had no doubt that taxi fare would be considered such, but streetcars are a fascinating reminder of a bygone era and unfortunately not commonly found today. So I rode it out to Duvivier Street and a walk of four blocks brought me to the Armorers' Hall.

It boasted a checkered career, according to the plaque outside. Originally a warehouse used to store ammunition during the War of 1812, it had been burned down — not by a well-aimed British shell, but by a careless smoker. It had been rebuilt as the three-story Bank of New Orleans and had an impressive gray granite front in what was called the Greek Revival style. The bank had been prominent in financing the digging of the New Basin Canal that connected with Lake Pontchartrain. When the bank moved its operations, the building fell into disuse for some years, then the Louisiana Central Trust Company bought it and added two more stories.

The building's exciting professional life continued as a part of the Board of Trade activity, one of many structures taken over by that board during World War One. More rebuilding followed and the federal government occupied it until they remodeled it in World War Two, but only just in time for the war to be over. It was then appropriated by the city, named the Armorers' Hall and used for veterans' functions. More remodeling and it became a convention center and exhibition hall.

Four Corinthian columns in front gave it a look of prominence and I walked between them through tall glass doors and into a large lobby where women sat at desks checking names and dispensing large red-and-white tags.

THE BIGGEST BOOK AUCTION IN THE SOUTH, proclaimed a large banner, and posters listed contributing organizations and charities benefiting from the auction. I walked into the main hall. It was big as a cathedral, huge with steel beams high across the ceiling. Chairs were neatly arranged and quite a few people were here already. A few were seated but most were clustered in chatty groups, clearly previously acquainted. Around the walls were racks and shelves. All were stacked with books where prospective buyers could examine them.

Stacks of catalogs were on tables and a woman handed me one. I found the section covering books on food, and after some difficulty, reached an item called *Kitchen Cook-*

book with the author given as "A. Belvedere." Not a very enticing entry for a book that required my highly professional services.

A number of other books in the category caught my eye and temporarily diverted me. Sandwiched between volumes by Martha Stewart and Burt Wolf was a book with that famous name on the spine, of the grandmama of all cookbook writers — Isabella Beeton. Alas, it was a 1940 reprint but the content remained. Morton Shand was represented by his classic *Book of Food*, I was glad to see. Shand is peevish and controversial, insular and argumentative and amazingly narrow-minded, yet all of these characteristics are swamped by his encyclopedic knowledge. *Those Rich and Great Ones* by Henri was on the shelf, too, not in very good condition but at least that showed how many people had handled it and, I was sure, enjoyed it. Dozens of good stories there and all told with unflagging verve and wit.

A copy of Marion Harland's *Common Sense in the Household* caught my eye. It is not exactly rare but it is a worthy addition to any culinary library and is exceedingly practical, full of genuine "common sense." Then there was Paul Reboux's *Plats du Jour* describing gastronomic adventures in Burgundy in the 1930s.

Edward Bunyard's *A Book About the Table* is not rare, either, nor is it expensive but it is another of those books that should be on every cook's shelf. Andre Simon's cleverly titled *Tables of Content* did not have a dust jacket but it had the self-satisfied air of a book that doesn't need one.

Dozens of other books on food and eating did not reach the same peaks of culinary knowledge but stood shoulder-to-shoulder on the same shelves anyway. Great names pressed against newcomers, East squeezed against West and old fought for space against new.

I pored through them all, looking for A. Belvedere. He was not among those present. I realized I must have missed him — perhaps the cover was worn and the name unclear. I was about to start the search again when I received a bump on the hip.

"Sorry," muttered the young woman who had bumped me. She didn't sound sorry and she moved to push in front of me. Always the gentleman — and determined to be such here in a city of such cavalier traditions — I allowed her to do so. She was intent on a search of her own and I allowed her to pursue it. She was attractive, an inch or two above average height, blonde hair cut short and expensively, a tan dress with an autumn-brown knitted sweater and sensible brown shoes suggesting an active life.

She ignored my condescending smile and frowned at the titles. I resumed my search, once again without success. The young woman was equally unsuccessful, it seemed, for our paths kept crossing. At the third one, she gave a peevish sigh of frustration and walked with a determined step toward one of the women acting as stewards . . . well, steward*persons*, I suppose. I could hear most of the conversation, which was one-sided — it was a complaint that a book in the catalog was not on the shelves.

I was about to make a third try for my book when I heard her say, "It's by A. Belvedere and . . ."

The book nearest my hand was Marcel Boulestin's *The Finer Cooking*. I have a copy to which I refer often but on this occasion it was a convenient mask. I wasn't looking at the words but concentrating on listening to the conversation.

"It should be there," said the woman, a lively white-haired lady with a strong Southern accent — she said "they-ar." She came over and perused the shelves, using a long forefinger as a probe. She came to the end, frowned and repeated the process. She looked at the catalog, frowned again and made a third attempt.

"Well, I don't know . . ." she said. "Just a minute." She hurried off and I focused on Boulestin's words so as to not to attract the blonde girl's attention. There did not seem to be too much fear of that — she was tapping an impatient foot, looking haughty and unconcerned about anyone else in the room.

By now, the room was fairly full. Many of the attendees knew others and old acquaintances were being renewed — perhaps an occasion that occurred every book fair. I stayed with Marcel Boulestin until the white-haired lady returned. She went back to the shelves and the blonde girl joined her. "Well?" she demanded.

"It should be here." The white-haired lady was getting flustered now. She was obviously used to everything being in its place and an advocate of good order. A book not being where it should be disordered her universe.

"But it obviously isn't. So if it isn't here, where is it?" The blonde girl was getting annoyed at the book's absence. I was equally concerned but the blonde was being forceful and displaying all those American feminine qualities that we have come to admire in women from Belle Starr to Eleanor Roosevelt to Ethel Merman to Germaine Greer. For the moment, I thought it better to let her spearhead the "where is this book?" movement.

"Let me go talk to Mrs. Gracewell." The lady was eager to snatch at the opportunity to shift the problem to a higher level of administration.

Foot tapping continued. The blonde glared at anyone within range and I stayed at the limit of that range. She let out a periodic sigh of exasperation. At last, the white-haired lady came back accompanied by another white-haired lady, this one tall and commanding. I watched closely. This was going to be interesting.

"I'm Mrs. Gracewell." She introduced herself politely but the blonde was in no mood for niceties.

"What is the matter with this place?" she demanded loudly. "I want to see a book you've put in your catalog. All books in the catalog are supposed to be on the shelves. This one is *not* on the shelves. This person has confirmed that." She pointed an accusing finger and the unfortunate white-haired lady spread her hands in a gesture of admitted failure.

"So where is the book?" came the final broadside.

Mrs. Gracewell withstood the blast commendably. "I regret to say it's been sold," she replied.

The answer certainly hit me between the eyes. I even forgot to use the copy of Boulestin as a cover and lowered it. The blonde girl gave Mrs. Gracewell a withering look.

"Sold! How can it have been sold! The auction hasn't started yet!"

The auction was, in fact, just about to start. A gray-haired man in a tuxedo had tested the microphone and adjusted it on the dais. Others went to and fro, bringing books and papers.

Mrs. Gracewell had clearly been on more committees than the blonde girl had eaten po'boy sandwiches. She remained unruffled as the blonde girl's look turned on her. It would have curled the edge of a steel plate but Mrs. Gracewell was as unperturbed as if she had just heard that a coffee spoon was in the wrong place.

She gave the other a slight smile, not apologetic but with a tinge of commiseration. "This is a charity function, as I'm sure you know. It seems that earlier this morning, a person came in and made one of our volunteers an offer for the book. This lady reasoned that the amount offered was considerably more than might be realized at the auction. She sold the book."

There it was, concise and unarguable. Well, it should have been but the blonde's need for the book seemed to be immense. She harangued poor Mrs. Gracewell, who gave tiny nods of agreement and mini-smiles of sympathy. Finally, a shortage of breath produced a short break.

"The least you can do is give me the name and address of the person who bought it," were the first words after the break.

Mrs. Gracewell hesitated. "Well, it may be considered confidential, I'm not sure —"

"Nonsense!" snapped the blonde. "This is an open auction. If the book were to be sold here, everybody in the room would see who had bought it. Give me the person's name and address!"

Mrs. Gracewell thought for a couple of seconds. "Very well," she said. "This book is clearly important to you so I see no reason why you shouldn't know. Please come with me."

The blonde followed Mrs. Gracewell with an angry but elegant stride, leaving me standing there with the copy of Boulestin in my hand. I had several points to consider. Who was this blonde and why was Arturo Belvedere's book so important to her? It had a certain historical value, that was sure, especially here in New Orleans — perhaps book historians were after it. But why this sudden interest in it? Presumably it had been lost for some time after Ernesto's faculties had declined — so why now? The next question was, how could I get that name and address too?

I went out of the room just as the auctioneer was rapping his gavel and welcoming everyone. Several cubicles took up space in the anteroom. All were filled, noisy and busy. I stood for a moment, then the blonde came out of one of the cubicles. Mrs. Gracewell was saying something to her but I couldn't hear what it was — no doubt a polite excuse or two although they were being wasted, as the blonde stalked out without a word or a backward glance. She was stuffing a piece of paper into her handbag as she left so she had presumably got what she wanted — well, after losing the book.

Mrs. Gracewell returned to the main auction hall to attend to other duties. I waited a suitable length of time, realizing during that time that I still had the copy of Boulestin in my hand. I went to the lady in the first cubicle. On her desk was a check with engraving in light purple. It was the only one I could see so I was sure it was payment for the Belvedere book and the one from which she had just copied an address.

The lady was tiny, birdlike and with a soft smile. She didn't seem too devastated by the blonde typhoon who had just swept out; nevertheless, I gave her my best sympathy smile.

"Wow, glad to see her leave! What a terror!" I waved the book in my hand, a badge of authentication.

"A very dynamic lady. She must want that book very badly." Her voice was soft too.

"Yes," I agreed, then, as if I had just become aware of why I had gone into her cubicle: "Oh, Mrs. Gracewell is sure you got full ID on that check. I told her I was sure you had but said I'd confirm it with you."

"Oh, that isn't necessary," the lady said in her delicate voice.

"It isn't?"

"No. See —" She turned the check around so that I could see it. " 'Michael Gambrinus, Bookseller' — well, I mean, he's one of the biggest booksellers in the city, isn't he?"

chapter three

The taxi wove a dizzying route through the city. At least, it was dizzying to me because most streets seemed to be one-way and laid out like a crazy chessboard. So I just sat back and enjoyed the ride — well, I sort of enjoyed it. Many of New Orleans' street signs are missing and the ones remaining are either hard to read or faded beyond sight.

Some old blue-and-white tiled signs had names that could be read only by pedestrians. In some neighborhoods, thin vertical metal strips nailed to telephone poles carried the names. These are *really* unreadable. A few street signs even point *away* from the traffic stream. All this seems to be carrying urban secrecy too far.

Riding a vehicle through New Orleans is a novel experience. We passed a mule-drawn buggy and almost terminated a zigzagging drunk. Drivers appeared to have their own rules and seemed to be determined to keep their intentions to themselves. The few times they used signals, they were completely misleading.

I was glad it was a short ride. I had a suspicion that I had been driven in two concentric circles and arrived in a location very close to where I had started but I said nothing as I was happy to alight safely.

The bookshop was on Carondelet Street. During the boom days of the mid–nineteenth century, this was the center for cotton. Shipping companies had their offices here, near the Cotton Exchange. New Orleans' first skyscraper was built on Carondelet Street and, when bank after bank went up, the thoroughfare became known as the Wall Street of the South. I had learned all this from the pamphlets in the hotel and knew, too, that the street was named after the first governor of the French Province of Louisiana in 1791.

It was an upmarket location for a bookshop. The shop itself looked almost as venerable as its prestigious neighbors, with its dark-green–painted wooden-framed windows and imposing door. The name, Michael Gambrinus, was in faded but legible gilt lettering and an old trigger-type bell pealed out with a tinny clang as I entered.

The atmosphere was musty but not ancient. It was a museum but not a mausoleum. Avalanches of books were everywhere. The basic layout was orderly and sections were marked by subject, but uncontrolled influxes of volumes had flooded the shop and exceeded sales. Many books looked quite valuable, and morocco-bound editions were prominent.

I could see no one, but a doorway led to another room that turned out to be almost as crowded and chaotic. Beyond it was a third room — the building seemed to go on and on. I saw yet another room and it seemed less crowded with books but more folders and files. Perhaps it was an office. Someone must be there.

"Anybody here?" I called, but no answer came. A massive carved desk had a large brass lamp, a brass-and-wood antique-style phone, and was piled with papers. A brass-and-mahogany plaque read, MICHAEL GAMBRINUS. Behind the desk, a computer screen was blank but beside it stood attendant equipment like a printer, a copier and a fax. But it was the desk that instantly reclaimed my attention . . .

A man sat in a large armchair, sprawled back. I went farther into the room — a patch of red gleamed in the soft light of the desk lamp. It was in the center of his chest.

I felt his wrist. It was warm but when I felt for a pulse, there was none. A round black hole in the patch of red on his chest was patently the cause of death. He had been shot, and very recently.

How recently? I wondered. Recently enough that whoever had shot him was still here? It was at that inappropriate moment that I heard a slithering sound . . .

The hair on the back of my neck prickled. I froze, waiting for the sound again. If I could figure out where it had come from, I could move hastily in the opposite direction. All was still, though into the silence crept the faintest buzz of street traffic.

A door slammed. Trouble was, I couldn't tell where. It took me a moment to realize that if it had been the front door, I would have heard that tinkling bell. So there must be another door — well, obviously, there had to be a back entrance for unloading all these books.

I went back into the third room and there it was — it opened to a turn of the knob. An alley went all the way to the next street. Trash cans lined up and there were piles of cardboard crates and boxes. But no person or persons.

Going back into the room with the dead

man wasn't particularly pleasant but the body acted like a magnet. I thought about wiping the doorknobs and getting out of there, like any non–law-abiding citizen would. Had I picked up any books? I wondered. But leaving fingerprints would not be incriminating unless I did, indeed, duck out of there.

Being non–law-abiding is something I cannot readily contemplate. Besides, a check of cab drivers would turn up the one who had driven me here and, though he had not paid much attention to me (or the traffic, for that matter), he would probably be able to identify me. I reached for the phone, stopped.

A box of tissues stood on the edge of the desk. I took one and used it to lift the phone. At least, I wouldn't obliterate any fingerprints that might be on it.

The food business is a multibillion-dollar industry and even the sedentary aspects of it that involve me often have contact with the seamier side. Crooks and criminals can be found in there just as in any business — a small percentage of those involved can always see a way to make more money by doing something illegal.

Unwittingly, I have been mixed up in a few of these and some have even involved a corpse or two. It was very rare that I had been in the position of calling the police upon finding one of them, though. The operator was polite and helpful and when I was promptly connected with the police department, they were the same. I confess I was disappointed. It was the first time I had ever had the opportunity to say, "I want to report a murder," and the sergeant who introduced herself was about as excited as if I had told her that my pet Pekingese was missing. She asked me to stay where I was until the police arrived, adding that they would be there in a few minutes. She was as cool as a dentist's assistant making an appointment.

It was under five minutes, in fact. Two patrolmen in uniform came, looked at the corpse, checked my identity and made a phone call. They moved around, looking at doors and windows, though one of them was in the room with me at all times. About ten minutes later, two plainclothes detectives came in.

"LieutenantDelanceyHomicide," said the foremost of the two. The way he said it, it came out like one long word. He was short, light build, with a face that looked worn and tired. He had light-blue eyes that improved his appearance a bit and untidy dark hair that didn't. He wore a gray suit that was far from new and a dark-blue tie that he probably got as a Christmas present. His ears were prominent and he moved his hands in an expressive way that was almost Italian. "Stickaround, I wannatalktoyer," he said, and I knew he was not from Louisiana.

He motioned to the two uniformed men and they all huddled together. It did not take long for observations to be passed along and the uniformed men left. "Sergeant Zukowski," the lieutenant said, jerking a thumb in that direction. I gave the sergeant a brief but friendly nod. He might have returned the nod but the energy it must have used was immeasurably small. He was a big, beefy man with an unexpressive face, though that might have been part of the job.

The lieutenant moved around the room, looking at the corpse, at the desk, looking at everything as if he were photographing it in his mind. Maybe he was. He went into the other rooms but the sergeant stayed with me. He was not too obvious about it but I was seldom more than five seconds out of his vision.

Lieutenant Delancey had no sooner rejoined us than the doorbell tinkled. Delancey ignored it but the sergeant went

41

and came back with two men and one woman. They carried equipment of various kinds in leather sacks and pouches, and soon flashes filled the room while the other two were poking around all over, performing mysterious functions.

"Overhere," Delancey said to me, moving his hands toward the other, book-filled room. We went into the comparative quiet, leaving the technicians with the body.

"Whaddayerknowaboutthis?" It was going to take me a little while to get accustomed to this condensed speech, I could see that. The general drift of his question was obvious, though, so I was saved from having to ask him to repeat it.

I told him about Van Linn first, hoping that the name of a prominent New Orleans lawyer would weigh in on my side. Too late, I realized that Van Linn might well be a defense lawyer and persona non grata with a police force that had been thwarted by him countless times. I went on anyway, telling him about the book, the auction and the reason for my being here in Gambrinus' shop.

It did not sound too convincing to me — and I knew it was true. I could see why the expression on Lieutenant Delancey's face was turning into a frown that, if not outright doubt, was certainly heavy on skepticism.

"A book? Telling me thisisallaboutabook?" There it was again, skepticism in his voice as well as his look. At least I was able to detect a couple of breaks in the continuity of his speech.

"Not just a book, Lieutenant. It may be a fairly valuable book. There may be a great story in it — how the Belvedere family built a restaurant dynasty —"

"But stillabook."

"Some of the recipes could be valuable. One of the recipes was for oysters Belvedere, which was the one dish more than any other that made the name of Belvedere famous."

I was losing ground with him, I could see that — at least, losing ground as far as convincing him that the book was important. Getting him to accept the concept that a recipe could be worth money might be an uphill battle. On the other hand, as far as communication was concerned, I was making rapid progress in learning to understand the lieutenant's staccato approach to the English language.

"How valuable?"

"Hard to say. A thousand dollars, maybe, give or take a —"

"Murdersbeencommitted for less."

Another couple of minutes and I would have broken the code.

"I suppose so."

"Thiswomanwhowasthere, at the auction. Gethername?"

"No, I didn't."

"But you thought she was coming here."

I had it! Bletchley Park could not have been more elated the day they solved the Enigma puzzle. I was understanding every word without having to examine possible variants. The lieutenant and I were on the same wavelength!

"I thought she was. She got the name and address and she certainly left hurriedly."

"Tell me about you."

The lieutenant was not a native of New Orleans, that was plain. I would have guessed New York but that didn't matter at the moment. We were speaking the same language. A fleeting thought went across my mind that perhaps he was having as much trouble with my speech as I was with his, so I kept it simple, fairly slow and enunciated carefully. I probably sounded like a Cotswolds shopkeeper determined to sell a priceless antique to a Japanese tourist.

I handed him a card. Better get this over as quickly as possible. The session began as anticipated.

" 'The Gourmet Detective'! You're a detective?"

"No, I'm not a detective, I'm a food-finder . . ." I went through my whole explanation. "— Somebody gave me the nickname of 'The Gourmet Detective' and it stuck. It's good for business but it causes problems when something like this happens."

He seized on that like a hungry terrier on a meaty bone. "Things like this happen often, do they?"

"I wouldn't say 'often,' but food and restaurant businesses turn over billions of dollars. That kind of money attracts criminals and even normally law-abiding people are tempted. Inevitably, some crimes are committed — thefts, substitutions and —"

"— And murders?"

"Well, yes, once in a while." I thought it was time to give myself a plug. "I have been able to be of help to Scotland Yard on more than one occasion."

"Is that right?"

"Yes. I have worked with Inspector Hemingway, among others."

Delancey kept his light-blue eyes on me as he gave a slight nod. "You helped them."

"Yes. They were cases involving food, and my job means I accumulate a lot of specialized knowledge. That's how I was able to be helpful. I also helped Inspector Gaines of the Unusual Crimes Unit in New York not long ago."

"Is that right?"

He said it again and I was about to assume it was rhetorical when he said, "Hal Gaines?"

"Yes. You know him?"

"Worked with him once or twice. I was with the NYPD."

So I was right. He was from New York, and if he knew Hal Gaines, that could clear me.

"If you talk to him — you know, when you're checking on me, give him my regards and tell him I hope the King's Balm is still working."

"King's Balm?"

"It's a herbal remedy I recommended, cured his stomach problems."

"Yeah, well, about this book . . ." He combed his fingers through his untidy hair. It did not improve it. "You're sure it's not here?"

I looked around the room, thousands of books on racks, on shelves, on tables, stacked here, piled there. "I haven't looked," I admitted.

He gave me a rueful grin. "Guess not.

Labor of Sisyphus, huh?"

That surprised me. He went on: "Give the sergeant a complete description of the book and where you're staying. Meantime, you can go."

"I'll stay around a few days," I volunteered. "Then you won't have to ask me not to leave town. I'm at the Monteleone."

"Nice hotel." He gave me a nod of dismissal. "I'll be in touch."

chapter four

My first action upon returning to the "nice hotel" was to phone Van Linn. His response was predictably incredulous.

"Dead? Gambrinus? How can he be?"

"Not only dead but apparently murdered."

Some spluttering came down the line. I told him the rest, such as it was. "You can expect a visit from a detective," I told him. "I had to give him your name."

"Well, yes, of course you did. But — my goodness, I can hardly believe it!"

"I couldn't either. It was a shock, you can imagine."

"Yes, yes, it must have been —" There was a pause and when Van Linn considered it had gone on long enough, he asked the question. "It — ah, well, it's a little indelicate to ask, but I suppose there was no sign of the book?"

"Why do you suppose that?"

"Why? Well, I mean it's what you went

there for, wasn't it?"

"Yes," I said, and probably sounded testy, "but I wasn't expecting a murderer to go there for the same reason."

"Certainly not!" Van Linn said, and sounded emphatic.

"Tell me — did you have any idea that this book was going to prove this important to somebody?"

"No, absolutely not, but — are the police sure that the book is the reason for the murder?"

"You'll have to ask them that."

"I'll do that."

"In the meantime," I said, "do you want me to keep looking for the book?"

There was a pause. "Yes, I'd appreciate it if you would. Be careful, though — I mean, it's not so important that it's worth risking your life for."

"I have to stay in New Orleans anyway for a few days — so I'll definitely keep my ears and eyes open. And I'll be careful. Just one point — is there anything else you want to tell me?"

He didn't hesitate with his answer as far as I could tell. "No, nothing. I assure you that I had no idea something like this could happen. I mean, murder . . . it — it's inconceivable."

★ ★ ★

I dined alone that evening. I felt I deserved some civilized sustenance after a shock like that. Having heard so much about the outstanding qualities of New Orleans cooking, I found myself in a quandary trying to pick a restaurant. I need not have worried. My first choice, Commanders' Palace, was fully booked. So was my second choice, Brennan's. The fact that I was a lone diner was not, I knew, to my advantage. Restaurants don't like to put single diners at a table, it simply is not efficient for them. My third choice, the Court of Two Sisters, accepted my reservation.

It was a short and easy walk from my hotel and the leaded windows allowed a peek inside at a room filled with what looked like happy diners. Being alone, I did not expect one of the best tables and, in fact, I was seated in what looked like the Garden Room, next to the large courtyard — the largest in New Orleans, I recalled. A noisy group of Asians was doing their best to disprove the inscrutability label — at least it did if "quiet" came under the heading of "inscrutable." I was at the next table.

The first course I ordered was turtle soup and, although I expected it to be clear like a broth, which is normal, it was thick with small bits of turtle meat. This was considered to be an aristocrat among soups in earlier days and was served at great ceremonial banquets and diplomatic dinners. The turtle was delivered live to the kitchen where a chef's helper would wait until the turtle poked its head out from under its shell. The helper would then lasso the turtle and, with help, hang it from a high hook. The help was necessary, as turtles often weighed a hundred pounds.

The hanging, however, was not for killing purposes but for exposing the neck, which was slashed — all other parts of the turtle being so leathery as to turn even the sharpest blade.

Hammers, chisels and saws then reduced the creature to meat which was blanched and chopped fine, added to consommé with herbs and vegetables and cooked for hours. Modern kitchen technology has turned this procedure into a more clinical and less bloody scenario and taken all the drama out of it.

The shrimp rémoulade for the main course was blander than I anticipated but I reminded myself that every dish in New Orleans was not spicy. It is, of course, usually served as an hors d'oeuvre, but as the restaurant is widely known for this dish, I was determined to have it and at the same time, I was not prepared to give up the idea of the turtle soup. Creole mustard and Tabasco sauce are standard ingredients of this rémoulade but the spice chef must have had a light hand with the spices today.

The next morning, I came down to breakfast and was making my way across the brown-and-white-tiled lobby to the Breakfast Room when a folded newspaper waved at me. It was not unattended, of course. A police lieutenant by the name of Delancey was on the other end of it.

"Good morning, Lieutenant." I pronounced it in the American way. It was too early in the day for even minor complications.

"Heading for breakfast?"

Surely I was not going to have to go through this learning curve all over again!

"Yes, I am. Care to join me?"

"Nice of you, yeah, we can talk."

Well, that was a relief. I had reestablished a common language already.

When we were seated, the lieutenant said, "I talked with Hal Gaines last night. He said you were okay."

"Okay." Was that all? But I just nodded.

"Scotland Yard said about the same thing

so I wanted to tell you that."

It wasn't a rave review but it should keep me out of a lineup. "Good. I appreciate your telling me."

The waiter arrived, poured coffee for us both and I ordered a half grapefruit, ham with two eggs over-easy, hash browns and whole-wheat toast. The lieutenant wanted only coffee and waved away my invitation to eat. "Had a couple doughnuts at the station earlier." He settled back in his chair and regarded me.

"Know Mr. Van Linn well, do you?"

"No, I only met him through this assignment." I explained how it had come about and he nodded. The scalding-hot coffee did not bother him at all and he sipped it as if it were tepid.

"How about Mr. Gambrinus?"

"I had never seen him until I saw him dead yesterday."

He sipped coffee and appeared contemplative for a moment. Then he gave me a sharp look. "What would you say if I told you I talked to him last night?"

I stopped with my grapefruit spoon halfway to my mouth. "What did you use — a Ouija board?"

He shook his head matter-of-factly. "Just like I'm talking to you right now."

"But you couldn't have!" I protested. "He was dead, I'm sure of it."

"How sure?"

"Well . . . certain sure."

"Got any medical training?"

"No, some first aid . . ."

"Yeah, well . . ." summed up his opinion of my first-aid training. "No, I talked to him right enough. Point I'm making is, the body you found isn't that of Michael Gambrinus."

I ate more grapefruit. I needed it. "Ah, I see. The man I found was dead, though?"

"He was dead."

"I suppose I jumped to the conclusion that the man I found was Michael Gambrinus," I confessed, "because it was his shop and the man was sitting in his chair."

"And you had never seen him before," contributed the lieutenant. "I mean, neither of them?"

"Right. I was hasty. Sorry if I misled you."

He shrugged. "It's okay. I had a nasty moment when Gambrinus wanted to know what I was doing in his shop — but we straightened it out."

"You're being extremely civil about this, Lieutenant. Some detectives of my acquaintance would be livid."

"Livid, yeah, well . . ." He seemed to be trying to decide if a better word would be more appropriate but either couldn't think of one or didn't want to correct me.

"But then I can see that you New Orleans police have many of the courtly and polite mannerisms of the South." Was that troweling it on too thick? I would see.

"I may be *in* New Orleans but I'm not *of* New Orleans, if you get my drift."

"Really. With a great name like Delancey? How can you get more Southern than that?"

"Ever been in New York? Yeah, sure you have if you know Hal Gaines. You know Delancey Street?"

"Anybody who's a fan of Ella Fitzgerald knows Delancey Street," I told him.

"Well, that's the Delancey I'm named after."

"I see." I didn't quite, but I have found that if you put the right uncertain inflection on the words, you can usually extract more information.

"I was found in a crate in front of the Salvation Army welfare station on Delancey Street. There was no clue as to who I was, so they called me Patrick Delancey. It was St. Patrick's Day."

"So you're a native New Yorker — and

that's another song."

"Sure am."

"And now you're in New Orleans. How did that come about?"

"My wife was killed in a driving accident — Sixth Avenue — hit by a taxi trying to avoid a pedestrian out-of-towner."

"I'm sorry. Was that recently?"

"Three years. I'm okay now but at the time I just couldn't stand the thought of staying in the city any longer. I made a nuisance of myself till the commissioner agreed to a transfer to wherever the first opportunity came up. Happened to be New Orleans."

"I see." I did, a little, but I was still wondering why he was telling me this.

"And now you're wondering why I'm telling you all this . . . Well, Hal Gaines said you were all right. Said to be straight with you and you'd be straight with me."

"Wouldn't have it any other way —"

"Hal also said you could be helpful."

Aha, here it came. "You mean we make a deal?"

He gave me a reproving look. "I'm a cop. I don't make deals!"

"What about a quid pro quo?"

He nodded enthusiastically. "Now you're talking my language."

"I am?" I asked faintly.

"Reason I know what that means, I'm in my third year of law school. I get some time off for day classes, attending court, sitting in on legal briefings and stuff — and I take evening classes, study on weekends."

"A tough schedule," I sympathized. "I had to do my studying under similar circumstances."

"Is that right?"

"Yes, fortunately, cooking is an activity that goes on all over the world so I worked as a chef on a cruise ship. I stopped off at various ports and spent a few months in each, learning the local cuisine, then picked up another ship and went on. Made my way round the world that way —"

"Must have learned a lot of different cuisines."

"I did."

"Not Cajun or Creole, though." He finished his coffee and waved for a refill.

"I know them from cookbooks, but this is a great chance to sample them firsthand — and from the masters."

"Okay, now, speaking of cookbooks . . ."

I grinned. "You did that very cleverly, Lieutenant."

"I didn't need to. I could have just asked you. Hal Gaines said you were the right guy

to tell me all about food and eating and restaurants."

"Some detectives I've met wouldn't have
asked — they'd have told."

"Run into some toughies, have you?"

"Yes, and the toughest was a woman."

Delancey nodded. "Figures."

"So what do you want to know about the
cookbook?"

"Anything that'll help."

"Well, many cookbooks go back several
hundred years. The oldest of all is probably
the one written by Apicius giving the recipes
of Ancient Rome."

Delancey looked fascinated. "Is that
right? Gee!"

"The one we have here isn't in that category, of course. It's not being sought because of its age but probably because it tells
the story of the early days of the Belvedere
family in the restaurant business. In the
trade, it isn't called a cookbook but a 'chef's
book.' "

"Why are chefs' books that interesting?"

I looked up from my eggs and ham. "Lots
of chefs write down recipes. They are always
making changes while they're cooking,
trying to improve, wanting to squeeze out
that little extra bit of flavor. Eventually, the
book becomes a compilation of their own

favorite recipes, plus the ones that the restaurant features, and all the tricks, shortcuts, things like that." I returned to the ham and the second egg. I had told him most of this at the bookshop but I was familiar enough with police procedure to know how they love repetition.

Delancey's worn face didn't exactly light up with understanding. "So what's so great about it? Why would anybody kill for it?"

"The motive might not be that simple. The book could have value from a historical viewpoint. The Belvedere family is famous in New Orleans, after all."

He shook his head. "Try harder, you don't convince me."

"Not enough motive for you?"

"No. Oh, I know people do funny things, get fanatical about stamps and coins, paintings and sculpture — even had a case when I was in New York where a guy killed a woman because she was going to blow the whistle on him. Know what he'd done?"

"No," I said obligingly.

"Stolen a design — a fashion design. Oh, sure, it was from a famous fashion house but imagine — committing murder for a skirt!"

"When you put it that way, yes, it sounds absurd. But it's a good comparison — people do get extremist about their job or their hobby, their business, their passion."

"They sure do," the lieutenant said emphatically.

"Did you solve the case?"

"Sure," he said laconically.

"Put him away?"

"Judge gave him seven to ten, he was out in four."

I finished the ham and eggs. I had just enough egg yolk to go with the last morsel of whole-wheat toast. I hate it when the final portions don't balance out.

"Must be infuriating when that happens — but then that must be why you're studying law — why you want to switch from the investigative to the judicial side."

"Something like that." He seemed uncommunicative on the subject. "Back to this book . . . it's been in the family for generations, right?"

"From the beginning."

"Okay. Now, how come it's such a mystery — what's in it? Somebody in the family's gotta know."

I explained how Arturo originated the book, how Edgardo and Alfonso had continued it and then so had Ernesto until he had his medical problems and the book had gone missing. I told the lieutenant of the fame the restaurant had achieved.

He listened attentively and nodded.

"Oysters Belvedere — that was their specialty, huh?"

"That's right. One of the great dishes of American cuisine."

"I'm a meat-and-potatoes man, myself."

I had thought he might be. Hal Gaines had had similar culinary tastes and had tolerated me in New York because my knowledge of spices had been critical to the case. Gaines had suggested that Lieutenant Delancey should make use of me for the same reason — making it my part of the quid pro quo.

"Think of oysters Belvedere as a Supermeatloaf to Die For."

He gave me a sharp glance to see if I was making fun of him, then his creased features eased into a small grin. "Now you're talking my language." At least he had a sense of humor. That would make it easier to work with him.

"I take it you're not yet into New Orleans food, then?"

"All this Creole and Cajun stuff? Nah, tried a few but they don't grab me."

"Maybe they'll grow on you."

"Doubt it — anyway, tell me about that broad at the auction."

I told him all I knew.

"So you think she went straight to Gambrinus' bookshop?" he asked. He had asked me that before, too, but I was not going to remind him.

"She was all steamed up to do just that."

"But you didn't see her again?"

"No, I didn't —"

He caught the slight hesitation in my voice. "Go on, what were you going to say?"

"When I first found the body and was still staring at Gambrinus — well, I thought it was Gambrinus — I heard a noise —"

"What kind of a noise?"

"A sort of slithering . . ."

"What, like a snake?"

"I don't know, it only lasted a few seconds. Then a door banged. I went to look. It must have been the back door, but whoever it was had gone."

He studied me keenly as I was talking.

"The rustle of a woman's clothes maybe?"

"Could have been, I suppose."

He gave the slightest of nods. "We dusted the doorknobs," he said. "The back door had smears, not enough to pick up. Nobody in the neighborhood saw anything useful. They're all used to seeing people go in and out of Gambrinus' shop and the other shops on the street."

"No trace of the book?"

"Plenty of cookbooks but nothing like your description."

"What does Van Linn say?"

"Mostly what you told me."

"The weapon?"

"A thirty-two — no record on the rifling."

"Don't some people call that a woman's gun?" I asked.

"Yeah, some do." He looked longingly at his coffee cup. "Gotta go easy on this stuff. Sure would like another, still —" He pushed the cup out of temptation range. "Not much to go on, huh?"

"The body," I said. "You haven't told me about the body."

chapter five

"His name's Richie Mortensen. He used to work for Gambrinus in the bookshop, then times got tough and Gambrinus had to let him go. That was a coupla years ago. Since then, Gambrinus has used him on a temporary basis now and then. He got him to go to this auction when something more important came up —"

"You've checked on that, I'm sure."

"Yeah. A large library was up for sale in Biloxi so Gambrinus went there and sent Mortensen to this auction. Mortensen's been to a lot of these, knows the ropes."

"Yet Mortensen was sitting in Gambrinus' chair —"

Delancey shrugged. "Looks like Mortensen went to the auction early to get a jump on the crowd. According to accounts, he was kind of a brash kid and smart at that stuff. Brought the book to the shop."

"And he was sitting in Gambrinus' chair when someone else came in, shot him and took the book," I said.

The lieutenant eyed the coffee cup again but a steely look came over his face and he nodded. "Looks that way."

"You don't sound like you're a hundred percent convinced," I said. In fact he didn't, but I felt it was the right thing to say in order to get him to tell me more — if there was more.

"At this early stage in an investigation, there's lots of questions and theories. When we've got more information, I'll know better."

I had to be satisfied with that. "Stay and finish your breakfast," he told me, getting to his feet. "I'll be in touch."

After he had gone and I had finished, I went out onto the sidewalk and surveyed the day. It wasn't particularly bright. In the gutter across the street, green and gold glittered incongruously. I had to walk over and look. I realized what they were — the strings of beads that were thrown to the crowds from the Krewes on the Mardi Gras floats.

Some gray clouds were hanging around up there, looking for a polo game to spoil. The passing traffic included a man standing on a two-wheeled cart drawn by two large Dobermans. Nobody seemed anxious to get in his way.

A Jeep Cherokee with flames painted on the side thought about it, but discretion prevailed.

I thought I heard my name called. I was deciding I had to be mistaken when I heard it again. It was a female voice but I couldn't tell where it was coming from, what with people coming in and out, staff wheeling trolleys of luggage and drivers ushering passengers out of the hotel.

Taxis were lined up outside. Valets were helping owners climb in, a taxi was pulling away, then I heard the voice again. Back down the line of parked cars was a stretch limousine — one of those hybrid vehicles that look like two normal-sized ones welded together. It was of a cream color, and the windows were the kind of glass that looks dark from outside. A hand waved, beckoning.

I walked down to it, puzzled. Perhaps Eric Van Linn had commandeered it or borrowed it — maybe he even owned it. I could not think of anyone else I knew in New Orleans who might be here to pick me up — or, more to the point, anyone who knew me.

An attractive young woman in a trim suit stood by the open door of the limo. As I approached, she smiled gaily. "We've been

66

waiting for you," she said, and motioned me into the vehicle. I peered inside. Four other women were in there, all just as attractive, and all were smiling a welcome. The woman on the sidewalk took my arm and eased me through the car door. Willing hands inside grasped me and drew me in. I sank onto a soft leather seat in the spacious interior, arranged so that there was lots of legroom and we all faced each other.

Conflicting perfumes from the ladies mingled pleasingly with the lemongrass aroma that was evidently dispensed by the vehicle's air-conditioning system.

The young woman who had called to me climbed in beside me, the door slammed and we pulled out of line and snaked out onto Royal Street as smoothly and silently as a Rolls-Royce. In fact, it probably was a Rolls-Royce; the engine was softer than the purr of a week-old kitten.

I looked at the faces. The woman who had called me from the sidewalk had light-brown hair, a wide mouth and restless brown eyes that looked as if they might betray every emotion. Another was a shiny-haired blonde with an ample figure and a come-hither look, while the next had an almost Asiatic appearance, smart clothes, carefully coiffured dark hair and a self-confident demeanor. The fourth had black hair and long black lashes and an almost perfect array of features. The fifth had the stylish look of the Italian females you see stalking past the fashion stores along the Corso in Milan.

"Delighted to meet you all," I said. "To what do I owe this pleasure?" I looked at them in turn, wondering which was going to be the spokeswoman.

It turned out to be the fourth one.

"We have just kidnapped you," she said.

After the understandably protracted pause, I laughed. It was a very short laugh. "I can't think of anybody who would pay anything for me," I said.

"We think you have considerable value," the Asian-looking girl said in a soft voice.

"That's nice of you." Naturally, I wasn't going to antagonize any of these charming creatures, certainly not until I found out whether they were pussycats or tiger cats.

Whatever brand of feline they were, they were eyeing me as if I were a particularly delectable species of mouse. I was growing more uncomfortable by the minute as I waited for them to burst out in fits of giggles and tell me it was all some kind of joke; I didn't really care what kind — any kind was fine with me as long as it was a joke.

But no giggles came and they all looked so serious — smiling but still serious — that my nervousness ballooned. I had to say something. I said, "You know, I've never been kidnapped before." Not brilliant but anything would do as a trigger.

"Not many people have," said the shiny blonde.

"Do you do this sort of thing often?" I asked. It sounded like a question that P. G. Wodehouse would have Bertie Wooster ask, and I was aiming for an effect a lot more solemn than that.

"We've done it two or three times before," said the brown-haired, brown-eyed damsel, and the way she said it was almost convincing.

It was time to break this deadlock. "Now, come on, ladies . . ." I tried to avoid a cajoling tone and did not want to be patronizing, either. "You don't look or act like kidnappers, and anyway, kidnapping went out of style with the Lindbergh case. In my instance, it would be downright unprofitable and you all look like you know the NASDAQ from a backpack. Now, tell me what this is all about."

While I was giving this spiel, an unnerving thought was creeping in. I was already involved in a case where a man had been murdered over a cookbook. Was it the kind of case that might support a kidnapping as well? Could this incident possibly have some connection with the Belvedere chef's book? If it did, it was no joking matter.

"Here we are," said the girl who might be part Asian, and the limo stopped. All the time we had been chatting, the vehicle had been sliding almost noiselessly through the New Orleans traffic, almost without a tilt or a bump, as smooth as warm cream. The girl who had ushered me in from the sidewalk was the first out. I was motioned to follow her, and the other three followed in such a manner that, without seeming to, they surrounded me. It was not exactly militaristic but it was certainly efficient. If it was true when they told me they had carried out two or three kidnappings before, they were fast learners.

We were in . . . well, not exactly an alley but a street as narrow and unimportant as it can be before it is designated an alley. It was neat and tidy, though, and looked to be the backs of buildings which must front onto a larger street. The shiny blonde opened a steel door that was not locked although it had a formidable padlock. We went in, our circular formation transforming into a line order, then, inside the door, I inhaled . . .

There was no mistaking that odor — we were in a restaurant. It had that solidly comforting smell of a superior restaurant, too — no garlicky overtones, no rancid-fat undertones but a nicely rounded, richly satisfying, good food smell.

I was instantly reassured. This was familiar territory. I felt I was on safe ground and I couldn't wait to see what happened next.

Our squad marched past the kitchen but I didn't get enough of a glance inside to see much. I got a glimpse of the main dining room and it looked pretty classy though it wasn't open yet, shrouded in a curtained gloom. We went up a flight of stairs and into a private dining room. It was intended for banquets and had one large table that was fully occupied once we sat down — about fifteen women were already there.

The black-haired miss with the almost perfect features opened the proceedings. "You're probably wondering what this is all about," she said, and I didn't answer. It had been the understatement of the year.

"Each of us is a restaurant owner," she went on, and I breathed a huge sigh of relief though I managed not to let it show. If they

71

owned restaurants, they weren't real kidnappers. If not, though, why did they pretend to be? She was continuing, "We call ourselves the Witches."

I had been glancing at the faces at the table meanwhile, trying to get a clue. Not all were as good-looking as the quintet chosen for the actual snatch but a few smiled and none looked downright dangerous. Several were somewhat older, but again, none looked as if she came from the criminal classes so my tension was easing.

The shiny blonde muscled her way into the arena. "Let's get civilized here." She showed a magnificent set of gleaming white teeth that could have admen from half a dozen toothpaste manufacturers fighting over her. "I'm Jenny Kirkpatrick. I have a restaurant over on Swallow Street, it's called The General's Tavern."

The other members of the hit squad didn't want to be left out of the act. The black-haired, long-lashed, nearly perfectly featured number said, "My name's Marguerite Saville. My place is the Bistro Bonaparte."

The next contributor said, "I have a place on Waverley. My name's Leah Rollingson." She had a delightful smile that brought out two tiny dimples. They were a contrast to her almond-shaped eyes and as I wondered about some Asian origin, she added, "It's really Li — spelled *L-i*. My parents are from Singapore but everybody called me Lee until one day, a Louisiana native called me Leah. I've been Leah ever since, sounds more Southern."

The brown-haired, brown-eyed lass who had waved to me and started all this, tossed in her contribution. "I'm Emmy Lou Charbonneau, born and bred in New Orleans. My place is called Café Cajun — and it's authentic as all get-out." I could believe it. Her accent was as Southern as hush puppies.

"Della Forlani," said the refugee from an Italian fashion catwalk. "My parents brought me here from Italy when I was three. My mother taught me to cook and now I have the Villa Romana."

"So you all own and operate restaurants when you're not kidnapping people," I said. Most of them laughed amiably. I was about to add, *And the rest of you are accessories, presumably before the fact,* but bit it off just in time. The fewer references to crime, the better. I substituted, "And you call yourselves witches."

"*W-I-T-C-H-E-S,*" Marguerite corrected me, spelling it out letter by letter. "It stands for 'Women in the Catering, Hotel and Eating Services.' "

"From what I've heard of New Orleans and its history of voodoo, 'Witches' is very appropriate," I said.

"This is a male-dominated town," said Jenny. She really was quite attractive. Her blonde hair didn't look that shiny anymore and she had steady blue eyes. Her chin was proud and determined, especially the way it jutted out a little bit further now as she spoke up on behalf of the dominated class. They sure didn't look like they took any domination, I thought — but then, that was their point.

Jenny went on. "Men own this town, men run it. They think women should stay home and cook for the family —"

"— And mind the babies," added Emmy Lou. "Well, all of us wanted to cook, but not just for a family. We wanted to make it a career, we wanted to make a name for ourselves, to be known, recognized, applauded for our efforts and our achievements."

"We all wanted to become chefs and have our own restaurants," said Della.

"It caused a stir at the time." One of the women who had already been at the table took up the tale. She was in her fifties and looked as if she could run the kitchen at the

White House and be able to write half a dozen books about it. "I'm Harriet Vance. The culinary institutes round these parts had never had any women chefs. They were as masculine as the marine corps —"

"The marines take women now," a wispy girl with long hair, clearly a stickler for detail, interrupted.

"They didn't then," Harriet went on without pausing, "so we all had to go elsewhere. It just happened that several of us came back to New Orleans about the same time. A few of us knew each other and as we were all striving toward the same goal, we got together, informally at first, then we formed 'the Witches.' "

"And we've been using it to exert what leverage we can," another woman said. She had prematurely gray hair, very fashionably styled, and a smooth unlined face. "I'm Eleanor McCardle. I have a cooking school and placement bureau for the trade. As Witches, we've been able to help a number of women to advance in the food and restaurant trades."

"Very laudable," I said, "and now you want to improve your cash flow by going into the kidnapping business. I hope you're not helping those other women by advising them to follow your career change."

That brought numerous smiles, even a

few laughs. My comment was a bit snippy but I was still feeling the relief from learning they were not ill-intentioned, so I was sure I could get away with it. Marguerite was one of the smilers.

"From time to time," she said, "whenever someone comes to town who we think might help our cause, we bring them here and put our case. We like to call it kidnapping — I hope you didn't take it too seriously. I mean, I'm glad you didn't have a heart attack or anything."

"The only effect on my heart was being pulled into a limousine by five beautiful women," I said. "That sort of thing doesn't happen to me very often — in fact, I can't remember the last time."

More smiles greeted that, the first of them appearing on the faces of the Famous Five. It was still true, I reflected, you can never overdo flattery. "All that remains," I pointed out, "is for you to tell me what you want from me. Now I know that you're not going to throw me into a kind of harem-in-reverse, you can talk freely."

"It concerns the chef's book from the Belvedere." Jenny, the blonde, delivered this message.

I winced inwardly. Complications might be getting into this case.

chapter six

"How do you know about that?" I asked for openers. It was only one of several questions I was going to need the answers to before I committed to this particular female cause, no matter how worthy.

The older woman was ready for that. "First, all of us in this room are in the restaurant business. Second, New Orleans is not that big a town, it's hard to keep a secret here. Third, the Belvedere family is famous, anything that is connected with their name gets some visibility. When you put all of these together — well, you can understand how we know."

"You knew about the book already?"

"Of course we knew," piped up another voice. It belonged to a stern-looking woman who probably ran a very tight restaurant but had a warm smile when she wanted to use it. "Like Eleanor said, the Belvedere family is famous in New Orleans. In the trade, it's always been common knowledge that

Arturo Belvedere wrote a chef's book and that his heirs have carried on that tradition. Naturally, when we heard about the auction, we were interested in the book."

"A coup for the Witches?"

"We try never to miss a chance of getting our name out there. Besides, the book could get more and more valuable. It could increase in value faster than any stock, so we were able to justify the idea financially. Of course, we had to set a limit."

"That's why we decided to bid on it." This was Della, the dark-haired, Italian-flavored beauty. "Oh, we knew we didn't stand a chance if the bidding went way up, but we thought it was worth a try."

"So one of you went and bid on the book? Which one?"

There was a pause. "Actually, it wasn't one of us," said Jenny. "Well, she used to be one of us. She gave up working in the trade and started her own agency doing publicity for food fairs, food trade conventions, TV and radio, putting out a newsletter, setting up Web sites — that sort of thing."

"Why not one of your own members?" I asked.

"This lady has a . . . well, let's call it an aggressive personality. We thought she was so much better suited to handling an auction than any of us."

I asked the question slowly. "Is she blonde, pushy, impatient, loud, big-mouthed?"

"He's already met Elsa," giggled the wispy girl with the long hair.

"Attractive," I added hastily, "late thirties —"

"She says she's thirty-two," a new voice called out indignantly.

"I'm bad on women's ages," I explained.

"Her name is Elsa Goddard," said Marguerite. "She managed to get her name in the newspaper report —"

"The bookseller who was murdered," said Della. "Maybe some of you saw it on the TV news."

"I missed that, I was working late," said another, and two or three of the other members gave her a composite account. "So the Belvedere book hasn't been found?"

"Not yet," I said.

"What were you doing there?" It was Della asking.

"I was hired to do the same thing as Elsa Goddard, apparently," I answered. "Go to the auction and buy the book."

"Who hired you?" asked Della.

"I can't answer that," I said.

"So you can't act on our behalf, then?" Della sounded disappointed.

"Of course he can," Marguerite said firmly. "There's no conflict of interest. He was unable to carry out his assignment and buy the book at the auction. So now he can work for us."

"I have to wait and see what my principal wants me to do," I said, getting all official. I went on quickly. "You may well be right, in which case I will be glad to do what I can."

Nobody seemed to have an argument with that.

"Am I released from captivity?" I asked.

There was a titter or two then Della said, "We hope you'll visit our restaurants, sample some genuine New Orleans cooking, get to know us."

A few assenting murmurs came, then business cards fluttered across the table like a cloud of white butterflies. I gathered them up. "Thank you. I'd like to do that. Tell me something — have you really kidnapped two or three others before me?"

"Oh yes," Harriet said.

"Get anything for them?"

There was a laugh at that. "They were kidnappings in the same sense that yours was," Jenny said. "They were all people we wanted to help us."

"In your fight for recognition as Witches?"

"That's right."

"Did it work?"

"We're still fighting the good fight," Marguerite asserted firmly.

"One unpleasant subject I have to bring up," I said, "and that's the matter of a fee." That brought absolute quiet to the room. "I'm prepared to be reasonable and I'm well aware that the restaurant business isn't as lucrative as people who eat in them think it is."

"Unless you're Wolfgang Puck or Alain Ducasse," said Jenny.

"And we're not," Della said. "We're not even Alice Waters."

"But we will be, one day," Harriet said bravely. Then she spoiled it by saying, "I think the best way would be a flat fee for getting us the book — say, a thousand dollars."

A woman who had not contributed until now chose that moment to add, "Of course, there would be no payment for failure." She looked like one of the Witches, I thought; all she needed was a bubbling cauldron to stir. Still, it was a convenient approach for me to fall in with, as it avoided any problem I might have with serving two masters. If I didn't bring the Witches the book, they didn't have to pay me. Besides, I still had these niggling doubts about Eric Van Linn, who might not have told me everything.

"Eating at any of our restaurants would naturally be without charge," Jenny said brightly. "That's worth quite a lot of money."

"How about expenses incurred during my investigations?" I inquired.

A few dubious expressions showed around the table but Della, who had clearly paid close attention to the financial part of the curriculum when she had studied cooking, said, "Up to twenty-five dollars a day; anything over that to have prior approval. All fully receipted."

I tried to get that up but without success. I had done business with women before many times, but it had been in the singular. How different they were when pluralized.

"Reporting," said Marguerite. "We will want frequent reports."

"How do you want me to do that?"

"You can do it through me," Marguerite offered, and I saw nothing wrong with that idea but Jenny said brightly, "Or I can be the contact." This was good, now they were fighting over me.

The discussion continued briefly, then Harriet broke the deadlock and said to the group, "If he's going to be eating at our restaurants, let him make the reports then. We're all in touch with each other frequently."

That was deemed a good solution by all.

"Am I released from bondage, then?" I asked.

"Paroled," said Eleanor. "Be on your best behavior."

"The poor man," Emmy Lou said. "Here in New Orleans!"

The stretch limo had gone when I went out but it was easy to get a cab. Before leaving, I had asked which television station Elsa Goddard worked for and learned that it was WKNO. I had phoned and asked if she was there. She was indeed and I hung up and went for the cab.

The driver was from Minnesota, a farm boy who had got sick of farming and wanted to sample the wicked ways of the Big Easy. "Enjoying them?" I asked him, and his languid "Yeah, I guess," sounded as if he was tiring of the wild life already or else had not yet found any.

"Were you here for the Mardi Gras?" he asked.

"No, I missed it by a couple of days."

"Too bad. It was really great."

"It's a big football game or something, isn't it?"

He flashed me a skeptical look. "It's a parade. Floats and stuff, bands, costumes."

"Oh, yes, I think I've heard of it."

We had traveled only a few blocks when he called out to me, "Hey, you with the CIA or something?"

It was an unusual query and though my culinary investigating occasionally engenders suspicions about my connections to the authorities, I don't think the CIA has been mentioned yet. "No, I'm not. Why do you ask?"

He glanced at his rearview mirror anxiously. "Car back there seems to be following us." I looked back but all I could see was a black car, ordinary looking.

"Want me to lose him?" the boy asked, hopefully. He probably hadn't had this much excitement since he left the farm so I said, "Sure. Go ahead."

He made a couple of sharp turns, one on a very dubious yellow light. He glanced back and grinned. "Lost him!" he said triumphantly, but after two more blocks he looked back in disbelief. "He's back!"

Perhaps Lieutenant Delancey had someone protecting me, I thought. Or maybe he wasn't entirely satisfied with my story or was having me followed. The thought I had after that was one I didn't like at all — it brought in the possibility of a person or persons unknown.

"When we get to the TV station, sit in front of it for a couple of minutes," I told the young man. "See if that black car pulls in behind us."

He nodded eagerly, and five minutes later he slid in behind a short line of vehicles. "He'll either have to cruise on by or pull in behind us," he said. We waited but no such vehicle appeared. I paid him and kept an eye open as he drove off. No sign of a tail.

WKNO was a remodeled building in a business part of the city and its roof bristled with a hedgehog arrangement of antennae of a dozen varieties and satellite dishes like a mushroom forest.

The receptionist took my name while answering the phone, pulling a roll of paper out of the fax machine, glancing at her computer screen and alternately nodding and shaking her head to questions tossed at her by staff members going by. She did it all without frenzy and I hoped she was getting paid well for all these jobs. I hoped she was being paid better than I might be, but then I pushed that sour thought aside.

A little lady came into the lobby, bright-eyed and lively as a cricket and the receptionist called to her and asked her to take me to Studio Five.

We went through a maze of passages and elevators and the little lady pointed to a large double-door with STUDIO 5 written on it in large letters. "Know Elsa Goddard, do you?" asked the little lady, and I said, "Oh yes, I know her." The doors thumped behind me.

An awful lot was going on. The studio was enormous and cleverly designed to accomplish many functions. There was a stage ringed with lights, a large polished table of the type that interviewers like to sit behind, and several small rooms with panels of lights and switches and microphones. Tall screens, light reflectors, lamps on high poles and snaky black cables were all over the floor. I wondered how many people tripped over one or another of the cables every day.

Plenty of people were there to be tripped. Mostly young and earnest, roughly equal numbers of each sex, many bespectacled and many more wild-haired and all moving pieces of equipment or carrying sheafs of paper or in earnest discussion or staring into cameras or pushing switches and juggling rheostats.

Were there any budding Ed Murrows or Milton Berles or Dan Rathers here? Hard to tell at this age, I supposed. I watched the blurs of movement for a while, fascinated. Nobody really took any notice of me. One young girl asked me politely if I would step aside as I was blocking the light. I did and nearly knocked over a ten-foot lamp stand.

I had expected to walk in and see Elsa Goddard somewhere but there was no sign of her. I saw a figure with its back to me inside one of the small rooms with lights and panels. It seemed to be the only one of the several rooms that was occupied and I moved closer to see if it was her, as jeans and a dark windbreaker jacket were no iden-tifying help whatever.

Then the figure turned. It was a man. Not only that but . . . My breath caught in my throat.

It was Richie Mortensen, whom I had last seen sitting at the desk in the bookshop of Michael Gambrinus.

It couldn't be. He was dead. He was, wasn't he? Yes, he had to be; Lieutenant Delancey had told me that he had been identified. So if he was dead, what was he doing in a television studio? Several smart answers to that might be around but I could not lay hands on one at that moment.

I looked at him again. He had moved a bit and was now looking at me through the glass. When I had seen him in that chair in Gambrinus' bookstore, his eyes had been closed in death. Death, I thought. What about that bullet hole in the middle of his chest? That was a sure sign of death, wasn't it?

But now the eyes were staring at me with a feral intensity that I didn't like. I moved to make sure and his eyes followed me. It was unmistakably me he was staring at, and now I saw his hand move inside the jacket — to come out immediately . . .

There was a gun in the hand. I was paralyzed. I tried to find a rational thought that would explain this. I was in a television studio — a man with a gun must be as common here as housewives at a Macy's sale. Where were the cameras, though? None on him, that was for sure. On me? Yes, that must be it, they were filming me for a sequence that said, *Pan to victim, show face full of terror.* They had made a good choice with me — I must be showing more terror than all the Vincent Price movies ever made.

No, forget that, not a camera was on me. Hidden cameras? Don't be paranoid. It didn't leave me with much and none of that was reassuring. It meant that there was a man with a gun and he was looking at me. Worse yet, he was moving to the door of the tiny studio and coming out . . .

chapter seven

The double doors closed silently behind me as I made an exit in what must have been record time. I hurried along a corridor, made a turn and hurried along another. I didn't recall the geography of the place from when the little lady had escorted me in, but it didn't matter. When you're escaping from a dead man with a gun, all roads lead to safety.

I was puzzling over that paradox as I narrowly evaded a wheeled cart piled with mysterious-looking equipment. He couldn't be dead or he wouldn't be chasing me. But he was chasing me — ergo, he couldn't be dead. But I had seen him dead and Lieutenant Delancey had confirmed it. . . . Was the lieutenant playing some devious game? The thought brought to mind recollections of a Charlie Chan movie in which the Honolulu detective had an actor impersonate a murder victim so as to get the murderer to confess.

No, I decided. That didn't sound like

Delancey's style. He just wasn't the Charlie Chan type. On the other hand, there was more to him than met the eye. *Pay attention to getting out of here,* I told myself. REFRESHMENT CENTER, said a large sign, and a group of men and women clustered around several vending machines.

It was far from a madding crowd but it would have to do, and as a temporary refuge it wasn't bad. I squeezed in among these people who gave us all our news, our education and our entertainment. None of them paid me any attention.

My breathing was returning to normal and I was even contemplating getting a cup of coffee so that I could stand with it and really look like I belonged. The line was long — it must be that good New Orleans coffee — and I was looking for the end of it when I saw my nemesis down the corridor.

He was coming this way.

His hand was inside his windbreaker so he wasn't attracting any attention — except from me. I looked for an escape route. Emerging from the crowd was not a first step that appealed to me and even after that, I didn't know where to go. I huddled deeper into the coffee and Coke drinkers and edged over to get some extra cover from the potato chip, nacho, peanut and cookie buyers.

He was looking this way and that but as he came closer, he turned and disappeared down a side corridor that must have looked like a probable hiding place for his quarry. I seized the opportunity and dashed off in the opposite direction.

I didn't really have a plan — other than my primary strategy of avoiding being killed. Several approaches suggested themselves. For instance, I could find a security guard and complain about a man with a gun running loose in the building. The only problem with that would arise if the guard asked if I knew the man and I replied, *Yes, he's dead.*

I could just get out of the building and save Ms. Elsa Goddard for another day, when the outlook for escaping violence was more favorable. The faintest reek of timidity accompanied this — some might call it cowardice although I preferred "prudence."

I could confront him, disarm him and — no, no, that was ridiculous. In the midst of all this mental turmoil, I found myself facing a bank of three elevators. This was not the way I had come in but that did not matter. I pressed the button and a door opened. I stepped in and went down to the ground floor.

People were coming and going and generally pursuing their business. It looked safe to get out of the elevator, but, before I could do so, a hand grasped my arm. I turned to see the one face I didn't want to see.

"You killed my brother."

The accusing voice should have terrified me but the funny thing was that the words came with a significance that was reassuring. His brother! So I had not been pursued by a dead man, after all! Well, of course not, that was absurd. Now, looking at this face, though, I could see that the mistake was understandable. This fellow and the one in Michael Gambrinus's office did look very much alike. After all, I told myself, I had only seen Richie Mortensen dead and with his eyes closed. This man was a little different but the brotherly resemblance was clear.

The first thing to do was establish was my innocence. "I didn't kill your brother," I said to him firmly.

A young woman entering the elevator gave me a strange look.

"This is a funny place to rehearse," she snapped. "Can't you find a studio?"

"He was already dead when I went into the shop," I said, putting all the conviction into the statement that I could muster and trying to ignore the young woman who was shaking her head and tut-tutting at my breach of broadcasting etiquette.

"Anyway, I had never met him, I had no reason to want to harm him."

"That book." That was all he said. At least he didn't pull out the gun, although one hand remained menacingly inside his jacket. I looked him in the eyes. They were dark and, at the moment, threatening. He had the slight stubble of a beard on his face, a long but strong chin, and was in his mid-thirties.

The woman got out of the elevator at the next floor and shot us a final look of reprimand. "I had been to the auction to buy the book," I went on, determined to get in all the points of view that might save my life. "I was told it had been sold already. I found that it had been sold to a Michael Gambrinus so I went right away to his shop. I found your brother dead in Gambrinus's office — I didn't know who he was, of course. In fact I thought he was Gambrinus — I called the police right away and told them that."

His eyes searched my face. I must have looked honest to him; at least, his aggressive attitude relaxed a little. Most satisfying, he still did not pull out the gun. "Look," I told him, "let's sit down and talk about this." I didn't wait for him to agree. I just went to the one of the oases that dotted the lobby — a small round table with chairs around it. I sat in one of them. He hesitated then did likewise, half facing me.

I went over my story again, filling in bits like Van Linn's name, emphasizing his importance as a New Orleans lawyer, telling who I was, why I was in New Orleans — trying to submerge him in corroborative detail that might help push me out of the line of fire.

I must have been more convincing than I had even hoped. He asked a question or two, nothing relevant to the death of his brother or my possible culpability, which was encouraging. I thought I saw a glimmer of doubt in his expression.

"Were you close to your brother?" I asked.

He looked away. "We didn't see each other too often."

I toyed with the idea of suggesting that he might be considered a suspect himself, but some very wise person writing mystery novels once said, "Never antagonize a character with a gun," so I didn't say that. The more I talked to him, though, the less resolute he seemed. It began to look increasingly as if his original attitude had been strictly impulsive.

He didn't strike me as the type to want to kill someone in revenge for his brother's death on sentimental family grounds, and I started to wonder if there was something else, some other reason for his attitude.

"You know about the book?" I asked conversationally.

He looked, well, not alarmed but certainly nervous at the question. "Most people in New Orleans know about the Belvedere family," he said.

He was about to go on when a voice called out, "Why, hello, Larry! You're early."

It was a voice I had heard before and I was putting a name to it as she came into sight. It was Elsa Goddard — she of the combative attitude at the book auction, the designated buyer for my favorite group of lady chefs and kidnappers, "the Witches."

She looked very fetching yet businesslike in a blue silk blouse, a russet-brown skirt and a short, darker brown jacket. She wasn't the type to surprise easily but she looked just a touch taken aback as she saw me. I watched recognition creep into her face.

"My goodness!" she said. "Isn't this fortunate? How did you know about the show?"

"Hard to keep anything quiet in New Orleans," I told her heartily. "You know how this stuff gets around!"

"This is great," she replied in a tone that didn't quite reinforce her words, but then her professionalism kicked into high gear. "I was only expecting Larry for the show, but now I can put the two of you on!"

She was looking from one to the other of us. She sensed the tension and a mounting amusement showed on her face. "Oh, Larry, don't tell me you accused him, too, of killing your brother!"

He looked slightly embarrassed. "I had the idea it might startle one of you into admitting something incriminating," he admitted, and Elsa laughed.

Meantime I was wrestling with another angle. "Show?" was the best I could manage.

"The story of the Belvedere chefs' book, its place in New Orleans cooking history and the startling murder which may be connected with it."

"Oh, I can't contribute much to that," I said modestly. "You've got the right man in Larry here, though. I know he has some strong thoughts on the murder of his brother."

It was a cat-among-the-pigeons idea. I

could have added *Larry is ready to shoot anybody he thinks is a suspect,* but I didn't want to toss in too much drama and break up any intelligent aspect the show might have.

Larry Mortensen looked vaguely uncomfortable but said, "I didn't really want to do the show but Elsa convinced me that it might bring new information on Richie's murder."

Elsa seemed to relish the effect her summary of the show was having on both of us and said enthusiastically to me, "But of course we want you on the show, too. At the auction, I didn't know you were a food expert. You can be helpful in telling the people out there all about the book from the point of view of an outside authority."

She glanced at her Rolex. "Less than an hour. We'd better get along to the studio, get you into makeup right away." She looked at our clothes with a touch of disdain, Larry's then mine. Her nose wrinkled. I already knew that tact was not her strongest point so I was not surprised when she said, "I'm sure we can find something for you to wear."

A murder is the caviar on the toast for the media — for a couple days after it happens, at least. The technical crew was efficient, the wardrobe lady was accommodating and the makeup people did the best they could with the two of us, spending most of their time on Elsa. She looked radiant when they had finished, almost overpoweringly glamorous at close personal range but certainly just right for the cameras.

When we were properly positioned, the cameraman and the young woman with authority over the lights had a few minutes of moving and jiggling so as to get rid of shadows and glare. Another young woman threaded a cord up our sleeves and clipped a mike onto our lapels. There was a countdown, red lights flashed, and a musical fanfare blared out then died away as a plummy, unseen voice introduced Elsa.

She was good at her job — poised, charming, eloquent and exuding a completely different personality from the brassy broad who had been at the book auction. She began by outlining the history of the Belvedere family in New Orleans and relating the success story of their restaurant. "The Book" she described briefly and went on to refer to the murder in Gambrinus's bookshop.

From then on, the program slid downhill on a slippery slope. I was asked to contribute on the theme of chefs' books and I mentioned a few. Elsa asked me about famous recipes and I explained that the concept had all been well exploited by today's marketers. I mentioned Kentucky Fried Chicken which contained only a mix of common seasonings, then went on to an account of Coca-Cola and the alleged "secret" formula that was kept in a safe and was known only to two people. I talked about the sauce on the Big Mac, which is really only Thousand Island dressing, then Elsa eased me out of the spotlight for a commercial break.

Larry Mortensen went into the hot seat next, but Elsa didn't give him a roasting; it was more of a "heat gently at very low temperature." Some TV interviewers would have torn him apart but she was surprisingly gentle — another contrast to the abrasive personality I had seen at the auction.

Elsa wrapped up with a couple of police comments about "pursuing valuable leads" and a promise to TV watchers that she would continue to follow this "fascinating real-life crime."

Television cameras don't move around; their subjects do. When we went dark for another commercial, Larry and I were whisked out of our chairs and replaced by a couple of local politicians and an engineer to discuss some problem in which the Mississippi River was threatening part of New Orleans. Elsa was focusing on the effect on the river's supply of seafood and what was being done about it.

Larry and I watched this from another corner of the studio but before this segment was over, he touched my arm and whispered, "I'm outta here. Sorry if I scared you back there. Maybe my method wasn't so good." Before I could tell him that — subject to a count of possible gray hairs which I didn't have yesterday — no harm was done, he was gone.

I stayed for the remainder of the program. Lights and chairs were being dragged into position for the next hour's startling revelations and the studio looked temporarily forlorn. Elsa exchanged a few words with a man with Rastafarian whiskers then caught sight of me. She came over. At close range, her makeup looked garish but exciting.

"Not a bad start on that story," she said breezily. "Let's hope there are more developments in the next few days."

"Just no more murders," I said fervently.

She nodded but I didn't think her heart was in it. "Well, I'm glad you came," she said. "Your contribution to the program was great."

"Good," I said. "I stayed on mainly to ask you one question."

She smiled brightly. "What's that?"

"When I went into Gambrinus's office and found that body there, you were just leaving. How long were you there and what did you see?"

chapter eight

While I had been watching the argument over the Mississippi River and its fish, my thoughts had been straying to the imbroglio in which I was caught. A bold stroke was needed if I was going to achieve any progress and make Lieutenant Delancey proud of me.

Someone had been in Gambrinus's office seconds before me, I was convinced of that. I had heard a door slam and that door led to an alley and a quick escape. Had that person been the murderer? It was not certain but that person had not waited to be caught in the same room with a dead man, whether they were innocent or guilty.

A point on which there could be no doubt was that Elsa Goddard had left the book auction all steamed-up to go to Gambrinus's shop. She had evidently not told the police this, which suggested a fear of being accused. So I settled on this bombshell tactic and stood waiting to see what her reply would be.

She was cool as ice. "What did I see? The question is what — or who — did *you* see? It couldn't have been me, I wasn't there."

How far did she want to carry this? I went a little further. "I just caught a glimpse of you leaving," I prevaricated. "You were in a great hurry — and no wonder! Found in a room with a recently deceased man! I presume you got the book?"

"I didn't kill him, and I didn't get the book." Just in time, she remembered to add, "— And I wasn't there."

"So who did kill him and get the book? If we assume it wasn't you?"

"I don't know." She paused then said, "You haven't told the police about this wild idea of yours. Why not?"

"Lieutenant Delancey and I are working both sides of the street on this." I thought I had heard that expression on television once and it sounded appropriate now. I hoped I was using it in the right context so I added, with an undertone of pomposity, "He's pursuing some lines of investigation and I'm pursuing others."

Her eyes narrowed. "You're working with the police?"

"Within my limited capacity," I said modestly.

That didn't intimidate her — she wasn't

the type to be intimidated by anything less than a starving tribe of cannibals. She did regard me with a little more respect but she wasn't going to let go easily. She said, "How do I know you're telling me the truth?"

"Ask the lieutenant."

She looked as if she had every intention of doing so but her voice was sharp as she asked, "How are you so sure it was me?"

"Your perfume," I said.

"I don't believe I was wearing perfume that day, I —" She stopped.

"It doesn't matter. Just tell me about it — and let me say I don't think you killed Mortensen."

"I heard the front doorbell and I thought you were the murderer coming back," she said, and her voice was normal now. "I wanted to stay and get the story but the body had a bullet hole in the chest and I didn't want to be caught by the murderer."

"What did you find when you came into Gambrinus's office?"

"Must have been exactly the same you found; you were only a couple of minutes after me. I had time to see him, realize he was dead. I looked over his desk to see if the book was there. I couldn't see it, then I heard the door — that must have been you."

It sounded reasonable and I had been telling the truth when I said I didn't think she had done the shooting. Television personalities are not above murder but she didn't seem likely to kill for a book. Unless there was something else. That called for another question.

"Did you know Gambrinus?"

"No, I didn't."

"How about Richie Mortensen?"

"No, neither of them. I assumed it was Gambrinus when I saw the body. I hid in the alley for a few minutes, not knowing if you were the killer. Then the police began arriving. I didn't want to appear on the scene too soon so I didn't show up until enough time had elapsed that it wouldn't look suspicious."

"How did you meet Larry?"

She smiled. She looked quite human despite the heavy makeup. "He accused me of killing his brother."

"You, too?" I returned her smile.

"It seems to be his investigational technique. He accuses everyone."

"Do you have any thoughts on what happened to the book?" I asked.

"No. Oh, I didn't go to the auction to buy it for myself. I went on behalf of a group, they wanted —"

"You mean the Witches." I nodded and she stared.

"You know about them?" she said, genuinely surprised.

"Oh, yes, we know," I said in an off-handed way, shamelessly allying myself with the New Orleans Police Department.

She eyed me, obviously wondering how much else I knew. In my turn, I wondered how much more she knew that I didn't. I waited to see where else this trail might lead, but she didn't offer any help.

"Is there anyone else who might want the book?" I asked her. "Enough to kill for it?"

She seemed about to answer but thought better of whatever she was going to say and instead said, "It could be valuable enough that a number of people would be after it."

"Because of its intrinsic value? Surely not."

"There could be . . . something else."

"Such as what?" I asked.

"One of the recipes?"

I tried to analyze how much importance she attached to this idea. "Seems a bit far-fetched, doesn't it?"

She shrugged. "Maybe."

"Are you going to follow this up?" I asked her.

She nodded vigorously and her blonde

hair, though not long, danced a little. "The book is still a good story — it has to be when it involves one of the greatest names in New Orleans cuisine."

"Exclusively?"

"Oh, no, I always have lots of stories going. This one isn't likely to bring developments every day so I'll probably come back to it every two or three days. I'll keep that up as long as it's still live."

I nodded, waiting for her to show some spirit of cooperation in that endeavor, but she only gave me her professional smile. It was obvious that she'd like to know anything I found out, but I didn't intend to reciprocate.

"Well, good luck," I told her.

"Tell me one thing . . ." Her voice was unusually moderated.

"What is it?"

"Have you been to St. Cynthia?"

"Who?" I was baffled by the question.

She studied me, looking for signs of concealment. She evidently didn't see any. "No, I guess you haven't."

"Who is she and why —"

She was already talking over my question. "It doesn't matter. You can find your own way out, can't you?"

I could and did.

★ ★ ★

I was ready for some sustenance after the morning's excitement and it was approaching lunchtime. I dug into my pockets and came up with the cards I had been given by the Witches. One of the first that came to hand said VILLA ROMANA, and had the name of Della Forlani, one of my erstwhile kidnappers.

It was on the edge of the French Quarter and the cab ride was uneventful — no pursuers, tails or gumshoes. It was a little disappointing, really, to be forgotten already.

A drunk was singing "New York, New York" in a karaoke bar as I walked past the open door, and a few thin streams of tourists sauntered about. A man on a street corner was hawking packets of red beans and rice, and across the street a bearded, haggard young man was playing something mournful on a saxophone. It sounded like Hoagy Carmichael.

A lunch counter had a sign in the window, EAT LOUISIANA OYSTERS AND LOVE LONGER, and the Villa Romana was just past it, a pleasant building with green shutters and a wrought-iron balcony out in front above the entrance.

Della was in the restaurant, taking the first orders of the day, for it was still early.

She beamed at the sight of me. "So glad you could come. Would you like a table by the window?" Restaurants like to fill the window seats, as it makes the place look popular, and I wanted one so that I could watch the passing scene.

After giving her order to the kitchen, she came out with a young woman who took over as Della came and sat at my table. A glass of sparkling white wine appeared at my right hand. "Prosecco," I said, "one of my favorite wines."

She clapped her hands with glee. "Good, I hoped you'd like it." Then she became suddenly serious. "I hope we didn't give you palpitations when we — er, kidnapped you. I've suggested that we stop doing that, but I'm outnumbered."

"After the first few uncertain moments, it was all right," I said. "Gives me something unusual to talk about back home. I may be the only person in my circle of friends who has ever been kidnapped. I'll be the envy of Hammersmith."

"In the meantime, you're pursuing the book?"

"Absolutely. You wouldn't have seen me — Oh, no, of course, you couldn't, it was taped and will be shown tonight."

She was frowning.

"Elsa," I explained. "I went to talk to her and found myself on her TV show."

"Ah, she's a real dynamo, isn't she?"

"She certainly is."

"So what would you like for lunch?" she asked.

"First of all, tell me why an Italian restaurant in New Orleans of all places."

"But that's exactly why, don't you see?" She became enthusiastic in talking about her restaurant. I liked to see her that way. "It's all Cajun and Creole. They have French origins so I thought, Italian cooking is not enormously different and, besides, people might like a change of pace. So we offer great Italian dishes and also blends of Italian cooking with Creole and Cajun flavors."

"The best of all possible worlds," I nodded, "from the culinary viewpoint, anyway. Good thinking — how is it being received?"

"We've been in business four years and do better and better every year."

"That's great. Do you do the cooking?"

"I used to; now my husband does it — he's half Italian. I take care of the front of the house."

"I have a friend who says it's easy to be a chef," I told her, and her eyes widened as

111

she began to protest. But I went on: "He says all you have to do is combine the brain of a scientist with the heart of an artist, the ingenuity of a used-car salesman and the energy of a marathon runner."

She laughed merrily. "Anyway, what's for lunch?" I asked.

We discussed her offerings one by one, but for the first course I decided on the *ostriche appetitose*. "A few of our tourist customers want to be adventurous and order this because they think it's ostrich," Della said.

Ostriche is, in fact, Italian for "oysters" and she explained that a batter of breadcrumbs, garlic, pepper, parsley and thyme is used to cover the oysters in their shells. Their own juice carefully preserved, they are then moistened with a drop or two of olive oil, cooked on a hot grill and served with lemon.

I had eaten a similar oyster dish in Emilia-Romagna on an Italian assignment and I was sure that Della's enthusiasm would make this outstanding.

"Now for the next course —" she went on.

"Make this the main course, please," I asked her. "I know that any self-respecting Italian will have four or five courses for lunch, but I try to stay with three."

"All right," she smiled, "you must have our seafood Terrabona."

"You've got me there," I admitted. "I didn't think there were too many Italian dishes I wasn't familiar with, but you've found one already."

"I cheated. It's not strictly Italian. It's a New Orleans dish and was originated by Italians living here. Also, it's as traditionally Southern as you can get."

"Sounds terrific; tell me about it."

"It's catfish fillets, shrimp, crawfish tails and oysters. First, the catfish are bronzed in a hot skillet, then the shrimp are butterflied and bronzed under a broiler. The crawfish tails are coated with seasoned flour and deep-fried and the oysters are coated with a blend of seasonings and also deep-fried —"

"What seasonings?" I asked.

"Salt, pepper, onion powder, garlic powder, thyme, basil, oregano, cayenne and paprika."

"That's the New Orleans contribution, not Italian," I commented.

"Right. We serve it with red beans and rice."

"You refer to 'bronzing' — I suppose that's like blackening?"

"Yes, but using a spray of margarine to

113

cook in rather than lots of butter."

"You must have some pastas that are different from the standard Italian pastas," I said.

"We do," Della said. "We serve it Sicilian style, a cooking method that remains substantially the same as in Roman days. Fry lots of garlic in olive oil then add spaghetti already cooked al dente. We sprinkle chili peppers and Romano cheese and parsley on it."

"That's a very healthy way to cook it, too."

"Yes. Tell me, have you had redfish since you've been here?"

"No, I haven't," I admitted.

"It's a popular Gulf fish and you'll see it cooked lots of New Orleans ways. We cook it Italian style — dipped in seasoned flour, then egg and then seasoned breadcrumbs. The big difference is that the standard Italian breadcrumbs are too fine and you can't get the fillets crispy. You have to use the very coarse grade."

Trout Florentine was another dish popular in Italy but given a New Orleans twist here at the Villa Romana. Artichoke with garlic mayonnaise was yet another, and the plentiful supply of oysters had initiated a number of cross-cultural dishes — veal rolls stuffed with oysters and sausage was a good example.

My appetite was getting the better of me by now. "I think I'd better order," I told Della, and settled on the oysters she had described and then the seafood Terrabona.

"We have an excellent Gavi di Gavi if you like Italian wines."

"I wouldn't have any other kind," I told her.

chapter nine

"Just a small portion," I said firmly when Della pressed me to have one of their house specialties as a dessert. It came in a small cup and I slowly cut the spoon through the crunchy, crusty top and withdrew a spoonful. It was delicious — a slightly different version of the French crème brûlée, which also has a crusty top, or the Italian *panna cotta*, which does not. The texture was like silk on the tongue and the vanilla flavor was assertive, not the neutral taste we get used to in many ice creams.

"Is this a good time for you to make your report?" she asked, smiling.

"I talked to Larry Mortensen, Richie's brother," I told her. "He gave me a hard time at first, accused me of killing his brother."

"Goodness!" Her eyes rounded.

"He accused Elsa Goddard, too."

"He must have lost that argument."

"Ah, you know her well, I can see. Yes, I

think Elsa and I both convinced him of our innocence. He seems still bent on the vengeance trail, though."

"What about the Belvedere book?"

"We didn't get very far with that. We talked about the possibility of some family secret recipe. What do you think of that, from a professional point of view?"

Her features were not suitable for an expression of deep thought but she gave it a good shot. "It's possible, I suppose," she said at length. "But I'm not sure. If there were something else, it would be more likely."

"I agree. Trouble is . . . what?"

We batted that around without any conclusion and she said, "Well thanks for the report. I'll pass it along."

"Thank you for the meal. It was great. You deserve to be successful." The first and second courses had, in fact, been very good and I told Della she was achieving the blend of New Orleans cooking and Italian cooking with remarkable results.

"You'll have to come again and have our gumbo Milanese," she said. The twinkle in her eye led me to believe that she was kidding but she insisted she was serious. I had to suppose that the possibility of liaisons with the two cuisines was unlimited.

★ ★ ★

A thought was nagging at me as I was leaving. Had the farm-boy exile driving the cab been right, and we had been followed by another cab on the ride to the TV studio? In the first scary moments of being chased by a dead man with a gun, I had assumed that the pursuit had been a continuation of the cab incident. But that didn't make sense — Larry Mortensen could not have been following me because he had been scheduled to be in the studio for Elsa's show. Either the boy was wrong or someone else had been in that other cab.

The implications were not pleasant, and, anyway, another query was arising. If there was something in the Belvedere chef's book that made it vital to get a hold of, why hadn't someone already seen that entry? I thought back to the lawyer, Van Linn. Whose lawyer was he? Did he know more than he was telling me?

I phoned him. I expected a polite brush-off — nothing total, but at least stressing how busy he was, et cetera. I was surprised therefore when he agreed promptly. "I have an appointment in town in a couple of hours," he said. "We can meet before that, say in an hour. Let me see . . . there's a coffee shop near the Convention Center.

It's on Lee Circle and on the St. Charles streetcar line. It's called Minky's."

Understandably, I had to ask him to spell that. "I haven't thoroughly mastered the New Orleans language yet," I told him. I found the nearest streetcar stop, still disappointed that the car called Desire had been taken off the line. (It had not even been replaced by one called Passion or Ecstasy — possibly the result of some local religious influence.) The ride was pleasant and only a dollar and a quarter. We passed grand residences and rattled along oak-lined avenues. We passed a cemetery and I recalled that these play a major role among the city's sights. I supposed it was too early but I saw no vampire hunters, no wooden stakes or mallets and no rosary wavers.

Minky's was a quirky mixture of styles. To some extent, it resembled the coffeehouses of seventeenth-century Europe, catering to a few students, several locals and some tourists. A bakery in the back was sending out a stream of beignets, cakes, pastries, sugar pralines and fudge balls bigger than golf balls. Two girls were eating ice cream and a waitress was bringing an omelette to the next table. The powerful aroma of freshly brewed coffee overwhelmed all others.

The restaurant had both booths and tables but as it was early, both were available, so I took a booth and ordered a café au lait. I watched people come and go and was ordering a second coffee when Van Linn arrived. He looked smooth-faced and prosperous. He sniffed as he sat down. "Still drinking the chicory, I notice," he said, and I agreed.

He ordered coffee, specifying regular, and regarded me with just a little curiosity. "So," he said, "you have some progress to report?"

I hated to disappoint him so I didn't reply directly to the question. "Do you know there are other factions trying to get hold of the book?" I asked.

"Other book dealers? I wouldn't be surprised —"

"No, not book dealers. A group of women who call themselves 'the Witches,' for a start."

"Bah!" His face showed his reaction. "Women's-lib crackpots! Always complaining they're repressed and excluded. Want to sue every time they think they have been mistreated or overlooked or discriminated against or —"

"They must make good clients for you," I said slyly.

"I wouldn't represent them. Oh, they've asked me once or twice, but I turn them down. So they're after the book, are they? Do you know why?"

"They like the idea of the prestige of having it — they think it would enhance their image. Also, they say the secondary reason is its monetary value."

"Value to whom? You mean they just want to sell it and make a profit?" He snorted derisively. "I don't believe that for a minute." He eyed me keenly. "Are you sure they don't have any other reason?"

"Not that I'm aware."

"They must have." He drummed well-manicured fingers on the tabletop. "Anything else to tell me?"

"Yes. Richie Mortensen's brother is involved in this, too."

He frowned. "Involved how?"

"He's looking for his brother's killer. He accused me but I managed to persuade him otherwise. At least, I hope I did. I heard he's accused others, too, so I suppose he's not just focused on me."

"You've talked to him?"

"Yes, I have." I didn't think it necessary to go into details.

"Do you think he's looking for the book, too?"

"I didn't get that impression. He seemed mainly intent on avenging his brother's death."

Van Linn's coffee arrived. He stirred it but it must have been for thought-stimulating reasons because he didn't put anything in it. "Did you have something else you wanted to ask me?" He was sharp — but then I hadn't doubted that.

"You still don't want to tell me who your client is?"

The keenly disapproving expression on his face answered my question and I said quickly, "No, you don't — well, all right, but tell me this . . . Is there any possibility that it would help me find the book if I knew who your client is?"

"Wouldn't help you at all." He shook his well-groomed head firmly. "I'm quite sure of that."

"The person who spotted the book, realized its worth and got it into the auction — have you talked to that person?"

The question surprised him. "No, I haven't. Why — do you think they know anything?"

"Just a thought. It seems that between the time the book was found and its being put into the auction, someone must have looked at it and seen its contents."

"One of the people running the auction could put you in touch, I suppose." He drummed fingers at the side of his coffee cup. My question seemed to be raising thoughts that had not occurred to him. "Mrs. Gracewell, for instance."

"Good," I said, "I can try her."

I waited. He didn't appear to be forthcoming with any revelations and we chatted for a while longer without anything emerging of note. He excused himself to go to his other appointment and insisted on paying the bill.

"No Time Like the Present" was my motto of the moment. I phoned the Armorers' Hall; they gave the name of the organization that had run the book auction, and a few minutes later I was talking to Mrs. Gracewell. I did not identify myself but told her I was interested in contacting the person who had put the book into the auction.

"Perhaps you could tell me the reason for your interest," she said cautiously.

"I believe it would make a very good story," I said, and paused to give her time to draw the appropriate conclusion.

"Which magazine are you with?" she asked, and then saved me from prevarication by adding, "— Or are you freelance?"

"I'm freelance," I said, "but there is interest from several quarters."

"I see. That's fine, then. Enid Pargeter is the lady you should talk to." She gave me the address.

On the way to it, I was still mulling over my talk with Van Linn. It seemed fairly obvious that he was the Belvedere family lawyer so it followed that he would be representing the family in this matter. I wondered why he didn't want to say so. Keeping the name of a client confidential was a theme of many of the private detective stories I had read; Van Linn was a lawyer, though. I knew they had the same rule, but under these circumstances, surely it wasn't that critical to keep silent?

Enid Pargeter was a slim, willowy woman, probably in her forties, and with a charming and graceful attitude. She was widowed three years ago, she told me, and had moved into this apartment building a year later. It was in a quiet neighborhood with a park across the street where she walked her dog twice a day. Elmer, she called him. He was a large terrier, blended from various origins, an indeterminate shade of brown in color. He sat by the television and regarded me with a tolerant but not too curious air.

"I've been fascinated by books all my life," she told me. "Still have a lot of them, as you can see." She did indeed have them spread in several different locations, on shelves and racks, in bookcases, on tables. A few were new but most were not. At a glance, they represented a variety of tastes, ranging from current affairs to history to biography to art to travel, with a fair representation of mysteries and romance novels.

I used Mrs. Gracewell's name liberally and Enid said, "You seem to know her very well."

"I would like to think so," I said and came to the point quickly. "As a matter of fact, when I was talking to her a short while ago, she agreed what a good topic this is for a magazine article. The connection with a well-known restaurant with so many years of serving New Orleans —"

"Oh, I agree, too, absolutely. Well, you can imagine how surprised I was to come across the Belvedere book —"

"Just how did that happen?"

"I've been an avid book-buyer for years — just for my own satisfaction, you understand. So when a committee was set up to collect books for this auction, I was happy to volunteer — I saw it as a labor of love."

"Have you done this before?" I asked.

"Oh, the committee was set up four years ago and I've done it every year since. I'm pretty good at it now and several people know me and offer books — collections sometimes and private libraries, even. In addition, I scrape around — library cast-offs, bookshops' can't-sells, charity shops' overstocks . . ." She beamed proudly. "I know all the sources."

"You certainly do. Tell me, did you know the source of the Belvedere book?"

"I've had books from him before, so yes, I did."

I was closing in now and had to word my questions carefully. "Just the one book, was it?"

"Goodness, no. Two large boxes — and I mean *large*. I couldn't lift them in or out of the van."

"You collect the books yourself, do you?" I asked her.

"Oh, yes. I had to have them loaded in the van for me."

"Who donated the books?"

"He gives to several charities but likes to remain anonymous."

"His secret is safe with me," I said, hoping that I would be able to hold to that. "Is he a collector?" I added casually.

"He's a bookbinder. Of course, he loves

books, too. Well, in that business, he'd have to, wouldn't he? He gets in masses of books, he uses bindings off old books, restores them and puts them on other books — oh, he's a real artisan of the old school, very few like him around anymore."

I agreed wholeheartedly. "So after you got these boxes back here —"

"I had to have young Erwin from next door bring them in for me."

"Yes, and then you went through them to pick out the ones worth putting in the auction."

"That's right. It was quite a thrill to find a book by one of our famous local chefs."

I noted that she said "*a* book" — she didn't say "*the* book." "Did you know it was a valuable book?"

"Why, no, I had no idea. I certainly didn't know that someone would kill to get it. I heard that on the television news." She regarded me with some doubt. "Don't you think they're wrong there? That wasn't the real reason for the murder, don't you agree?"

"You may be right."

We talked a while longer, first about the auction, then about books in general. I commented on several photographs on the walls showing a distinguished-looking man, who turned out to be her late husband and she talked about him. The two of them had shared a love of books and he had been the president of the Southern branch of the National Publishers Association. She was proud of his accomplishments in that position and showed me a framed certificate of achievement awarded him by the association. She went on to talk about her dog, Elmer, named after Mrs. Pargeter's favorite cousin who had died only recently in St. Paul. Elmer came across, wagged his tail and waited to be patted on hearing his name.

I didn't want to place any conversational emphasis on the bookbinder who had given her the book, as it should have been easy enough to find him in the yellow pages. There were only two of them and one was a business run by two sisters. That left only a Herman Harburg. His address was in the Riverbend area of New Orleans, just up the Mississippi River from the French Quarter. Folks with money evidently lived here, for there were some charming houses. But they rubbed shoulders with apartments where students lived.

I saw signs for artists' studios as well as bars, restaurants and "music clubs" and among these was a row of small cottages next to several Victorian shotgun houses. One of the cottages had a brass plate that read, HERMAN HARBURG, BOOKBINDER, on an old hand-carved wooden door. I banged on the brass doorknocker twice with no result so I walked around to the back. An addition had been built onto the cottage, an awkward-looking extension that must have been practical because it certainly wasn't aesthetic.

Another handmade wooden door was there though not nearly as elaborate as at the front. Knocking brought no response here, either. I tried the knob and the door was open. I called out Harburg's name but could hear no reply. I went in.

This added structure was a workshop and had all the materials that might be expected in a bookbinder's — stocks of paper of all kinds, pots of inks and glues, packs of cardboard and thin sheets of leather. This was a dying art, I knew, and only a handful of craftsmen, mostly from Europe, still plied the trade. That Herman Harburg was one of those, I had no doubt, and the conviction was re-inforced by the various pieces of equipment. They were old, built of iron, well-used but still serviceable — printing presses, guillo-tines, collators, stackers and binders.

The walls were hung with examples of Herman Harburg's work, covers, first sheets, spines, letters describing satisfaction with a difficult rebinding job, certificates and diplomas that were brown with age and curling at the corners.

I called Harburg's name again but still there was no response. I looked around more carefully and noticed a door set flush into one wall that I had not noticed before. I knocked without expectation of any reply. There was none. I tried the door and it was locked. A shelf nearby had several old iron tools on it and I moved one aside — sure enough, behind it was a key. It was the old-fashioned kind and so was the door lock. I tried it, it fitted and I went in.

The small room was equipped like a draftsman's office before they became computerized. Tilted drafting tables, bright spotlights, a glass-topped bench with lighting underneath, shelves with ink bottles and racks full of pens and engraving tools. A tiny electric furnace was in one corner and beside it were two ceramic crucibles in stands and a stack of small shiny metal ingots.

I looked over the benches. Sheets of paper, some new but mostly old. Several books, all with different bindings, again some new and some old.

Somewhere, a door banged. I hastily exited, locked the door and put the key back. I just had time to be standing, looking idle, when in came a figure.

chapter ten

I rode the St. Charles streetcar line back into town, my head buzzing with conflicting thoughts. I had had at the back of my mind the nasty idea that I might be about to find another body. Two in a row would be hard to explain, even to a cop as friendly as Lieutenant Patrick Delancey.

It was Herman Harburg who had almost caught me in his inner sanctum. A small, frail man with wispy, gray hair who was probably close to eighty, he moved with a little difficulty, probably due to arthritis, but his mind was alert. He was none too pleased at my intrusion.

"I go over to my neighbor's and come back finding you in my workshop!"

I apologized as profusely as I knew how, tossing in the names of Mrs. Gracewell and Mrs. Pargeter and referring to the charity book auction. I managed to convey the impression that I knew both ladies well and was closely connected with the auction committee. He was partly placated but I saw his eyes stray to the door to his other room. He seemed to be satisfied to see it still locked.

I began to explain why I was there and he was shaking his head long before I had finished.

"Bookbinding is my business. I get lotsa books — all kindsa people." His words were German-accented, the softer German, probably of Bavaria. "Sometimes I look at names of books but not much. This time, I gotta lotta work. I didn't look, just called Mrs. Pargeter to come get 'em."

"You might have noticed this book," I told him. "I don't know exactly what it looks like but it was a chef's book — the kind a chef writes recipes in — so it might look different from all the other books."

He shook his head resolutely. "Didn't see it. No, sir. Didn't look at all. Nothing like that."

He hadn't been inclined to small talk and he didn't even want to talk about bookbinding, which had to be a passion with him as well as a vocation. He just wanted to get me out as fast as possible.

The streetcar squeaked to a stop and we scooped in a few more passengers. I returned to my cascading thoughts. I was relieved at not finding a dead body, but the live one I had found was giving me a lot of reason for conjecture.

A bookbinder he might be, and probably a very experienced and able one.

He was also a forger.

I had no doubt on that score. Everything in that inner room pointed to it. No wonder it had an inconspicuous door and was kept locked. The key was not in the cleverest hiding place but it looked as if he seldom allowed anyone access to it. The paper, the books, the furnace and the metal for casting type on a small scale — all indicated a cozy little forging operation.

Nothing ambitious like hundred-dollar bills or bearer bonds. Herman did it on a scale that would merit little investigation even if any suspicion were aroused. That was unlikely, too; an expert might spot the difference between a genuine Edgar Allan Poe and a forgery but how many people — even book lovers — could tell a forgery of say, P. G. Wodehouse? Many of his titles I knew to be worth ten to twenty thousand dollars, while early copies, not even first editions, of Agatha Christie or Conan Doyle could bring much more than that.

Forging books was a safer proposition, as it didn't provoke investigation by the Treasury Department as did the reproduction of currency or bonds. Herman looked like the kind of man who would want to minimize the risk of scrutiny from authorities.

So why was a book forger involved here? To produce a copy of the Belvedere chef's book seemed to be the obvious answer — but why was a copy put into a charity auction? There was no profit in that. That puzzled me but, setting it aside for the moment, it meant that if Richie Mortensen's murderer had taken the book that Mortensen had bought at the auction — he had a forgery in his hands! Another question was, what had Herman Harburg used to copy from? The original and genuine Belvedere book? If so, where was it now?

We bounced over a non-uniform section of track. My brain needed shaking up after all these questions but it didn't help much. I decided I needed mental stimulation, and that meant food.

I took the St. Charles streetcar into town as far as it went. That was Canal Street where it U-turns and comes back. I walked back to the Monteleone along Royal Street.

The lobby was busy as always, the overstuffed couches were full of people. Stacks of luggage awaited removal and guests were browsing in the glass-fronted cabinets.

Electronic door keys in hotels have made the old practice of stopping by the front desk obsolete and I was heading for the elevator when a figure came up beside me.

"Why, Lieutenant Delancey! What a coincidence!"

We shook hands.

"Nah, not really," he said. He still had that look that was on the edge of rumpled. His eyes looked tired, but then they always did, it seemed. His hair was not untidy but its acquaintance with a brush or comb was fleeting at best. "I figured you'd be here about this time, getting spruced-up to go out to dinner at one of our celebrated spots."

"You're right," I said, "I am. But you wanted to chat."

The lobby was not only busy but getting busier so we went into the Oyster Bar adjoining and ordered coffee. "I'm glad you're here," I said. "I have an interesting development to report." I told him of the visit to Herman Harburg while minimizing my information-gathering talks with Mrs. Gracewell and Miss Pargeter. From previous experience, I knew that the police get annoyed at private citizens acting in a way that leads others to jump to false conclusions. If they get extreme about it, the police

136

call it "impersonating a police officer."

"Interesting," he murmured. "Didn't leave any broken locks or anything like that behind you, did you?"

I was appalled. "Of course not! I didn't break in or even pick any locks."

He nodded affably. "Know how to get in without that, do you?"

"I've read about it," I conceded. "They do it with a library card, don't they?"

"Credit card, the way I heard it."

"Oh yes, American Express, isn't it?"

"I don't think it makes a lot of difference."

"Oh, really? I'll have to remember that —" I caught his expression and added hastily, "— in case I ever get trapped in a locked room."

"Wouldn't work from the inside. You gotta read more books." He shifted his position. He was one of those people who never look comfortable in a chair. "So you think this guy Harburg forged a copy of the real Belvedere book?"

"I do, yes."

"So where's the real copy?"

"That still puzzles me. Of course, Harburg wouldn't have to have an original in order to make a phony."

"That's true, I suppose —"

137

"But it does raise a further point," I said. "Unless Harburg is a connoisseur of food, he would be unlikely to know what to put in the forgery to make it convincing."

The lieutenant nodded. "Meaning that whoever commissioned him to make the copy must know plenty about food."

"Exactly. Of course, that doesn't help a lot in this city — there are plenty of people like that. Have you been making progress?"

He sighed. "Not enough. We've been checking out this Larry Mortensen. Seems he's been rooming with his brother for the past few weeks so that raises the possibility that the two of them were involved in some scam. It's a ratty sort of place they live in and neither seems to have either money or income — and that means motive to make money."

"Does either of them have any police record?"

"No, they're clean."

"What about Gambrinus?"

"Don't have anything on him. We're combing the other bookshops in the city but no sign of the book. Ballistics didn't come up with anything useful, either. It was a nine-millimeter automatic, one of those small foreign jobs, probably made in Eastern Europe." He gave me a searching look. "So what's your next line of investigating?"

"I'm keeping in touch with the Witches —"

"The Witches . . . Oh yeah, those women's-lib broads."

"They're all in the restaurant business so they might hear things. They wanted the book in the first place so they have a stake in this."

He nodded though he didn't look as if he expected great results from this approach. I decided this was a good time to butter him up a little. "I must say, Lieutenant, that I appreciate your liberal attitude on this, I mean, letting me help in the investigation."

"Ahh," he said, "good way to keep an eye on you." There was almost a grin there. "Anyway, I never could understand why Lestrade didn't accept Holmes's brilliance and make more use of him to further his career. Then, too, why didn't Inspector Cramer accept that Nero Wolfe was a genius and just tag along with him instead of always trying to jail him?"

"Is that what you're doing with me?" I asked. "Making use of my brilliance and genius?"

He shifted in the chair again. It was comment enough. "After all," he went on, "John F.-X. Markham, the New York DA, not only grabbed on to Philo Vance's coattails and hung on, they were buddies. Even had breakfast together —"

"Fillet of white perch, tied with silk cord, dipped in batter, rolled in chopped almonds and sautéed in butter," I contributed.

"Yeah, I guess you would remember that. I remember the murder methods."

"You astonish me, Lieutenant. Not many real detectives read about fictitious ones."

I recalled his previous comment, about a "labor of Sisyphus." He was an unusual detective. "How are the law studies coming along?" I asked.

"Okay. I'm on schedule. I'm on torts now. Used to think they were something to eat." He rose to his feet. "Gotta get along."

"You going to do anything about Harburg?"

"I'm in Homicide, not Forgery — and the T-men have got enough on their plates without tossing a cookbook onto one of 'em. Still, I need to know who hired him to forge the book."

I showered, then, while I dressed, watched part of a cop show on television but there was too much violence for it to be real. I took a taxi to the Café Cajun where Emmy Lou Charbonneau welcomed me. "Was hoping you'd come," she said warmly. She looked delightful in a trim blue dress that avoided ostentation but had a distinct flair. Her brown hair and brown eyes were almost the same color, I saw now, and her complexion was smooth and feminine.

The restaurant had something of the intimate style of a Parisian sidewalk café, perhaps the kind that is more of a brasserie. Large black-and-white photographs on the walls depicted the New Orleans of the past and the red-and-white-checked tablecloths added to that impression. Tables were close together but that only helped the intimate atmosphere, and the noise level was tolerable.

It was early and seating was not a problem. "How about a New Orleans cocktail?" Emmy Lou asked.

"What do you recommend?"

"Sazerac? Ramos gin fizz? Mint julep?"

"Do people still drink mint juleps? I had the impression they went out with Scarlett O'Hara."

"A few ask for them."

"Tourists, you mean?"

"We try to call them 'visitors,' " she said with her gentle smile.

I settled on a gin fizz and Emmy Lou sat with me after she put it on the table. "If it's named Ramos, it must have a story behind it."

"Oh, it does," she assured me. "Henry Ramos came to New Orleans in 1888 and opened the Imperial Cabinet Saloon. This gin fizz was his specialty and it made him so famous that he had to sell the saloon and buy a bigger place. They say that during the Mardi Gras of 1915, he had thirty-five bartenders making this drink and the lines were out into the street, day and night."

"You still make it the same way?"

"Certainly. Mix the white of an egg with an ounce of heavy cream, the juice of half a lemon, the juice of half a lime, two ounces of gin, and fill up with soda water. It needs shaking for at least three minutes to get this consistency."

I looked at it — it was thick. "Everybody makes it pretty much the same way?"

"Pretty much, yes. Some put in a few drops of vanilla extract, some add a few drops of orange flower water. We don't use either."

I tasted. It was delicious. The gin fizz used to be popular in England but its popularity has declined. As I recalled, it was very similar to Henry Ramos's drink but the heavy cream and considerable shaking made the latter richer and thicker.

She seemed inclined to chat so I asked, "Tell me about Cajun cooking."

"I'd be glad to — but first, let's talk about the Belvedere cookbook and the murder."

chapter eleven

I tried not to look startled and the best way to do that was to have another sip of the luxuriously rich gin fizz. I hoped it gave me the right air of nonchalance. "What do you want to know?" I asked in my best impersonation of Lord Peter Wimsey.

"It's not what I want to know — it's what I want to tell you."

That surprised me, too, and I looked more carefully at the quiet, brown-eyed, brown-haired girl who had lured me into the limousine and into the Witches' den. She sat there, demure as could be, hands clasped in front of her and leaning across the table to look at me intently.

"I will admit that progress in the case is not as rapid as it could be," I told her. "Consequently, anything that you can tell me could be helpful, even important."

"I'm sure that you got the impression when we — er, kidnapped you that we have a number of very talented women in the Witches."

"Yes indeed, I certainly did get that impression."

"Not only talented but successful."

"You would all have to be," I concurred. "I've spent enough time working in restaurants to know what a tough profession it can be."

"And to achieve a level of success, it's necessary to be determined and — at times — ruthless." Her tone was still conversational but I felt a touch of ice in these words. I had another sip of Henry Ramos's stimulating gin fizz. The direction her remarks were taking was becoming evident. It was not fully clear as yet but her final words had a sharp edge.

"Go on," I encouraged her.

"We've been talking, the girls and I —"

"Inevitable."

She smiled, showing her excellent white teeth. "Yes, we talk among ourselves a lot at all times, but now, with this happening, we talk a lot more. It's more serious, too, now that it involves murder."

I nodded. I sipped gin fizz and said nothing. Maybe that would bring her to the point.

"This isn't easy to say and I suppose I'm not doing it very well but, well, here it is . . . We think that one of the Witches is mixed up in this."

So there it was. No wonder she found it hard to say. They appeared to be a sociable and integrated group, all with a common goal, friends as well as part of the same service community. It would be hard to accept that one of them was . . . Was what? A murderer?

She must have seen in my expression some inkling of what I was thinking. "Perhaps not the murder," she said quickly. "Well, not directly, anyway, but at least the plan to steal the cookbook."

"What makes you think that?" I asked. Another sip of gin fizz was needed. This might turn out to be a three–gin fizz problem.

"It's hard to say. Nothing specific — though maybe one or more of us does know something specific and doesn't want to make it known," she said with an apologetic smile. "When a number of women discuss a topic, it can be hard to know exactly who is saying what or how certain subjects came up."

Either that was true, or suspicions had been voiced and Emmy Lou didn't want to clarify them. "Do you want to identify any of the Witches? Any that might be mixed up in this?"

"Not right now. It's too vague — but I

thought you should know."

"Anything else?" I asked her.

"Not at the moment," she said cautiously. "If more concrete evidence comes to light, I'll tell you." Her brown eyes searched my face intently. "You're working closely with the police, aren't you?"

"Very closely," I said confidently — for the sake of her confidence as well as mine. "Just left them, as a matter of fact."

"Do they tell you anything new?"

"Oh, I guess I'm supposed to give you a report, aren't I? Well, there may be forgeries of the Belvedere book around."

"Is it that valuable?" She sounded surprised.

"Maybe."

She caught that implication immediately. "You mean there could be another reason for wanting it?"

I repeated the "secret recipe" idea but she didn't look impressed. "I suppose that could be — I don't know. It is said to contain the famous oysters Belvedere recipe. What else could someone want it for?"

"I don't know, either — yet. But I'm working on it."

"Good, now I can come to your question about Cajun food." She sounded relieved that the difficult chore of receiving my report was over. "First, you know who Cajuns are?"

"Early French settlers, weren't they?"

"That's right. 'Acadians' originally, farmers from the south of France who emigrated to Nova Scotia in the early 1600s. They were driven out by the British a century later and made the long trek south to Louisiana. They settled along the bayous to the west of New Orleans and took up their traditional trades of farming, fishing and trapping.

"So they were accustomed to living off the land and they were adaptable at making use of whatever was there to cook and eat. They found the slaves cultivating okra which they had brought with them from Africa so the Acadians incorporated that into their cuisine. They eagerly took the peppers and spices that the Indians used and they kept their French roux and their French method of cooking everything the long, slow way. Being from the south of France, they tried to grow grapes but the soil and climate weren't suitable so they grew sugarcane instead."

"Fascinating," I said. "Now, tell me, how does Creole fit into this?'

"The French and Spanish took turns in governing Louisiana and were concentrated in New Orleans — their cuisines blended into one, and by the turn of the nineteenth century, that had become Creole cooking."

"Didn't some West Indian influence creep in there, too?"

"Into Creole cooking, yes, it did."

"But you prefer to specialize in Cajun?"

"Yes. Creole cooking has had a lot of exposure and lots of people outside of New Orleans cook that style. Cajun isn't as well known."

"Paul Prudhomme has done a good job promoting it, though."

She smiled. "He certainly has — his blackened redfish is one of the more famous Cajun dishes."

"Tell me about it."

"Fish from the Gulf of Mexico are coated in hot spices and then seared quickly on both sides in a very hot cast-iron pan. This blackens the skin and seals in the flavors, leaving the fish moist and tender."

"What's his secret?"

"Two secrets; the first is the spice mixture and the second is to have the pan extremely hot, much hotter than is usual in pan cooking."

"Do you cook this?"

"Oh, yes, it's become a part of New Orleans cuisine. Customers would ask for it if it weren't on the menu."

"And the secret of the spices?" I pressed her.

She smiled again. "Ah, the spices! We use a mixture of garlic, paprika, cayenne pepper, chili powder, celery powder, onion, basil, oregano, marjoram and salt and black pepper. Every chef here uses these basically. The proportions vary only slightly."

"The cooking itself is very simple, isn't it?"

"All Cajun dishes are. Some people think that for a dish to be good, it has to be complicated. Cajun cooking has disproved that. We tended to forget that the early Cajuns — Acadians — were very simple people. They lived off the land and spent virtually all their days getting food either by hunting or trapping or fishing and then spent the rest of the day cooking it."

She sounded passionate on the subject and I told her so. Her brown eyes glowed with pleasure and she went on. "It's such a shame to lose the beauty of Cajun dishes by adding powdered onions or powdered garlic — they taste of chemicals. And you can't use commercial blends of herbs — you have to mix your own. What's the point in taking the trouble to find fresh fish if you're going to spoil it by using powdered and dried ingredients?"

She stopped abruptly. "Enough! You want to eat, don't you?"

"I have to admit that you've got my taste buds quivering for Cajun food," I said. "Now what's really, typically Cajun?"

"Well, I suppose you should start with a gumbo." She was emphatic, didn't hesitate a second.

"I've had gumbo a few times," I said. "The last time was in Florida."

"Florida! Pah! They can't make gumbo in Florida!"

"How do you make it?"

"There are basically two types," she told me. "Okra gumbo and filé gumbo. Okra is used for flavoring and for thickening both. Filé is ground sassafras; this does both of those two but it also darkens and enriches. Many chefs use only one or the other but we often use them together."

"Right, I'll start with a gumbo. Is it always seafood based?"

"Good heavens, no! We use alligator, rabbit, raccoon — depending on what we're able to buy."

"You're kidding! Do people eat those?"

"Tourists — visitors — love to go home and say they ate alligator gumbo," she giggled. "Beef, chicken, veal, turtle, ham too, of course — and oysters by the ton."

"What's on today? Anything exotic?"

"Oh, you're adventurous? That's good but I'm sorry to say today's choice is limited to mixed seafood or oysters."

"Okay, I'll take the oyster gumbo."

"Good choice. Now, for the next course — take a look at the menu." She handed me one, it had large cardboard sheets of a yellowing color that looked convincingly antique and was printed with elaborate curlicued lettering. The dishes included Crawfish Pie, Speckled Trout in Rum, Fish Stuffed with Rice and Pecans, Cajun Chicken with Yams, Meatloaf Abbeville, Jambalaya with Andouille Sausage. "And today," said Emmy Lou, "we have Smothered Quail."

"You'll have to explain that one," I told her. "The society for the protection of birds might object to that technique."

She smiled. "Smothering is a New Orleans technique of cooking. It's really braising, first quickly and at high heat then very, very slowly for a long time at very low heat."

"Just my style," I said. "It's rare these days to find slow food. I'm sorry to say fast food has outstripped it."

"Good choice." She rose to her feet. "I'll

pass your order to the kitchen. Another gin fizz?"

"I believe so."

With the gin fizz, Emmy Lou brought me some Cajun Paté. It was different from most French patés, more like Jewish chopped liver. Thyme, bay leaf and Tabasco sauce gave it a savory taste and with it came Melba toast strips.

The oyster gumbo was excellent, the oysters just beginning to curl at the edges and there had been no skimping on the oyster liquor. Regular onions as well as green onions and chopped green peppers swarm in the gumbo. At the table, a little rice was spooned into the serving bowl, the oysters were placed on that and the gumbo ladled over them. I knew that it was standard to use three kinds of pepper in the cooking — red, white and black.

The smothered quail was more than up to expectation. The cooking technique had brought out sweet, subtle flavors in a way that no other method could match. The gravy was naturally thick and far superior to the usual prepared gravy. With it, I had a side dish of red beans and rice, another Cajun specialty.

Emmy Lou came to the table afterward

and pulled up a chair. "Louisiana is sugar-cane country," she said, "so we have wonderful raw sugar that we can make use of — pecan pie, bread pudding, chocolate fudge cake and calas are the most popular Cajun desserts."

"What is that last one? I don't think I know it."

"Calas are rice fritters, made with sugar and eggs."

"I'd better try those."

I did, they were tender and sweet, and their golden-brown color made them very appealing.

I congratulated Emmy Lou on a superb meal and she glowed with pride. As I finished my thick black coffee — with chicory, of course — and said good-bye to her, I could not help wondering how much more she knew than she had told me. If she didn't know more, she — and perhaps some of her fellow Witches — had suspicions. Were they too loyal to voice them?

chapter twelve

On the way back to the hotel, I found myself periodically assailed by strains of jazz spilling out on to the sidewalk. Some of it was down-home traditional Dixieland stuff, some if had to be more R&B but there was also what sounded, to my not-well-accustomed ear, like the cutting-edge contemporary variety. As New Orleans was claimed to be the birthplace of jazz, I had to do a little sampling.

Funky Butt's on Rampart Street was the first to bring me in and I stood at the bar nursing a beer while a cornet player blew his heart out. Jason Marsalis, youngest member of the talented musical family, came on then with a vibraphone, an instrument I didn't recall seeing since Ritz Brothers movies.

Down near the river, the Dragon's Den enticed me with its unusual location above a Thai restaurant. An Eastern theme prevailed and it looked as if it was pretending to be a turn-of-the-century opium den.

When I finally got back to the Hotel

Monteleone, it was after midnight but it was as busy as midday. Cars were arriving and leaving, limos were gliding to and fro — although none drew me in — and people were gathered in knots and groups in the lobby and outside.

A saxophone wailed somewhere — do saxophones ever do anything but wail? A woman plaintively waved a sign for a tour group, looking like a Bo-Peep who had lost her flock. A man in an old gray suit and a straw hat was handing out leaflets and a couple swayed, hanging on to each other for stability.

The man with the leaflets thrust one at me and I shook my head. I had to sidestep a quartet arguing over their destination for the evening and there he was again — the man with the leaflets. This time, he pushed one into my hand before I could refuse.

I maneuvered my way into the lobby and walked across to the bank of elevators. The lobby, too, was busy and all the elevators were on other floors. Someone ahead of me was impatiently pressing the button so I waited. Idly I glanced at the leaflet. Then it grabbed my full attention and I read it carefully twice. An elevator came, emptied, refilled and departed. I think another came but I was intent on the leaflet.

BE ON THE DELTA DUCHESS
10 A.M. SAILING
TOMORROW WEDNESDAY
TOULOUSE STREET WHARF
IF YOU WANT THE BOOK

I turned the sheet over. The other side was blank. I hurried back outside and most of the same characters were still there, with one exception — there was no sign of the man handing out the leaflets. I read it again. It was crudely printed in block capitals. I tried to remember the face of the man who had handed it me but all I had was a vague impression of an elderly, nondescript face.

I breakfasted on Texas grapefruit, two eggs over-easy, bacon, sausage and grits with two cups of well-chicoried coffee; I needed fortification for whatever the morning ahead was going to bring. I arrived at the wharf to stand in line and buy a ticket for the *Delta Duchess.*

Two hundred feet long, carrying over a thousand people, the paddlewheel alone weighs nineteen tons — how could I be unable to find a vessel that size? The lady who sold me the ticket said the *Duchess* was moored behind the Aquarium but all I could find there was the Mississippi River. I tracked down a portly young woman in a semi–police uniform and with a formidable-looking revolver in a bulging holster on her belt. "The *Delta Duchess*?" she said. "You'll find her in front of the Imax theater." I walked to the theater but again, no boat. I was at the stage now of calling her a boat when I know they liked to be called ships.

A young woman in the ticket booth at the theater said she thought I might find the *Duchess* "farther up." This was not any nautical term I was familiar with but I assumed she meant farther up the river. The twists and curls of the Mississippi make it impossible to see which way is up, but there was a paddlewheeler tied up by Abercrombie and Fitch's store and I walked close enough to see the name.

At last! She looked magnificent. The scene was like one from a hundred years ago — a giant behemoth from the past, tall as six stories, with flower-bedecked balconies, gingerbread trim and feathery-crowned smokestacks. I recalled seeing an impressive display of information on this and other vessels in the lobby at the Monteleone. Harbor cruises, river cruises, gambling cruises, dinner cruises, jazz cruises, dancing cruises, as well as others visiting plantations, battlefields and zoos — all were on offer. The gambling cruises seemed to be an exception in that they never left the dock. Presumably, gamblers don't like to be confined.

All the others left the dock, though, some for two hours, some for half a day, others for the evening and some for three or four days.

The crew were all in smart white uniforms with blue piping though I looked in vain for cigar-chomping card sharks and a fiery Ava Gardner trying hard to hide her Creole origins. All the passengers stayed on deck as the steam whistle hooted and the vessel throbbed as the engines came to vibrant life. Orders were shouted, warnings against falling overboard were given out, lines were cast loose and we pulled away from the wharf. We leaned on the rails and waved good-bye to loved ones we might never see again — well, it didn't take a lot of imagination to make that mental adjustment. The PA system belted out "Ol' Man River" just to help us and, on the Promenade Deck, a steam calliope was happily piping out other tunes from *Showboat* through several dozen brass pipes.

I wandered around inside. The bars were open and a piano player was rolling his way through some soft jazz. Slot machines outnumbered passengers ten to one and dining rooms had window views of the river. We sailed blithely along, getting farther and farther away from the coast though still able to enjoy its endless panorama while the engines throbbed their faint but reassuring vibration.

The decor, I presumed, was that known as Steamboat Gothic and perhaps for the first time I could appreciate Mark Twain's comment that "when I was a boy, I had but one permanent ambition — that was to be a steamboat man." Outside, Stars and Stripes fluttered everywhere, shiny brasswork glistened in the occasional sunbeam, and wandering minstrel groups played mostly jazz. Inside, cut-glass doors and huge chandeliers sparkled like showers of raindrops while the parquet wood floors gave a comfortable homey feeling.

Now that we were "under way," as we seafarers put it, I was able to give some thought to why I was here, especially as it entailed the next step. I viewed everyone on the vessel as a potential writer of the note that had "invited" me aboard but no one accosted me. I went back on deck where a number of passengers were taking photographs and using binoculars to spot landmarks. About a dozen cameras clicked away furiously in the hands of a Japanese contingent and I heard smatterings of Swedish from another group. Accents from all four corners of the United States contributed to a constant background.

We pulsed along. A half hour had passed and this was a two-and-a-half-hour cruise. I made myself available to being accosted on all the decks, in all the lounges and bars and rooms. I alternated between the inside and the outside. I loitered by every bank of slot machines. A weak sun was doing its best and the only breeze was that generated by the boat's passage so it was pleasant on deck.

I did not expect to see such bustling activity on the Mississippi. Ships were everywhere, ships of all kinds. Tiny tugboats were heroically pushing long vessels, deep in the water, their decks crowded with long, green cylinders. Oyster dredgers, oil tankers, Liberty ships taking grain to the East, container ships — we passed them all. Some were coming into port and some going out — whichever way port was. I made a mental note to increase my knowledge of matters nautical.

Another half hour went by and I was beginning to wonder. I picked out the busiest bar and had a glass of California Chablis. I drank it as slowly as I could, trying to be obvious. This was a distinct role reversal for me — most times when I am on a case, I am trying to be inconspicuous.

I went back on the Promenade Deck and made a circuit of the boat. I went on the next deck and did the same circuit but in reverse. I did not allow any possibility that I was not accessible to anyone on the boat. One man wandering alone caught my eye. He had a string tie and a Western-style jacket. Was he the one? I made sure he could see me but he made no move.

Did it have to be a man? A considerable number of women were already involved in this affair via those who called themselves "the Witches." Could my mysterious contact be one of them? No one could have missed me. I had to be one of the more clearly apparent people on the *Delta Duchess*. I had gone everywhere I could to be seen.

The PA system fed us a steady flow of information on the vessels we were passing. One was a Ground Assault Transport Carrier just back from the Middle East and looking severely businesslike in its drab-gray paint job. Six railroads came into New Orleans, said the PA, and all brought goods in and out of the port. We passed more container ships and freighters, most flying the flags of Liberia, Cyprus and Malta. "Flags of convenience," said the PA. Rust stains smeared their once-fresh paint and indicated countless thousands of ocean miles.

Twenty-five-foot-high levees protect New Orleans from flooding, as the city is below water level, we were told. Behind them, mile after mile of warehouses and wharves looked deserted but still saw use.

Some passengers were inside eating lunch — very Cajun and consisting of gumbo, jambalaya and red beans and rice. Most, though, were on deck and there were cries at the sight of red-and-orange flames flaring into the sky. A natural-gas plant, said the PA assuringly, burning off excessive gas pressure.

About an hour and three-quarters had elapsed and I was turning away from this pyrotechnic spectacular to head for one of the cafés to have a snack when a hand caught my arm.

"Let's sit over here."

It was a man's voice, slightly grating and not overfriendly. I turned. He was in his forties, with a face that had seen a lot, hard eyes and a tight mouth. He wore a plaid shirt, lumberjack type, well-worn jeans and heavy boots. A leather bag hung over one shoulder.

I followed him inside and he went toward

a quiet corner but I motioned to a table that was surrounded by occupied tables. "This is better," I said, and sat. I might not have been so affirmative but I was entering an impatient period and was still aware that one person had already been shot.

He hesitated then sat opposite. "Need to make sure I've got the right guy," he said.

"If you're a book lover, then you have." I emphasized the "book lover."

He gave a miniscule nod. He reached into the leather bag and came out with a book. It had a black cover and was about the same size as a hardback but not as thick. It looked worn and the cover was dog-eared.

"This is what you're looking for," he said.

"Is it?" I asked. "I'd have to see it first."

He hesitated then put it on the table, opened it and turned it to face me. He held it down tightly with both hands, one on each page, but so that I could see most of the text.

It was not easy to read but I could see that it looked exactly like a chef's book. The recipe on the pages that he had opened was for Venison Chaurice.

"What's 'Chaurice'?" I asked.

"What?"

" 'Chaurice.' " I pointed. He looked. A dubious expression came over his face. He shook his head. "Don't matter." It mattered to me. The word was a corruption of *chorizo*, Spanish for "sausage." Why didn't he know that?

He turned pages. The next recipe was for Baby-Back Ribs with a Clover Honey Sauce.

"That's not a New Orleans recipe," I said. I made it sound conclusive even though I knew that it most definitely was a New Orleans recipe.

"Sure it is." But he looked uncertain.

Did he really know? I pushed a little further. I read a few lines and shook my head. "It's good but it's not authentic."

He was confused. "Whadda you mean, not authentic? Sure it's authentic."

I adopted the pained look that experts use when someone challenges their authority. I half rolled my eyes to heaven in a gesture that intimated all the culinary secrets were up there. I added a shrug for good measure.

"Show me some more." I felt that would be establishing who had the control in this encounter, important as it was to do that early.

He turned pages. I read and shook my head. "More." He turned more pages. This was a method of cooking red beans and rice.

165

I looked bored. "Anything on shrimp?" I asked.

He shook his head. "I don't know." His eyes narrowed. "Listen, do you want this book or not?"

"I don't think so," I said. "I think it's a phony."

He sat back, closed the book and pulled it out of my reach. His eyes burned.

"Do you have the real one?" I asked. It was pushing my luck but it seemed like a good move.

"This one's real," he said harshly.

"Let me see it again."

He debated then put it within reach but again kept both hands on it. I motioned for him to turn pages. Gumbos, jambalayas, oysters, muffalettas, smoked fish, stuffed eggplant — all Cajun dishes, certainly. I went through it as fast as I could. One page had only notes that were a reminder to change the cooking sequence on a recipe for redfish and add certain spices.

"Someone's fooling you," I told him. "This really is a fake." I waited.

"You don't want to buy it?"

"Of course not. Why should I buy a fake? Bring me the real one and we're in business."

This was not going according to plan — I

could see that in his face. Whoever had briefed him had not done an adequate job. Of course, I would have been less certain if I had not been in Herman Harburg's forgery room, and therefore was half prepared for this, but I still would have been highly skeptical. I put on a rueful, sorry-about-this expression.

"We can make a deal on the price," he offered hopefully.

"No way," I said. "This book isn't worth anything. You must know that."

He glared, looked at the book, then grabbed it and stuffed it back into his leather bag. He stood up angrily and stalked off.

When we docked, I looked but saw no sign of him. I found a public phone and called Van Linn. "Do you have news?" he wanted to know.

"Negative news," I said. "I was just offered the book —"

He was sputtering congratulatory words before I could stop him.

"— Unfortunately, it was a phony."

"A phony?"

"A fake, a forgery."

The temperature of his voice dropped. "Are you sure?"

"Yes, about as sure as I can be."

"Who was this person who offered it to you?"

I explained the circumstances. "But how could you know it was a forgery?" he demanded.

"I have had occasion to talk to people in the forgery business," I said delicately. "I am sure of it."

"But maybe you should have bought it," he argued. "If it's a copy, it could still contain the . . ."

"Go on," I urged. "It could still contain what?"

"Why, the original contents." He was covering up well.

"No. I would say that this copy was forged by a person who did not have the original."

"Then how could you know that it was not the original?"

"That's what you hired me for."

"I think you should have bought it," he said sulkily.

"Believe me, it was a phony."

He heaved a sigh of great dissatisfaction. "So here we are, no further ahead."

"I wouldn't say that. It's possible that whoever has this phony copy also has the original."

He thought that over. "What makes you think that?"

"I've been very busy on your behalf. I've gathered a lot of information. Most of it suggests that the person who commissioned the forging of the copy I saw this morning, also has the original."

Van Linn digested that for a moment. "I was going to call you anyway," he said. "My client is very anxious to get that book. My client is increasing pressure on me and I'm passing that pressure on to you."

"I'm doing all I can —"

"My client is willing to increase his fee considerably and I'm willing to pass much of that increase on to you."

Was he repeating "my client" because he didn't want to identify his gender? Perhaps he didn't want to say "he." I thought back to Emmy Lou's words. Perhaps it was more likely that he didn't want to say "she." There were, after all, more women involved in this than men so wasn't "she" more probable?

"I'll press harder on this," I said. "I'm going to talk to Michael Gambrinus today. I have a suspicion he knows more than he has told."

"You think he's involved in the crime?" Van Linn sounded doubtful.

"Maybe not. I hope to find out."

"Very well. Keep me informed."

He hung up before I could pin a statistic to his mention of an increase in my fee.

chapter thirteen

The bookseller didn't sound ecstatic when I told him I wanted to come over and talk to him but I didn't leave him much choice.

He was a burly, bearded man and his fuzzy old green sweater added to his bulk. His hair, once red, was now faded and heavily streaked with silver.

I came right to the point once we had exchanged introductions. He was sitting in the same chair where I'd found the body that I had presumed to be him. I sat opposite and looked at him over several small piles of books older than the two of us put together.

"As I found the body, right in that chair where you're sitting, I feel a certain responsibility to clear myself of any complicity." Perhaps that wasn't altogether true but I felt it better not to claim too close an association with the police. I might learn more this way.

"Richie Mortensen had previously worked for you, I believe."

His voice was deep and mellow: "He came to me a couple of years ago. He'd worked for a small publishing firm here in New Orleans and was fascinated by books. I hired him and he was very useful — at that time, I had a lot of business overseas and organizing the packing and shipping was getting to be too much for me. Richie took care of that side of the business."

"You found him reliable, honest?"

"Yes, I did."

"Why did you get rid of him?"

"Currency exchange rates shifted the wrong way and my overseas sales dropped. I didn't have enough work for him here in the shop so I had to let him go. It wasn't exactly precipitous. I had to cut him down to four days a week, then three, then when I told him of the possibility of going down to two days, he said he'd rather leave altogether and look for another job."

"He did that?"

"Apparently he had a hard time finding just what he wanted. I called him in for special occasions — when I had a signing to put on, when I was going to be out of town for a book fair, that kind of thing."

"He wasn't doing anything else, then? He hadn't found another job?"

"Just a few days here and there, apparently, temporary jobs." He ran his fingers through his thick hair.

"On this occasion, you had already planned to go to the book auction and bid for the Belvedere book, hadn't you?"

"Yes."

"You specialize in cookbooks?"

"No — oh, we have quite a number in stock but I've lived in New Orleans all my life so I knew about the Belvedere family. I thought a book that was so much a part of New Orleans' history would have considerable value."

"But you went out of town when you knew the auction was about to be held?"

I half thought he might take umbrage at that provocative deduction but he didn't. "I had made a bid on the private library of a wealthy landowner in Biloxi," he said. "I bid low but, to my surprise, I was the lowest. I was sure I could make a really good profit on it but naturally I wanted to see it before closing. The auction here was less important so I called Richie and had him take my place."

"You know that he went to the auction before it opened and pulled a fast one in getting the book?"

Gambrinus smiled. His teeth were yellowed from smoking and I saw that the wooden rack on his desk was full of well-used old pipes.

"Richie was sharp. He occasionally did that kind of thing."

"Do you have any reason to believe that he was not buying the book for you?"

Gambrinus' smile disappeared. "He was buying the book for me! . . . What do you mean?"

"I'm suggesting the possibility that he planned on selling the book to somebody else but that person shot him and took the book."

"You mean Richie was going to cheat me?"

"You must admit it looks that way," I said.

He absentmindedly picked up one of the morocco-bound volumes on his desk, studied the spine, then put it back.

"He never cheated me before."

"Perhaps he never needed money as much as he did this time."

"I said Richie was sharp, I never found him to be crooked."

"Know anything about his friends, acquaintances?"

"No. We didn't mingle socially," he said, with a touch of acid.

"No reason to think he might know some

dubious characters?"

"Not really. Still, New Orleans has at least its share of those, and maybe more."

"Did you ever meet his brother?"

"I didn't know he had one." His answer was prompt but then he added, "Is he involved in this, do you know?"

"He's involving himself. First, he was going around accusing people of killing his brother." I didn't add that I was one of the accused. I felt it was better to maintain my investigational status as above suspicion.

"Do you have any other scenarios to suggest?" I asked him.

"He could have got the book by his cute trick of avoiding the bidding and brought it back here for me. It could have been that someone else came in, demanded the book then shot him when he wouldn't hand it over."

"You believe the book is that valuable? Enough to kill for?"

He eased back in his chair, ran his fingers through his hair again. "It is only a chef's book, isn't it?"

"So I've heard," I said.

"You think it's something else?" He picked up my card from where it lay on his desk. " 'The Gourmet Detective,' " he read, holding the card by its edges.

"I'm not really a detective," I explained. "I'm more of a food-finder. I hunt up rare spices, lost recipes, advise on foods for special occasions — that kind of thing."

"And on this occasion?"

"I was hired to go to the auction and examine the Belvedere book and make sure it was genuine. If it was, I was to bid on it and, if I could, buy it."

"Did someone think it was not genuine?"

"You're in the book business," I told him. "Don't you occasionally run into forgeries?"

He looked pensive, probably wondering how far to venture out onto ice that thin. "Not very often."

I took a chance on pushing him further in that thought. "I've heard there are forgers active here in New Orleans."

"Currency, you mean? Oh, I —"

"No, not only currency. Books, old books."

"Really. I suppose it's possible." His carefully neutral tone said that he was more aware of it than he admitted.

"You must run into forged books now and then."

"Rarely," he said. "I suppose the purpose of having a forgery made would be to sell it and the original both?"

I nodded. I waited for him to pursue the point but he didn't. Instead, he changed the direction of the conversation. "I have some nice cookbooks back here," he said. "A few really old ones. Like to see them?"

He was closing out the interrogation but, lacking the authority of Lieutenant Delancey, I couldn't reserve that right for myself. So I looked at the cookbooks.

He had Eliza Leslie's *Directions for Cooking*, published in 1928, *The Carolina Housewife*, written in 1847 by "A Lady," and Mrs. Chadwick's *Home Cookery*, which was published in Boston in 1853. On open shelves were Pino Luongo's *A Tuscan in the Kitchen* and several modern writers including Betty Watson, Mary Fisher and Richard Olney.

In a locked, glass-fronted case, I saw *A New Book of Cookerie* by A. J. Murrell — not the original printed in 1615 but the 1805 edition. Next to it was the refreshing *Miss Leslie's Complete Cookery*, published in Philadelphia in 1837.

Vincent La Chapelle's *The Modern Cook* was dated 1733 and is renowned as the first cookbook to give recipes for making ice cream. This volume was in very poor condition and Gambrinus probably found it very difficult to sell but its detailed instructions made it valuable.

A copy of *The Canadian Settlers' Guide*, published around 1850, unfortunately had no date but is of interest for its account of cooking by the early settlers at the time the first versions of the modern stove appeared.

"Ever run across a cookbook by Scappi?" I asked him.

"Doesn't sound familiar."

"He was personal chef to Pope Pius V. It was published in 1570 and it's surprising that there are still a number of copies around. It's in Italian, not Latin, and has some wonderful engravings. I saw one once."

"I picked up a copy of *The Sportsman's Cookery Book* a while ago," Gambrinus said. "Didn't realize how many eager buyers would show up. Could have sold a copy to all of them." He must have realized the inference in that statement — at least, he hurried on to say, "Then a good customer of mine asked me to track down a copy of Mrs. Frances Trollope's *The Cook's Own Book*. Do you know it?"

"Published in Boston, wasn't it?"

"Yes, in 1845. She had some amusing comments on dining etiquette — a far cry from 'grabbing a po'boy sandwich,' I'm afraid."

"You have some old volumes in that case over there," I said, pointing to the glass-fronted and locked cabinet.

"They are the more valuable items," Gambrinus said. I thought he wanted to terminate the conversation and get me out but his pride in his books got the better of him.

"*Tess of the D'Urbervilles*," he said with a nod to a leather-bound volume. "First edition, 1891. Probably worth four thousand dollars. This one next to it is Frances Hodgson Burnett's *The Secret Garden*. It has been described as the most satisfying of all children's books, worth two to three thousand."

"You have a Hemingway here," I said. "Is that a first edition? Must be — being in such illustrious company."

"Actually, it's a later printing but it's signed and inscribed by Hemingway so it would probably bring about five thousand. There are a lot of Hemingway fans who are collectors."

"*Lolita*," I said skeptically. "Should that be in this case?"

Gambrinus laughed, a deep rumbling laugh. "Worth more than all these others!"

"Surely not?"

"Oh, yes. It's a first edition, printed in 1955. You find it hard to believe that I wouldn't sell that book for under ten thousand dollars?"

"Very. Guess I don't know that much about the book business."

"Sold a first edition of *The Great Gatsby* the other day," Gambrinus said. "Three thousand. An even more recent book, *The English Patient*, brings a thousand — or even more if it's in top condition. First editions of Harry Potter books bring over twenty thousand," he added disparagingly.

All through these interchanges, he had been edging me closer and closer to the door and when I reached it, I made the required move. As the bell clanged behind me, I was thinking that Michael Gambrinus wasn't a hot candidate for the villain but I wasn't going to rule him out of having had some complicity.

Rain was threatening but didn't have enough conviction yet. A faint smell of marsh grass was in the air, presumably wafted in by breezes from the bayou country. Some seagulls were performing aeronautical maneuvers at low altitude and a man in all black leather clothes was tooting on a flute. He had silver buttons, silver beads, silver epaulets and a big silver buckle on his black belt. His face was darker than his clothes and his flute-playing was clearly influenced by James Galway although this fellow had not had as much practice.

I was standing in Jackson Square, not far from the hotel. It was one of the historic sights of New Orleans according to the guidebooks in the hotel lobby. I hadn't got to the history yet, having stopped to watch a mime while nearby, a spindly-legged fellow spun a bicycle tire on his head while tap-dancing a Bojangles Robinson number. A young woman, probably a music student, played a violin with a good deal of flair and I strolled on past the redbrick Pontalba Apartments, said by the guide book to be the first apartment buildings in America.

Shutters were snapping closed furiously for it was obviously among the most photographed sights in the city. A tour group from Scotland was listening intently to their guide explaining in a thick Glaswegian accent how the apartments had been built by the Baroness Pontalba after she had been shot and wounded by her husband who then shot himself dead.

The guide went on to fill in the details of the scandal that involved many famous names in New Orleans and in Europe. The baroness had been a fine businesswoman, though, she said. When "the Swedish Nightingale," Jenny Lind, performed in the city, she stayed in the Pontalba and after the singer departed for home, the baroness held an auction and sold off — at a handsome profit — all the furniture from the apartment in which Jenny Lind had stayed.

The statue of Andrew Jackson, general and later president, sits proudly on his charger in the center of the square. I edged close to the Scottish tourists to hear the guide tell about him. "If you visit South America," she was saying, "you will see this same statue in many cities. It was so admired by the dictators of so many countries there, that orders rolled in. The sculptor simply mass-produced the statue and put a different head on each one — that of the country's leader."

A bunch of chattering schoolchildren crossed the square, clearly excited at the release from educational captivity, while teachers at front and back watched in earnest desperation for stragglers.

As the afternoon drew on, more musicians came onto what had been, in turn, an execution square, a military parade ground and a town square. The chords of half a dozen instruments sort of blended into a harmonious cacophony even though the players were unconnected. Many of the benches were occupied and people sat by the fountain. A clown appeared and immediately attracted the attention of the schoolchildren while a tarot-card reader was getting a hard time from a dissatisfied customer who thought her future should be more glamorous than was being depicted.

At the Decatur Street end of Jackson Square were ranks of open carriages. They had a convincingly romantic look to them and appeared to be doing good business. I had assumed at first glance that they were horse-drawn but now I saw that the pulling power came from mules, not horses. The animals were decked with ribbons and flowers and a couple wore straw hats at jaunty angles.

The leisurely atmosphere in the square applied to both residents and tourists. No one seemed in a hurry to go anywhere or do anything. It was very relaxing, and that was how I came to notice a hurrying figure going by the fountain. He was the only person in sight who was in a hurry.

He wore a checked suit in light gray which appeared to be almost a uniform, and the light gray cap with a brim added to that impression. I was looking away when a third item brought me back to look at him again

— this time, his face.

How could he be familiar? Then I recognized him — it was the man from the *Delta Duchess* who had offered me the phony Belvedere book.

I watched his fast stride take him across the square. He was moving in the direction of the ranks of the carriages. To my surprise, he took down a sign advertising tours and dropped it out of sight in the passenger seat. He climbed into the driver's seat, took up a whip, flicked it and released the handbrake. The horse reared its head, stamped its forefeet to restore circulation and pulled away from the curb.

I dodged between musicians, tourists, mimes, clowns, schoolchildren, nurses, contortionists and hot-dog stands as I hurried toward the rank of carriages. In one of them, a West Indian driver with a luxuriant mustache was already sitting in the driving seat. He looked ready for hire and I jumped in behind him.

I couldn't believe it when I heard myself saying, "Follow that mule!"

chapter fourteen

A flight of pigeons took to the air, apparently small friends of the mule's. The *clip-clop* of the mule's shoes had a friendly rhythm and we rolled past restaurants and coffee shops that ringed around the square. We went west along Decatur Street then turned left onto St. Ann Street, which was apparently one-way.

A small painted sign said the driver/owner was Benjamin and as we made the turn, he asked affably, "Where you want to go, man? Don't seem like you really want to follow that mule." He flicked his whip, pointing ahead to where the other carriage was just in sight.

"I do," I told him. "He's a friend of mine. I just saw him pulling away but couldn't catch him in time."

He nodded as if satisfied, but after a pause that lasted two blocks, he asked, "What's his name, man?"

He had me there. I could have pretended

185

a memory lapse but didn't think it would sound convincing. I said with a laugh, "Oh, I'm sure you know him. You see him every day."

"Yeah." He sounded sour and cracked the whip loudly in emphasis. "Sixty bucks he owes me now. He ain't ever gonna pay me, man." He looked back over his shoulder at me. " 'Course, if he's a friend o' yours, shouldn't be saying that."

"He's not exactly a friend," I said. Maybe any man who was out sixty dollars was more of a friend than my quarry was.

"Figured that," said Benjamin, and spat expertly into the gutter.

"Know him well?"

"Nah. None of us do. He don't associate with us."

"What kind of a guy is he?"

"Not for me to say," Benjamin muttered. That meant he was going to say, so I waited. After half a minute, it came. "Owes a lot of the drivers; it ain't just my sixty bucks. If you ask me, he got his finger in a lot o' places it shouldn't ought to be."

"Trouble with the law?"

He looked at me over his shoulder. "You'd know more about that."

"I meant the local law. I just got into town."

"Don't know if he's ever done time, but guys come around asking questions about him. Some lawmen, some others."

We were still going north, through the French Quarter, and we crossed Rampart Street, one of the infrequent intersections to have a street sign. A large park loomed on the left and he saw me looking. "Louis Armstrong Park," he said. "Know who he is?"

"Everybody in the world knows Satchmo."

He grinned. "You right on, there." The mule trotted along happily. Ahead, the other carriage was just in sight. The driver read my mind. "He won't think nuthin' of us behind him — even if he sees us, which he probably won't. See us carriages all over the city."

He beat me to it, "You don't sound like a cop. Private?"

"Not from round here."

"Figured that. Interpol, I bet."

"You're a shrewd fellow. So what's his name?"

"Earl Whelan. Want him bad, huh?"

"Don't want to lose him."

"We won't. Don't you worry none. Myrtle's the best in the city — ain't you, old girl?"

A flick of the tail indicated that the mule recognized her name as she plodded steadily along. "Females make better carriage mules than male — you know that?"

"No, I didn't. It's good to know, though."

He laughed, a chuckling, half-wheezy laugh. We passed underneath State Highway 10, thick with traffic. Darkness was falling fast.

"Still heading toward the lakeshore, aren't we?" I knew the city from looking at maps and had a rough idea of the layout.

"Right, but we ain't goin' there."

"We're not? Why, do you know where he lives?"

"No, but he don't live lakeshore, you can be sure o' that. More likely, he live where we comin' in now. Old Metairie, got a famous cemetery here, lotsa folks visit it. You into cemeteries?"

"Not before my time — and that's not yet," I told him, and got a deep chuckle.

It was a marginal neighborhood, not downright slum but not too appealing: rows of small houses on narrow streets. We had moved closer to the other carriage now that the traffic was much lighter, and Benjamin slowed Myrtle's steady step. "Gonna nail him?" he asked eagerly.

"Not right away. I want to watch him a bit

longer. See who he's with."

"When you cuff him, can I get my sixty bucks first?"

"I'll do what I can."

"Wanna watch him so's you can get the rest o' the gang too, huh?'

"Something like that."

After a few minutes of slower progress due to the narrow streets and clogging traffic, Benjamin said, "He's stopped."

"Stay back but keep him in sight." I said it the way any Interpol operative would say it, crisp and commanding.

We stopped a full block away and across the street. The houses here were old and looked none too firm. The one that Whelan approached had a large building on the side. Whelan opened a door, then a bigger one swung open. It was a barnlike structure and he proceeded to back the carriage into it, disconnect it, then put the mule in there, too.

"Is that legal?"

Benjamin shrugged. " 'Round here they don't care. Long as they get the rent."

Whelan closed the larger door from the inside. We waited and watched. It was probably ten minutes or so and we were both feeling impatience. I had to prevent mine from showing — Interpol agents should be used to long vigils.

A door in what had to be the attached house opened and a figure came out. It was female and she wore a long coat. She strode off along the street, away from us.

"Follow her," I said. "Just close enough to get a look at her."

She was fairly tall and had a long swinging stride. She looked to have dark hair but I had to wait until we reached an intersection where there was enough light before I could see her properly.

"Slow down," I said urgently. "Don't get any closer."

"Get a good look at her?" asked Benjamin eagerly.

"Good enough," I said. It was good enough — for me to recognize her. She was Leah Rollingson, the part-Chinese beauty who had been one of the Witches' kidnapping team.

We followed, keeping nearly a block behind. I recalled Emmy Lou Charbonneau's words: "We think one of the Witches is mixed up in this." Did she — or one of her sister Witches — know or at least suspect more than that? Did one of them know who it was and what her involvement was?

Ahead, a wide street crossed the one we were on. It was lit, and traffic buzzed by.

Leah turned onto it and stopped.

"Bus stop," Benjamin said, slowing down his mule. "Number thirty-six, goes all the way 'cross town."

"Let's wait. She may have something else in mind."

We watched, and within a few minutes a bus came. She did not have anything else in mind — she got on the bus and we watched it until it disappeared from sight. Benjamin shook his head. "No way Myrtle can catch that," he said.

"I didn't think so. Let's go back to the house."

We parked a block away. "You'd better stay here. I won't be long."

He shook his head firmly. "No way, man. I'm comin' with you."

"You don't have to, you —"

"Ain't doin' it 'cos I have to, it's 'cos I want to. I ain't sittin' here alone."

"What? A big man like you? Afraid?" I chided him.

"This here's a dangerous city," he said, still shaking his head.

"What about Myrtle? Is she okay alone?"

"Can't take her with us," he said reasonably.

"True. Anyway, she looks like a brave mule."

Benjamin put on a hand-brake, patted Myrtle a few times and whispered something in mule language. We crossed the street and walked along to the house. No lights were visible.

"Let's find the back," I said. We had to go around the block and we located the house. A dim light showed in a downstairs window. The second story was dark.

It would have been exaggerating to call it a garden. We crossed a mini-wasteland of junk and rubbish. Benjamin tripped over an old bicycle then put his foot through the shattered spokes of one of the wheels and couldn't get out of it until several dozen swear words later. I kicked a can that clattered into several other cans. All must have been empty, the way they resonated.

We finally completed our crossing of the minefield, and reached the window. I peered into a kitchen, small and untidy with pans on the stove, cans and jars and boxes on the countertops. The light was somewhere else in the house and filtered through dimly.

Benjamin squeezed beside me to look through the window.

"We goin' in?" he breathed.

I hadn't seriously considered it but it was obviously the kind of thing an Interpol man would do and I wanted to maintain the image.

"Yeah," I drawled. "We're goin' in."

I tried the window. It didn't yield.

"There must be a back door," I said.

We looked and there was, hard to see in the darkness. But the knob didn't turn and when Benjamin tried, it still resisted. "Feels like a bolt as well," he said.

"The window might be easier."

We went back to it and I tried both panes, a top and a bottom. Neither would slide.

"Let me try," Benjamin said. He took out a sturdy-looking pocketknife and opened a wicked-looking blade. He probed here and there, then suddenly, there was a metallic clang. He eased the lower pane upward. I looked inside. There was a space alongside a cabinet below the window.

"Give me a hand," I told him. He cupped a hand and gave me a heave. It was tight but I just made it. I took the weight of my fall on my hands and rolled over. I stood and turned to the window where a big, black face stared at me.

"No way I can make it through there," he said, and I wasn't sure whether he was relieved or sorry.

"That's okay," I told him. "Stay there, keep an eye open."

I went into the next room. A floor lamp cast a dim light. The room was as untidy as the kitchen, with cheap furniture. Tattered carpet covered a stairway and I was starting to go up when I heard hurried footsteps. I paused, heart quickening, trying to determine where they had come from. I heard them again then a muffled *thump*. It was a door closing.

I saw now that there was another downstairs room, one that evidently fronted onto the street. The entrance to it was off a small hallway at the foot of the stairs. I went in.

A table lamp with a Budweiser shade threw off a few miserable watts of light. The room was poorly furnished like the other but I didn't notice any details. My attention was all on the body, half seated, half sprawled on the couch. Its awkward position was a bad omen, and a quick examination confirmed that he was dead.

I recognized him. He was the man we had followed. He was Earl Whelan, the man who had offered me the book.

chapter fifteen

He had been shot in the chest. That meant that the person with the gun might still be in the house. I hastily checked the front door. It was unlocked. I called softly to Benjamin and he came, his eyes big and shining in the dark. I wondered how much bigger they would get in the next few minutes.

"We're going to search the house." I told him.

He looked doubtfully over my shoulder. "Ain't nobody in there, is they?"

"Not a living soul," I told him.

We did it room by room. He stood at the door and I went inside, checking closets, showers and large cupboards. Finally there was only one room left.

"We won't go into that one," I said.

"We won't? Why won't we?"

"Because there's a dead man in there."

I was right about his eyes. They could get much bigger. "You Interpols don't fool around, do you!"

"He was dead when I found him."

"Hey, that frail we saw leavin' — you don't suppose she did for him?"

"I don't know but I'll have to call the police."

Benjamin shook his head in self-reproach. "Minute you said, 'Follow that mule,' I shoulda known. Man, I shoulda known. What a day!"

"Do you have any problem with the law?" I asked. "If you do, you can take off. I know you didn't have anything to do with this."

"Nah," he said emphatically. "I'm clean. It's okay, I'll stay. Besides," he added, "you'll want me for an alibi. Maybe the law think you offed this guy." He cast a curious look toward the room with the body but his curiosity didn't go as far as going in to look.

"All right. There's a phone in the kitchen. I'll use that."

"You supposed to hold it with a cloth or somethin' — you know, so's you don't get fingerprints on it."

I nodded. "Television does have an instructional value, doesn't it?"

Lieutenant Delancey's look was distinctly frosty. "You've already found more bodies than I've had hot dinners this week. Who's this one?"

196

We walked into the room. Delancey examined the body, poked around the room, then looked to me for answers.

"His name's Earl Whelan. He drives one of the mule-drawn carriages. So does Benjamin." I explained the steamboat incident and our all-mule pursuit. When I came to the part where we came into the house, he looked disapproving. "Breaking and entering! That's not —"

"Luckily, the latch on the kitchen window was broken and I was able to get in that way."

"Sure it was." He poked through the room again, examined the couch carefully, then the body. He looked at Benjamin, who had been standing silently by the door.

"Know this guy, do you?"

Benjamin was polite and cautious with his answers but, under Delancey's expert probing, it emerged that Whelan was a drug courier. Delancey knew that several taxi drivers made extra money that way and Benjamin reluctantly admitted that one or two carriage drivers did so, too. As Delancey dug further, it seemed that Whelan was into other illegal activities. "Anything to make a buck," Benjamin said contemptuously.

"So you didn't see anybody else?"

I had been awaiting that question with unease. I thought Leah an unlikely murderess but I had been wrong before on more than one occasion. I liked her but that was no basis on which to protect her in a murder investigation. A more pragmatic consideration was that I would be putting Benjamin on the spot. Either I would be forcing him to lie, or his contradiction would look bad for me. I had to tell the truth.

"We saw a woman leave the house a while before we went in."

The lieutenant raised an eyebrow. "Know who she was?"

I told him. I saw the look of surprise on Benjamin's face but managed to keep Delancey's attention on me so that he didn't notice it.

"How did you come to know her?" he wanted to know.

I explained but didn't refer to it as a kidnapping. I used the euphemistic description of "an invitation to attend a meeting of a chefs' association."

"Anything about the way she left? Hurried? Worried? Anything to indicate she might have just shot a guy?"

"No, she left normally," I said, "but after I went in, I heard someone in the house."

"And neither of you heard a shot?"

Negatives from both of us.

The lieutenant was still asking questions when Forensics people began arriving. The lieutenant finally told Benjamin and me that we could go, adding to me, "Call me tomorrow. We may need to talk some more." We left after Benjamin had told him of a mule in the adjacent building that needed consideration. "I'll see it gets taken care of," the lieutenant assured him.

"Want me to ride you back to Jackson Square?" Benjamin asked me. When we arrived, I gave him three twenties and he looked at them so strangely that I gave him another.

"Hope you don't need any more help, man," he told me, although he took another look at the bills in his hand as he stuffed them away and appeared to be tempted to change that hope.

"Not this kind, you mean. No chases, no break-ins and no dead bodies. Otherwise, you're available."

He grinned amiably. "Man, you got a nose for trouble — but okay, otherwise . . . I'm here."

Despite the late hour, Jackson Square had more than its share of itinerant musicians, late-night strollers, lovers, bizarre outfits, diners working off excess calories and even a night-shift mime. I walked back to the hotel and slept well, with only a minimum of hazy dreams featuring a dead body.

I was entering the breakfast room next morning when a blonde vision in gray and blue intercepted me. It was Elsa Goddard and she smiled brightly. "I hoped I'd catch you. How are you enjoying New Orleans?"

She listened with widening eyes as I told her of finding another body. "So you were there! I saw it on the early-morning news!" Her expression changed. "Does this have anything to do with the book?"

"It seems possible." I was being cagey, still not certain how much I could trust her. Even if she were not involved personally, her media personality made her one of those people around whom it is safer to be reticent.

"Let's sit for a minute," she said, and waved to a group of chairs and a table out of the stream of guests going in all directions. "I've come to the conclusion that I can trust you," she began as soon as we were seated. I almost said thank you. "It's this matter of the book. You see, one of the Witches has been offered it."

"Really?"

"Yes, and the shots of the dead man on

the news this morning — well, that must be the man who offered it."

"Which of the Witches was offered the book?"

She raised elegantly manicured eyebrows. "I'll let her tell you."

"All right. It's a coincidence, though."

"Coincidence?"

"Yes. That man, Earl Whelan, offered it to me, too." I described in brief the encounter on the paddlewheeler.

"You turned it down?"

"Yes. It was a fake, a phony."

I was watching her carefully. I didn't learn much, though. She showed more surprise than any other reaction.

"How did you know that?"

"I was able to examine it carefully." The answer was evasive but she didn't seem to doubt it. "What about yours?"

"She said she'd need time to raise that much money."

"How much did he want?"

"Twenty thousand dollars."

"Pity he didn't show it to you. You could always show up early and get it cheaper."

She smiled. "I was a little overbearing at that auction, wasn't I? But I was so furious at that woman, selling it before the —" She was getting angry at the memory but she

201

caught my eye and brought back the smile. "There I go again. But tell me, how did you really know the book he showed you was a phony?"

She was sharp. She had picked up on the one point I didn't intend to explain, as I saw no reason to bring up the story of Herman Harburg and his involvement. Without him, my omniscience stood out prominently. How to explain it?

"I've seen a lot of chefs' books," I said loftily. "This just didn't look genuine."

"How did he take it?"

"He seemed a little confused — as if he wasn't certain himself whether it was real or not."

"Just who was he? Do you know?"

"He drove a mule carriage — one of those that operate out of Jackson Square. Apparently he was a drug courier on the side."

"I know some taxi drivers make extra money that way," she said. "I suppose a mule-drawn carriage is even less suspicious."

"Evidently. He also had a reputation for dipping his fingers into other endeavors, not always legal."

"So if you think he didn't know if the book he was offering you was genuine or not, he must have been acting as a go-between? He may not have had anything to do with the theft — or the murder?"

"Looks that way. Tell me something —" I went on. "I presume you're no longer acting on behalf of the Witches?"

She shrugged. "Business is business. There's a story here that hasn't been unraveled yet. If I can get it, it could revitalize my whole career."

"Does it need revitalizing? You seem to be doing very well."

"Between you and me, my future at the studio is shaky. A great story like this could get me into serious TV journalism."

"I'm sure I don't need to tell you to be careful," I said. "Two people have died already."

I didn't expect my warning to be very effective and it wasn't. She nodded a brisk acknowledgement, as if I had told her to dress warmly. "Actually, it was another matter that I wanted to talk to you about," she said. "We're putting on a show featuring Creole and Cajun cooking . . . Well, these are pretty familiar themes around New Orleans, so we wanted a new angle. We're doing this show as a conflict, a battle between the aficionados, but we're going to goose them up to be more fanatics than fans."

"The Creoles versus the Cajuns?" I suggested. "Kitchen knives at two paces?"

"Something like that," she smiled.

"And which side do you want me to be on? The winning one, I hope."

"Oh, you'll be neutral."

"Shot at by both sides, you mean?"

"Oh, those days are over — besides, we don't allow firearms in the studio."

I thought of drawing her attention to the fact that Larry Mortensen had not been disadvantaged by any such rule but I didn't. Anyway, it sounded like fun. She gave me the details and I agreed to be there.

I escorted her to the door and watched her depart. As I turned back into the lobby, one of the desk clerks called to me. I had a call: would I take it in the first booth?

It was Marguerite — she of the near-perfect features; black hair, long black lashes — and she was calling to ask if I would like to be their guest for lunch today.

I accepted readily.

chapter sixteen

I wasn't too clear on the location of the Bistro Bonaparte but the taxi driver was. It was a neat, trim, very French looking place, and the awning outside and the window shade were both of the bright, turquoise-blue that had an immediate Parisian appeal.

I was conducted into the main dining room but I was told there were two other, smaller rooms. In here, the distinctive ambiance was enhanced by mirrored walls, soft antique lights, vases of fresh flowers and mouthwatering displays of fresh fruits. Touches of the Baroque were evident in the carved wood panels between the mirrors and the red velvet drapes. The snowy-white tablecloths and the glittering silver completed the picture of a successful restaurant. All in all, it was very tastefully done, and without going to extravagant expense.

Marguerite looked charming in a simple black dress with small gold earrings and a thin gold chain around her neck. Her black hair was shiny and smooth and her long lashes looked as if they had grown a couple of millimeters since my kidnapping by the Witches. Her skin was faultless and her red-lipped smile was welcoming as she led me to a table and pulled up a chair opposite.

"Bonaparte himself would have been delighted at the opportunity to eat here," I told her.

"My aim was to offer New Orleans food, but with the French flavor resulting from years under French rule," she explained. "I tried to embody that in the design, too, both outside and inside."

"You designed this yourself?" I was amazed. "It's so professional."

"Everything you see." She nodded. "Of course, the French influence is strong in the city and it prevails in many New Orleans dishes but we make a specialty out of that and keep as many traditional dishes as we can, but stay up-to-date at the same time."

A waiter in a smart white jacket came and Marguerite suggested Kir Royales. "Perfect," I agreed.

"You know," she went on, "classic New Orleans cooking is one of the most distinctive regional cuisines in the country. The Creole cooking is more haute cuisine compared to Cajun, which is more the country style. Creole cooking started with French cooking techniques and then they modified them in accordance with the Spanish, African and Indian seasonings that were already in use locally. We use only fresh ingredients and a dish is taken off the menu any day they are not available."

"The traditional local cooking must have been the very slow kind," I said. "Wasn't that a challenge — I mean, to fit it into modern restaurant demands?"

"It was. You're right, in the old days, dishes would cook for hours. Everything is cooked to order here. Pastas and vegetables are all cooked al dente. Meats are lightly grilled or sautéed. Most of our fish dishes are cooked at very high heat for a very short time."

"Of course, you're very fortunate in having such a huge variety of ingredients. You have an unusual amount of seafood plus lots of game."

"Which brings us to the matter at hand — what would you like today?" She smiled invitingly, clearly proud of her role.

I skimmed through the menu. "The crabmeat Louis catches my eye," I told Marguerite.

"It's extremely popular. A Creole twist on a classic French dish. The Louis dressing —

onions, green pepper, chili sauce, yogurt and mayonnaise — is blended till smooth. Salad greens and crabmeat are piled on top with slices of cucumber, celery, melon, carrots and pineapple."

"Sounds good — but then there's the crawfish bisque."

"We make it the authentic way, starting with live crawfish. It is mainly a conventional bisque except that we make a roux in the Creole style, cooking it till it is a rich mahogany color."

"Then you have here 'Buster Crabs.' That's a new one on me."

"They are a Gulf specialty, though similar to the soft-shell crabs from Chesapeake Bay. We fry them quickly in a little oil so that they are crispy outside, juicy inside. We usually serve them with Choron sauce."

"It's a tough choice." I meditated briefly. "I think the crawfish bisque, though."

She smiled in approval. "And to follow?"

I narrowed down the many pages to three possibles: Trout in Leek Sauce, Pompano en Papillotte, and Veal Creole. "I'm passing over the Duck in Cherries," I said. "Duck is a favorite of mine, but while I'm here I'm going for the more strictly local dishes."

She nodded. "The three you've selected are all in that class. The pompano especially is very typical of our Creole/French approach. You're probably familiar with the classic old French recipe in which the fish is heavily sauced. We've streamlined that into a technique where we steam the fish in its own juices in the paper bag, then serve a light hollandaise-type sauce with it."

"You've sold me on that one," I said. "Much as I hate to pass on the other two."

I sat back after that excellent meal and sipped the last of the wine, a fine Puligny-Montrachet. Marguerite returned and sat opposite me. "You've done an extraordinarily good job here," I told her, "In the cooking and the presentation as well as in the restaurant itself."

"You know," she said, "in the old Southern mansions, the lady of the house would put on banquets for fifty to eighty people, many times a year. She would plan and organize the entire affair, all while running the place — which in many cases was a plantation. I like to think that I'm carrying on that tradition."

"You certainly are," I said sincerely.

"I'll give you a few minutes before mentioning dessert," she smiled, "and that will give me the opportunity to talk to you. I had two reasons for inviting you. The most important, of course, was that I wanted you to sample my wonderful restaurant —"

"And it is," I agreed.

"Thank you — and second, I wanted to tell you that I have been offered the book."

"The Belvedere chef's book," I said slowly. I saw no need to tell her that Elsa had already told me of the offer.

"Yes. This man phoned me and offered it to me."

"What did you say?"

"I asked him questions about it."

"Did he answer them?"

"Yes, although not fully and not too convincingly. He wanted to meet with me and show me the book."

"Did he say how much he was asking?"

"He said twenty thousand dollars."

"Are you going to meet him?"

"I was — but I thought it over and decided I should talk to you first. Have you made any progress in your search?"

The waiter came and brought a complimentary entremet. These are very French, the word means "between courses" and they are intended to cleanse the palate of one dish before the serving of the next. The concept arose during the reign of Louis XV, for it was at his court banquets that as many as forty courses would be served. Many of these might leave a taste in the mouth that would linger and affect the taste of the next course. This "entremet" was just a small scoop of water ice with a watermelon flavor.

"A very civilized idea," I complimented Marguerite.

I ate it slowly, giving myself a chance to compose an answer. The waiter returned promptly just as I finished and took the glass.

"As a matter of fact, I've been offered the book, too."

She arched her eyebrows in surprise. "The same way?"

"No, I was shown the book."

"Then you saw the person who had it?" She leaned forward in rapt attention.

"Yes, his name is Earl Whelan."

"He told you that?" Her voice rose.

"No, it came out later."

"So what happened? Did you buy it?"

"No, I didn't."

"Why not?"

"It was a phony, a fake."

"How did you know?" There was that question again. I was ready for it this time, though.

"I've seen a lot of chefs' books before. I knew this one wasn't authentic."

Her eyes were searching my face intently.

She had been hanging on every word. "Amazing," she murmured.

"Yes," I said. "He's having a hard time selling it. Such a famous, valuable book and nobody wants to buy it."

"Nobody? Has he offered it to others besides you and I?"

She was a sharp girl. She'd picked up on that right away. I avoided the question, though, and instead of answering, I said, "He won't be offering it to anyone else. He was murdered last night."

Her mouth opened then closed. She shook her head very slowly. "Another murder?" she murmured.

"It was on the news this morning."

"Is that how you heard about it?"

"No. I found the body."

"Oh, you poor man!"

"It seems to be one of the hazards of my business."

"But if he was murdered last night, when did he try to sell you the book?"

I explained — all the way from the paddlewheeler to the mule-drawn carriage. Described that way, it sounded a little silly but I gave it as much gravity as I could.

"How terrible for you! Look, you need some fortification after that — no, no, you must," she was saying in anticipation of my head shake. "I have just the dessert for you. You've probably heard that bread pudding is one of the most popular New Orleans desserts. We have our own version of it. We make it into a soufflé and serve it covered with a bourbon sauce."

She excused herself then returned at once. "It's a dish that has to be served the second it comes out of the baking oven. But you won't have to wait. Two of them are in various stages of baking right now. You'll get the first to come out."

Her flawless features were accentuated by her serious demeanor resulting from the tragic news. She shook her head sadly. "It's hard to believe, so much bloodshed. Over a book, too. Tell me — if the book you and I were offered was a fake, where is the real book?"

"I don't know yet."

"Do you think it's still around?"

"I think it must be."

"Then why aren't they trying to sell it?"

"Maybe they are — in a different market."

"But surely this is the best market," she argued, "right here in New Orleans. The home of the Belvedere family."

"That's a good point. It should be the best market, you're right. Maybe we'll see it beginning to appear now."

The bread-pudding soufflé arrived at that moment, steaming gently. It was light and frothy and bourbon never tasted so good. It satisfied the desire for a sweet finish to the meal but was not cloying or overrich.

When Marguerite told me to be careful as I left, I was in too euphoric a mood to even contemplate danger.

On a corner near the Bistro Bonaparte was a drugstore and there I sought a phone. The lieutenant answered promptly. "Yeah, fewthings weneedto talkabout," he said, but his verbal shorthand no longer fooled me and I understood every word. I told him where I was.

"Lee Circle? It's not far from where I am. I'll meet you there in twenty minutes. There's a coffee shop by the northwest corner."

I was there first and had just had time to inhale the chicory aroma from my coffee when Delancey arrived. He sniffed. "You like that stuff?"

"Chicory? Yes, I do. I don't suppose it pleases your New York tastes, though."

"Not me," he said emphatically. He made sure that the waiter understood his desire for "real" coffee.

I leaped in with the query that was uppermost in my mind. "You've talked to Leah Rollingson, I take it."

"Just came from there. She says her husband was still alive when she left him."

"Husband!" It took me a few seconds. "She's married to him?"

"Yeah." He couldn't miss the inflection in my words. "They don't seem too compatible — that what you're thinking?"

"Funny thing, marriage," I said. "It's hard to see what some women see in some men."

"And vice versa," he agreed. "I never talked to him so I couldn't comment on a personal basis, but from his record, he sounds like a poor choice of a husband. Evidently she found that out but not in time. They had filed for divorce and weren't living together."

"So what was she doing there at his place? — if you can call it that."

"Yeah, it's a dump. She felt sorry for him, she said, went to see him once in a while, usually ended up giving him money. Speaking of money, there's a big fat life-insurance policy on him."

"So you're saying she had a good motive for killing him?"

"One of the best."

215

"But why would she shoot him when they were already planning a divorce?"

"Didn't I just tell you why?"

"The policy, you mean?" I was skeptical. "She doesn't seem like the type."

"Hey," Delancey said, "if I had to list all the nice ladies I've had to book for murder, when I got to ten, I'd have to take off my shoes and socks and still call for an abacus."

"So you really believe she's guilty?"

" 'Believe'? Who's talking about belief? I'm a cop, not a religion."

"Then do you think she did it?"

"I'm not a philosopher, either. I just collect facts and make deductions."

"The press must have a tough time with you," I told him.

"As do I with them. That's why the NOPD has PR."

"You must get gut feelings sometimes, though."

"No, Don't have the guts for it."

I grinned despite the seriousness of the subject. "Then you decline to make a statement at this time?"

"I'll make one to you: I don't think she did it."

That surprised me but I was quick to say, "I don't, either — and I did tell you I heard someone in the house."

"Sure. I don't work like Maigret or Poirot; I don't have the brain for it. But I get there."

That told me a lot about him. Most American cops know Columbo and Kojak but it would take a reader of mystery novels to be able to categorize the French and the Belgian detectives so readily. Not only that, but he pronounced their names properly. This wasn't the moment for a discussion of mystery stories, though I mentally filed the subject for a future date.

"I think that damn book of yours is behind this," he said.

"The Belvedere chef's book? Even before you know how much the life-insurance policy is worth?"

"It's not a matter of the amount. That's a bum lead. There's something in that book that you either don't know or are not telling me."

That took me by surprise. "I absolutely assure you, Lieutenant, that I have kept nothing back from you." I put my most assertive and honest demeanor into the statement. "I'm beginning to think you may be right. There must be more to this book than just a regular chef's book. I wish I knew what it is. I really don't."

"You said something before about a

217

secret recipe. Care to expand on that?"

"Oysters Belvedere — that was the dish that made the restaurant famous back then. Other restaurants have their secrets, too, of course. Antoine's had theirs for snails Bourguinon, Commander's Palace has theirs — they all do. Betty Crocker's cake mix, Arby's sauce — they're both supposed to be secret. Planet Hollywood's Chicken Crunch has been copied by dozens of competitors but none of them has got it right yet. Soy sauce was a revelation to the Western world when it was introduced in the late forties and early fifties. It wasn't just a flavoring sauce like horseradish or mustard or Worcestershire — in addition, it enhanced flavors, it didn't hide or subdue them. Kikkoman dominated the world market because they used a microorganism, a proprietary mold culture; they still do, in fact."

"A good chemist could analyze 'em," Delancey said contemptuously.

"No, no, it's not that easy. You can't analyze an inorganic substance that way. Oh, you can identify many of the chemical components but it's the way they are put together that is hard to reconstruct. Nor can you tell the cooking sequence. For instance, some herbs have to be added early so as to absorb their flavor, others must be added late or they give a bitter taste."

"I asked you this before —" said Delancey. "How could any recipe be worth killing for?"

"That's the problem. It doesn't seem likely."

"So there's something else — and the big question is what?"

"Right. I'm glad you brought up this subject of the book, anyway. There's something I wanted to tell you about it — it's turned up twice."

He wiggled fingers at me. "Okay, give!"

I told him of my experience on the *Delta Duchess* and of Marguerite's phone call. "So perhaps you're right and the book is the crux of this whole mess."

"But you said you thought the book was a phony."

"I still believe so."

"Did the broad from the Witches think so, too?"

"If she did, she didn't tell me."

He shook his head, perplexed. "That forger, Harburg . . . I told you we checked him out further, didn't I? Anyway, he's got a clean sheet. I talked to a couple of our people who have experience in that area. There was a time when a few forgers were operating in New Orleans —"

"You mean in areas other than currency?"

"Right. Naturally, stocks and bonds took priority so books didn't get a lot of attention — but don't tell any taxpaying book lovers I said that. A few of them were nailed, though, and I guess that discouraged others." He shook his head in aggravation. "Unfortunately, we can't ask the last Belvedere what was in the book."

"I haven't asked you about the gun yet," I reminded him.

"It's not the same weapon that killed Mortensen," he said. "We're still checking, but so far, it's not on record, either." He drank his coffee in one gulp. "Gotta go. Wanna tell me your movements so I'll know where to go to find the next body?"

"I sincerely hope that won't happen. Two bodies are enough. If I find a third one, even you will have difficulty believing me."

"You can say that again."

I left on that unpromising note.

chapter seventeen

The widow was misty-eyed but flashed me a wide smile. I concluded that the tears were due less to grief than to the more immediate and powerful aroma of freshly chopped onions.

"I'd better not shake hands with you," she said, "or you'll have the Monteleone smelling like an onion farm."

"You know where I'm staying?" I asked in surprise.

"Oh, your name comes up quite a lot in our meetings. We know a few things about you."

Leah was a very attractive woman and the Asian influence was just enough to give her an exotic look. She kept her hair straight but not cut too short, wore eye makeup that almost reduced the tilt to her almond eyes, and had a wide mouth that was rare in Asians.

"I came to say I'm very sorry about your husband. I don't know if the police told you, but I found his body."

She nodded soberly.

"I also wanted to tell you that I saw you leaving his place before I went in. I was obliged to tell the police that, especially as I had another person with me. He was a carriage driver and would have been able to identify you."

"That's all right," she said softly. "The police told me that I had been seen. I didn't know it was you, though. How did you come to be there?" She pointed to an office area near the kitchen. "I'm sorry, I'm forgetting my manners. Let's go in there and sit."

It was a working office and two people filled it, along with the usual office equipment for printing menus, correspondence, file cabinets, bookshelves and a cluttered desk.

When we were seated, I said, "Earl Whelan offered me the book —"

Her eyes widened. "The Belvedere book?"

"So he said. He showed it to me and I said it was a phony. I saw him by chance crossing Jackson Square later and followed him home."

"I see. Do you really think it was a phony?"

"Pretty sure, yes."

She looked down at her hands, rubbed her fingers together. "We hadn't lived together, Earl and I, for some time. We had filed for divorce."

"Was he obstructing the divorce?"

"Oh, no, not at all. We did have a life-insurance policy, though — on both of us. The police may think I killed him for that, wanting to get the money before the divorce was complete. But I didn't . . . I couldn't do that. I didn't love him anymore and I didn't like having to keep giving him money but I didn't kill him — I couldn't."

It sounded to me like a sincere statement and I would have acquitted her on the spot. But I know I'm a marshmallow when it comes to women. Delancey would have shaken his head in despair at me.

"He was dead when you got there?" I asked.

"Yes. I was afraid that whoever had killed him was still in the house. I hurried out. I suppose I should have phoned the police before I did that. As it was, I came back here — I live upstairs — and the police called me first."

It sounded logical to me, although I knew Delancey would have a tougher attitude.

"I had only been back here a few minutes

when the phone rang and it was the police telling me about his death."

"Where did he get the book? Do you have any idea?"

"No, I don't."

"Was he interested in that kind of thing?"

She was about to scoff but probably had been brought up not to speak ill of the dead. "The only thing he was interested in was making money," she said, and kept all rancor out of her voice.

"It's been suggested that he was a drug courier."

"I don't doubt it. He drove a cab for a while and I'm pretty sure he was running drugs then. He probably decided that a mule carriage was a better cover."

"You mentioned your Witches meetings," I said. "Are any of your members looking for the book, too?"

"Maybe all of them," she said with a slight smile. "Elsa is now more likely looking for it for her own reasons, you haven't been successful yet" — I blessed her for that "yet" — "so several of the Witches are trying a few approaches of their own." She thought for a moment; she seemed like a very honest girl. "I think it's all right to tell you this. I don't see why it should be a secret. Jenny is certainly looking, so is Marguerite . . . Emmy

Lou is not, I don't think. I'm not sure about Della but I wouldn't be surprised."

"A lot of lookers," I commented ruefully.

"What do you think is in the book?" she asked.

"I wish I knew."

"Some of the Belvedere family's recipes must have value," she said.

"Enough to kill for?"

She shuddered. "Surely not."

"I also wish I knew where the real book is — if this one that he was peddling is a phony. Do you think Earl had the real one, too?"

"Well, I haven't been able to go through all his things yet — the police won't let me. I suppose if it's there, they'll find it." She gave me a look of concern. "Have you eaten?"

"Very well. At the Bistro Bonaparte."

"That means very well indeed. Marguerite does a wonderful job there. What did you have?"

I told her and she nodded approval. "Good choices. Real French Creole, just the style that Marguerite tries so hard to go for."

"I hear great things about your place here, too," I said. It was an exaggeration, but a pardonable one.

"So when are you coming to eat here?"

"How does the day after tomorrow look on your booking list?"

"For you, it doesn't matter. We can accommodate you."

"Great."

"Lunch or dinner?" she asked.

"Let's say dinner. I don't know yet what my schedule is likely to be."

"Fine — dinner it is. We'll have some terrific specials lined up for you."

We came back with me through the kitchen. It was quiet. She was the only one working at this time. The evening crew would probably be here in an hour or so but in the meantime, as I left her, she was looking over at the preparation benches, trying to find something to keep her occupied. I knew this was not a normal day for her — the owner of a restaurant does not chop her own onions.

There was just enough time left in the afternoon for one more step in the investigation. This one was not following anything like a straight course. Not that many of them do, but few had strayed this far out. My next move might not be rewarding but it could contribute a few facts.

My train of thought had been initiated by

Lieutenant Delancey's words — "Unfortunately, we can't ask the last Belvedere what was in the book." I added to them the words of the lawyer, Van Linn. He had said, "My client is very anxious to get that book and is increasing pressure on me."

Who could be that anxious? The latest in the Belvedere line, Ambrose, was going to reopen the family restaurant. Did a competitor of the Belvedere dynasty want to pre-empt him and use their recipes? It sounded plausible. Or was it someone with a grudge against the family? That sounded just as plausible.

I had to start somewhere on this approach, so back at the Hotel Monteleone I looked through the yellow pages. ATTORNEYS covered dozens of pages but after them came all the specialists — accident, injury, bankruptcy, probate, estates, contracts, mortgages . . . The categories went on and on, even admiralty law and aviation. Several specialized in "Wrongful Death" which I supposed was a euphemism for murder.

I wanted to stay away from that so I settled on a Michael James and Associates and punched buttons. A pleasant female voice gave me a choice of several extensions but when I realized that she was strictly mechanical, I just picked one at random. I got the secretary of Mr. James himself and after making sure this lady was real, I asked to speak to him.

"May I ask what this is in regard to?"

Far be it from me to tell her never to end a sentence with a preposition, so I asked for Mr. James personally and said it was confidential.

"Much of our business is," she told me. "I need to know a little more before I can connect you."

"It concerns food."

"Food?" She was blindsided by that answer, I could tell.

I repeated it. "Just a moment," she said, coming back to say, "Mr. James is just leaving for a legal conference in Memphis. Can I connect you to his assistant, Mr. Purvis?"

I agreed. Mr. Purvis sounded like a young man but he had a confident tone and after we had gone through all that confidentiality business again, he invited me to come to their offices in the business district. He hemmed and hawed over a time but agreed he could spare me a half hour if I came right away.

It was an impressive office on two stories and I was led along a paneled corridor where Mr. Purvis was just replacing the receiver. He was young to middle-aged, some silver strands showing already but only adding to his prosperous appearance, and his college was Princeton, I noted on the diploma over his desk.

After we had dispensed with preliminaries, I began. "I was given Mr. James' name because he has handled cases involving food."

Mr. Purvis looked perplexed. "I wasn't aware of that. Please continue."

We did the confidentiality thing again. I came close to overdoing it but it worked. Mr. Purvis leaned farther onto the polished desktop in interest.

"You're aware of mad-cow disease."

That hit him between the eyes. "Well, yes, I've heard about it, on the television. It's quite a problem in Europe, isn't it?"

"Ah, that's the point — in Europe, yes. Up to now, that is." I sounded suitably concerned and appropriately reluctant to voice such a major issue.

He picked up as I had hoped. "You mean we have it here, too?"

"The FDA says no, meat-marketing authorities say no, the Department of Agriculture says no." I stopped there. Innuendo-loaded silence could sometimes be more effective than more words.

"But a problem is developing here?" Alarm tinged his question.

"I sincerely hope not."

"Please go on." His interest was bubbling away like a Cajun stew.

"I was given to believe that Mr. James' experience in the food business would be invaluable and —"

He rubbed a hand along the desk top. "Who recommended him?"

"You mean he doesn't specialize in the food industry? Mr. Martin James?"

He straightened. "Our Mr. James is Michael."

"Oh, good heavens! Do I have the wrong office?"

"Just a minute." Mr. Purvis picked up the phone and issued some brief commands. While we waited, we made some small talk about my recent arrival in New Orleans, how I liked it, the weather, had I been here before, then the phone rang. Mr. Purvis listened and replaced it.

"There is no Mr. Martin James listed as an attorney in New Orleans."

I looked distressed.

"Perhaps in one of the outlying towns," he suggested.

"Well, I thought —"

"But if we can help you, we'll be pleased to do so. I doubt if any attorney really specializes in the food industry, not that I'm aware of, anyway. We have an excellent reputation here in the city."

"Well, this could develop into an extremely important matter. The entire meat industry —"

I went on at longer length, though I could see that Mr. Purvis was hooked. Perhaps I was doing him an injustice but I fancied I could see large dollar signs flashing in his brain. Phrases like *class-action suits* were probably appearing in bright neon lights and newspaper headlines reading *Bigger Than Tobacco* were composing themselves.

Now I could get on with what I came for. "The restaurant belonging to the Belvedere family must have strong legal representation. Do you happen to have their account?"

He stared. "Surely they are not involved in the —"

"Not in any way — as far as I know."

He flexed the fingers of his left hand. It seemed to stimulate his brain processes. "They are not one of our clients, no."

"Who would be their competitors?"

"Surely you — Oh, well, you are new to the city, aren't you? The Brennan family, the Chase family, the Patouts —"

231

"Do you represent any of them?"

"Well, no. But I'm sure that doesn't matter. We may not have a share of the legal business associated with the restaurants in the city but we have an excellent reputation." He turned fractionally pompous and I cut him off at the pass.

"That's good to hear, Mr. Purvis. Then there will be no conflict of interest."

"Oh, that's right." He managed a professional smile. "One of my regular golfing companions is also an attorney and his firm happens to handle affairs for the Belvedere family, as a matter of fact."

"Really? Is he with an esteemed firm?"

"Oh, yes. You wouldn't know the name, they have been in New Orleans a long, long time."

"Really old?"

"Quite old, Van Linn and Associates."

I left Mr. Purvis a little confused. He had not expanded his knowledge of mad-cow disease or whether it threatened the economic future of the South. In fact, he had learned nothing of substance and what he had learned, I had had him swear to secrecy. Phrases like "a serious situation involving grave international problems" had been enlisted into my arsenal. A parting word about "stopping in Washington, D.C., on my way back" probably left him with a certain impression, as I didn't add that the reason was to change planes.

On the other hand, I had gained a priceless nugget of knowledge. I knew that attorneys were usually adamant in their reluctant to disclose clients' names, and that had been why I had pursued this circuitous route. It had paid off and I now speculated over it.

So, Van Linn was the Belvedere family lawyer. So Ambrose Belvedere was his client who had commissioned the search for the elusive chef's book — the book, supposedly full of secrets, that two men had died for. Ambrose Belvedere wanted to recover the book that belonged to his own family. That must mean he knew what was in it.

chapter eighteen

It was late in the day when I got back to the hotel, and I needed a little thinking time. I watched some mindless TV which did not disrupt my thinking in the least, had a leisurely bath and then faced the pleasant task of deciding where to eat.

I was trying to alternate the meals at the restaurants belonging to the members of the Witches and those restaurants for which New Orleans is famous. Tonight should be one of the latter. After reviewing the myriad possibilities, I settled on Galatoire's. One of the traditional old-line New Orleans restaurants, I had made a reservation in the newly renovated second-floor dining room. This was a recent improvement, I understood, for reservations had not previously been accepted, much to the chagrin of many diners.

The mirrored walls and the brightly lit room had the look and feel of a Paris brasserie and the service was smartly attired and efficient. I started with the Oysters en Brochette then had the Crabmeat Sardou, both perfectly prepared and presented. The filet mignon Bearnaise was not perhaps typical Creole but it was done exactly as I had ordered it. I was tempted by the dessert card but resisted and settled for an Irish coffee.

Next morning, when I decided the hour hand had reached the time for all good lawyers to be in their office, I called Van Linn. This time, I beat him to the punch. "Sorry I don't have definite news yet but I thought you should know that another copy of the book has been offered for sale."

"You said the copy you saw was a forgery."

"I'm pretty sure that the other is a forgery also."

He grunted dissatisfaction. "Did you get anything out of Gambrinus?"

"Nothing useful. He made Mortensen sound a shade unreliable. He could have been mixed up in it."

"My client is getting extremely anxious," Van Linn said. "As I told you, we are willing to increase your fee for an early and satisfactory result."

"You told me," I agreed. "You didn't tell me everything, though."

"What do you mean?"

235

"I might be able to operate more efficiently if I were to be put in possession of all the facts," I said, sounding stiff and huffy.

"I've told you all that is relevant —"

"No. You haven't told me that your client is Ambrose Belvedere."

I would have had a little gratification if he had paused or hesitated but I should have known that he was too smooth for that. Years in a courtroom had trained his mind to think on its feet — or whatever the expression is.

"I have no reason to believe that your task would be made any easier if you knew the name of my client," he said, slick as olive oil in a hot pan.

"I think it would. This is a Belvedere matter. It might become clearer if a member of the Belvedere family were able to tell us what could be in the book that is of such vital importance." I was trying to sound irate but I didn't want to go too far. That "increased fee" had not yet been quantified . . .

"I have discussed this with the client —" The son of a gun still refused to name him! I let him go on. "— and I am assured that the Belvedere family has no knowledge of what is in the book. Let me remind you — Ambrose had no interest in going into the restaurant business in his youth. He rarely visited it when his grandfather and his father ran it. He knew nothing about its operations. He thinks he may have heard mention of a chef's book, might even have seen it, but is not really sure. I see no way in which you might learn anything contributory."

"I still think there might be something — perhaps without any realization of the existence of that knowledge —"

"I see no possibility of that." Van Linn's dogmatic and uncompromising tone left no room for further verbal maneuver.

I knew when to quit. "All right. I'll be in touch." I couldn't resist one tiny face-saver. "If I do think of a question that he might be able to answer —" I could hear him preparing a negative and hurried to cut him off. "— I'll call you and you can ask him."

"Very well." His tone was accommodating.

I had a little time before heading for the television studio so I did some local sightseeing. The Old U.S. Mint was first on my list. This, I learned, was built in the Greek Revival style and that made me want to see it — if for no other reason than to find out what Greek Revivalists built. Apparently it used to mint money for both the United

States and the Confederacy, surely an open-handed policy.

The adjoining museum had a large exhibit featuring New Orleans jazz and it was inevitable that this should commence with Louis Armstrong's first trumpet. I had missed Mardi Gras but I was able to see costumes and regalias worn then by famous "Krewes" and other memorabilia of Carnival traditions.

St. Louis Cathedral is the oldest operating cathedral in the U.S.A., it is said, and has some beautiful stained-glass windows and murals, though it is otherwise disappointingly ordinary. The Cabildo used to be where the Spanish government sat and is a comprehensive museum of life in early Louisiana. Its attractions include a death mask made of Napoleon by his doctor.

One area I particularly wanted to see was the French Market. Located somewhat naturally in the French Quarter, it has been there since the 1700s. It was a riot of color and aroma. Sheltered by its colonnade and its graceful pillars, the market glistened with the greens of avocados, lettuce, watercress, escarole, peas, string beans, broccoli and okra.

In contrast were the banks of grapefruit, lemons, oranges, limes, bananas, squash and carrots. Slashes of red came from peppers and radishes and melons were cut in half to expose their luscious pink interiors. Strings of garlic by the dozen dangled enticingly, flanked by shaggy brown coconuts, purple eggplant and knobby potatoes. Mirlitons were stacked high; they looked like oversized pears. Rows of fresh-cut herbs offered further temptation to the buyer. Racks of hot-pepper sauces from a score of producers filled shelf after shelf and their heat intensity ranged, so the labels claimed, from "hot" to "devilish" to "hellish."

Next to it was the Flea Market, tables of jewelry, gleaming silver and gold ornaments, souvenirs, T-shirts, even life-sized wooden Indians and alligators. One whole section had colored beads and I watched one couple slipping necklace after necklace of these around the necks of two giant mastiffs. The two animals appeared to be watching each other to make sure they were not being outdone.

These inevitably triggered considerations of lunch, and one of the many friendly shopkeepers recommended the Quarter Scene restaurant on Dumaine Street.

I found it casual and unassuming, only a block off busy Bourbon Street and with wide windows for watching the passing scene. The walls were covered with old lithographs and paintings depicting scenes of early Louisiana while other walls had works by contemporary local artists. It all indicated Southern hospitality. I was seated just in time to hear the waiter explaining to people at the next table that it had been the favorite eating place of Tennessee Williams when he had lived just up the block.

Many favorite local dishes were on the menu and I decided to go strictly home-made Louisiana. I was learning, though, that even the so-called "strictly Louisiana" restaurants incorporated into some of their dishes influences of Caribbean flavors. Jamaican jerk dishes were the most popular of these and the tuna steak prepared this way and topped with tropical fruit salsa caught my eye briefly.

Ginger, bay leaf, allspice, garlic, thyme, cinnamon and chiles are the principal jerk spices and are blended with soy sauce, orange juice and vinegar to produce a very pungent marinade and sauce. Properly prepared, it is said to be so good that Jamaicans put it on everything including eggs.

Still, I concluded that, while in New Orleans, I should keep to Louisiana-style food so I ordered the catfish, encrusted with pecans and served with a crawfish sauce. It proved to be an excellent choice and I was even successful in preventing the waiter from explaining to me why those deep-fried, golfball-sized dark-brown accompaniments to it were called "hush puppies." That explanation must have been heard around the world by now.

Having had only the one course, I felt justified in having the Bread Pudding with Praline Sauce, a homemade house specialty. It was a real treat.

The television studios at WKNO were fizzing with eager young communications tycoons and a large number of young men and women pursuing mysterious and indefinable tasks. After I had received my badge, I was conducted through the building and marveled at the degree to which the public is absorbed with news and weather. Studio after studio was dispensing one or the other.

My experience of weather forecasting was that it was not much more reliable than betting on horse races. The most fascinating activities in this medium were those where the presenter was in one studio and the large screen showing the changing weather pattern was in another. The sight of the attractive girl pointing to an empty screen and telling us to watch out for "this cold front" or "this storm area" was surely the basis for a comedy show.

When I finally reached the studio where the Cajun-Creole confrontation was to take place, Elsa Goddard was already bawling out a hapless underling who must have been seeing her hopes of being the next Connie Chung fading rapidly. Elsa saw me, gave a wave and continued her harangue. The stage was being set with two rows of chairs half facing each other while microphone lines were being strung and pushed out of sight.

A dozen fifteen-inch television monitors sat on a shelf on each of two walls. Several different programs emanating from WKNO's numerous studios were showing on one bank and the other bank displayed programs from competing networks and cable stations — either to inspire or emulate. Ceiling-height black screens formed the walls and could be moved around. Noises from behind them suggested that other shows were being prepared.

In our area, a man in an outfit that looked like a musical-comedy version of a forest ranger accosted me. "You in this here show?"

I admitted it.

"You must be Georgie Redding," he said. "Howdy."

Before I could correct him, he was continuing. "Bird's my name — Eugene C. Bird from Greensboro, North Carolina. Originally, that is. New Orleans the last twenty years. Heard you was goin' to be with us. Glad to have ya aboard. Gonna have a lot of fun."

A dowager lady with a great deal of hair and a purposeful demeanor joined us. "Which team you two on?"

"Team?" I asked.

"Cajuns, o' course," said Eugene C. Bird.

"Me too," said the lady. She gave me a nod that included me in the "team."

Another woman joined us. I had seen her trying to get Elsa Goddard's attention and failing. The unfortunate assistant was wilting by the minute. "You all Creoles?" demanded the woman who was small and thin and wore a dark red dress with gold shoes.

Eugene C. Bird looked at her as if she had accused him of being a child molester. "We're Cajuns," he said ominously.

A gray-haired, gray-faced skinny man picked his way through the cables. "I'm a Creole," he said in a piping voice. "Lester Levison, from Burnside, Louisiana." He gave us a feisty glare as if challenging us to contradict him. I was beginning to think

243

that New Orleans folk were fiercely parochial, especially on this matter of origin.

Elsa Goddard's assistant had almost melted into a puddle of unresisting flesh and had been pushed off into some remote recess of the studio. Her vanquisher, the queen of the airwaves herself, came to greet us, checking us over. "Someone's not here," she announced accusingly.

"Tess Natoches," said Lester Levison promptly. "Her niece is in hospital in Biloxi."

"She could have told me." Elsa Goddard was appalled that her universe was being disturbed.

"Doesn't matter," said the thin lady in the red dress. "We've got three Creoles." She waved a hand that encompassed herself, Lester Levison and me.

"I'm not a —" I began, but the dowager lady pointed to me.

"He's Georgie Redding, he's a Cajun."

"I'm not Redding, I'm —"

"Of course you're ready. We all are," said Elsa Goddard, smiling her professional smile, the one that smoothed out all difficulties as being trivial. "Don't worry. We go on in ten minutes."

Seats were taken, Cajuns on one side and Creoles on the other. I tried to distance myself from both of them but space was cramped. Makeup people dabbed here and there, throat mikes were clipped on, tests were made and then Elsa's radiant personality beamed out over Louisiana. She introduced herself and the show then went on to speak about today's program.

"The Cajuns trace their heritage directly from the Acadian French who, after being expelled from Nova Scotia by the English, relocated in southern Louisiana. Creole culture had its roots in the early 1700s during the French colonial period.

"Here in New Orleans" — she pronounced it "N'Yorlins" — "we are familiar with these differences and we all have a pretty good idea of the differences between Cajun cooking and Creole cooking. We hear a lot about the merging of the two cuisines, but is everyone in favor of this?"

On the monitors, the camera panned along the two battle lines. They were glaring at each other and the answer to Elsa's question was clearly in the negative. She smiled in satisfaction, smelling blood.

"First of all," Elsa said, "I'm going to introduce the two teams." She did so, then said, "For the first question, I'm going to ask the Cajuns for their opinion of Creole cooking."

Oh, oh, I thought, *here we go.* And we did.

The little lady in the red dress spoke up. "African cooking — that's all Creole is. All the Africans knew was cook a long time over a little fire."

The dowager lady with all the hair couldn't wait to leap in. "Creole cooking is French, Spanish, African, Italian, blended together to produce —"

"A mishmash!" crowed Eugene C. Bird. "That's not a blend, that's a mishmash! Why, the only idea the Spanish contributed was to mix meat and fish! Can you believe it? Meat and fish together?"

Lester Levison elbowed his way into the argument. "Know why the Spanish let the Acadians into Louisiana? It was because they couldn't find any other people dumb enough to want to live in the swamps!"

"Cajun cooking," declared the dowager lady, "is a coverup. It relies on peppers that are hot enough to cover the taste of the food."

"Know what the Cajuns do?" cackled the lady in the red dress. "Put pineapple in cole slaw! Imagine anybody with any taste putting pineapple in cole slaw!"

Elsa Goddard was enjoying this hugely. The conflict had become violent right at the start of the program; she hadn't had to do any priming at all. But she still wanted to make it clear that it was her program and now she tried to grab hold of the swelling confrontation before it got out of control.

"Ladies and gentlemen —" She had to say it three times. "Isn't there a saying that 'a Creole takes three chickens to feed one family —' "

Lester Levison was ahead of her. " 'And a Cajun can feed three families on one chicken.' "

"All the Cajuns know is how to feed a lot of people on not much food," said the lady in the red dress scornfully, backing up Lester in fine style. "Talk about loaves and fishes!"

"What about gumbo?" demanded the dowager lady, raising her voice to cut through the melee. "That's what I want to know. What about gumbo? All it is is left-overs — bits of ham, scraps of duck, crumbs of sausage meat, shreds of bacon, flakes of fish! You Creoles call that food?"

"Stupid Cajuns!" shrilled the little lady in the red dress. "Spent twenty years trying to grow grapes 'afore you found out that the soil was all wrong."

Off camera, the dowager lady was making frantic motions at me. *Come on! Get involved!* was her message, I had no doubt. It would have been like stepping between two groups of dagger-wielding opponents or trying to make peace between the Hatfields and the McCoys while dodging the bullets. From the other side, Lester Levison was giving me dirty looks and waving, his exhortation certainly being the same.

Elsa also was making motions that meant she wanted me to enter the fray and I was suddenly alarmed when I glanced at the monitors and saw myself replicated up there several times. "As a comparative outsider," she was saying, and I caught querying looks from the Cajun team who had thought I was Creole and the Creoles who had thought I was Cajun. "As a comparative outsider, where do you stand in this fascinating discussion?"

"Mustard," I said. Relative silence reigned. They were waiting to find out whether it was a criticism or a question. "There's French mustard, English mustard, German mustard, Chinese mustard and kosher deli mustard. They cover the chef's range of needs very well, so why did the Creoles need one of their own?"

It wasn't that difficult a question but no one offered a reply. I fired a second salvo. "One thing I could never understand about Cajun cooking is why does it have no pasta dishes?"

Elsa smiled brassily and brought up the topic of jambalaya. The Creoles said it was red and the Cajuns said it should be brown. It was a more inflammatory theme and we were back on the verge of fisticuffs very quickly. The program ended in a verbal fusillade from both teams of combatants and if there was a musical playout, it was *The Ride of the Valkyries.*

Elsa came up to me afterwards. "Perhaps I should have told you we were changing the format of the program," she said brightly. "This seemed like it would provoke more discussion. I think it went very well, don't you?"

"Pyrotechnically speaking, yes."

She was trying to catch my eye and frowned. "Is something wrong?"

"Over by that reflector . . ." I said.

She turned. "What is it?"

"There's a man standing behind it."

"I don't see —"

A figure emerged. "It's Larry Mortensen!" Elsa said, surprised. "What's he doing here?"

"I don't know," I said, "but he has his hand inside that jacket again and the way it sags, I think he's brought his gun with him."

chapter nineteen

"Your badge," Elsa said accusingly as Larry Mortensen reached us. "It's the one you were issued the last time. It's not valid for today."

Mortensen looked irritated. His clothes looked as if they had just been thrown on and the ancient bomber jacket he was wearing must have been made long before bombers were invented. The garment attracted my attention particularly because it bulged where his right hand was inside it. He didn't seem concerned about Elsa's accusation. He looked from one to the other of us. "Which of you killed Earl?" he demanded.

He was tall and strong and had a gun — all of which made him dangerous. He had a more purposeful look now than before, which was disconcerting.

"You knew Earl?" queried Elsa. It was a good move. It diverted him from any immediate action and he clearly wanted to explain.

"He was a good friend of Richie's," he said. "Who killed him?"

"Let's get out of this studio," Elsa said briskly. "The staff will be in here in a few minutes to get it ready for the next show. We can go in the conference room. Let me close out my segment." She went to an instrument panel and pushed buttons and turned switches. I took the opportunity to engage Larry Mortensen. "So the three of you were friends, were you?"

"We were good friends."

"Then you must know something about the book."

"The book?"

"Yes. Your brother got the Belvedere cookbook from the auction and took it to Gambrinus's bookshop. He waited there for someone to pay him money for it. They had an argument and the person shot him, shot your brother. Do you know who that person is?"

He gave me a penetrating look. "Was it you?"

"Certainly not!"

His eyes roamed over to where Elsa was turning away from the instrument panel. She came over to us. She gave me a glance that seemed to have some hidden meaning but only said, "Let's go to the conference room."

251

We had reached the door when a uniformed man hurried in. Elsa's head moved fractionally in Mortensen's direction. The uniform had tags that said SECURITY and the burly guard took in Mortensen's appearance with a practiced glance.

"I'll escort you to the lobby," the guard said, ready for trouble but not inviting it. Mortensen had his hand out of the bomber jacket now. He gave Elsa and me a very annoyed look but went without any resistance. We exchanged relieved glances.

"That fellow is getting to be a nuisance," she said. "What was he saying to you while I was summoning security?"

"He was accusing me of killing his brother."

"Might be as well if you stayed out of his way."

"I agree but it may be more to the point if he would stay out of mine."

"Are you any closer at all?" she asked. "To finding out who's behind this, I mean?"

"Still chasing the story? The big one that could make you famous?"

"Sure." She was nonchalant with her answer but I could sense a steely determination underlying it.

"My answer is, I'm making progress but

not yet ready to announce an arrest. How about you?"

She was debating in her mind. Was it how much she should confide in me? To urge her along, I said, "Wasn't it one of us who suggested that we might make more headway if we pooled our knowledge?"

"Was it?" she said with the wisp of a smile. "Which one?"

I shook my head sadly. "And just when I thought I was going to hear a revelation."

"From me?"

"Yes."

She still had her clipboard in her hands She raised it and glanced at it but with an unseeing eye. "I'm not sure how much of a revelation this is, but I guess there's no harm in telling you. After all, we're both after the same end, aren't we?"

"I don't think so. I'm primarily looking for the book. You want a spectacular murder hunt with a dramatic ending."

She wagged the clipboard thoughtfully. "It's just this. I think one of the Witches is involved."

"Which Witch?"

She smiled. "I don't know. I have a few ideas but I don't want to say anything until I'm more sure."

"What makes you suspicious of the

Witches?" I was remembering the words of Emmy Lou Charbonneau. She, too, harbored the same conviction. Were they both suspicious of the same woman? And for the same reason?

"Oh, various aspects of this whole crazy business."

"Anything specific?"

"Not really."

"You're a big help."

"No, I'm not — and I know I'm not. I just don't want to throw suspicion in the wrong direction, that's all. If I can just gather a few more facts . . ."

"You know what I think?" I asked.

She gave me an amused smile. "No, what do you think?"

"I think that you may not be the only one who is suspicious of the Witches."

"You mean you are, too?"

"Not me. I mean, I wouldn't be surprised if other Witches aren't suspicious of the Witches."

"One of them has told you this."

I knew she was sharp so I wasn't surprised. I neither confirmed nor denied, in the classical tradition. She did the right thing and concluded that she was right as well as sharp. "And you're not going to tell me who it is. Okay, it's a standoff."

"For the moment. But we should cooperate. I'd hate to think of either of us being the killer's next victim."

For all of her tough exterior, there was an unmistakable flash of anxiety there. It was good to know that she was human after all.

Tonight was to be dinner with Leah but before I dressed for that, I sat down with the telephone books in the hotel room. I went through the section on employment agencies, looking specifically at the classification for the hotel and restaurant trade.

I had pondered over the problem of learning more about the Belvedere family and their restaurant. It was closed now, awaiting its reopening by the latest in the line, Ambrose Belvedere. Who better to tell me about it, I reasoned, than the people who had worked there? The problem with that was, where were they? Many must be working in other restaurants but some must be looking for jobs. The restaurant trade has a high percentage of floaters, itinerants, the gypsies of the business who can't stay put in one job or one place for very long.

It is not always easy to spot these when they are hired. The restaurant prefers more stable employees but can't be sure when they are hired that they are going to stay.

Even as reputable a place as Restaurant Belvedere might hire staff that seem to be reliable only to have them leave a couple of months later. It could be a little tricky getting the information I wanted but I could face that tomorrow. In the meantime, I was able to compile a list of employment agencies who might be able to provide the information I wanted.

Leah's place was just outside the French Quarter and I had an appetizer in the Carousel Bar before I left the Monteleone. It is well-named. It revolves just like a carousel — well, perhaps not quite as fast but in just as circular a motion. It is an odd sensation and I tried to picture the effect on an imbiber after partaking of two or three drinks. The television screens were the only jarring note.

Leah had not overdone the Asiatic theme, I was glad to notice. A few touches showed, such as Chinese-style lanterns, wall scrolls inscribed with large, scrawling characters, and hibachi-type cookers on some of the tables, but the overall influence was subdued. Leah looked every inch the Asian hostess in a *chamsung* that fit her tall, exquisite figure perfectly.

It was in a lustrous material and had a

flowered pattern in blue on a white background. Her shiny black hair was drawn back and held with a dull gold ring. She seemed genuinely pleased to see me and gave me a table away from the kitchen with my back to the wall and a view of the room.

"My menu is descriptive," she told me in her musical voice as she handed one to me, "and we note the characteristics of both New Orleans and Asiatic cooking. Each has its own typical style and constituents so you will be able to see how I have chosen to blend them into a different and original dish."

I examined it. "Not an easy task. Looks as though you have done very well."

"I am sure you are aware of how important ginger is in Chinese cooking," Leah said. "It is used in many dishes and particularly seafood. The aroma of ginger not only neutralizes the odors but in China, it is believed to absorb any evil in the food."

I was still looking at the menu as she was talking. "There are a few unusual dishes here," I said. "Stir-fried Stomach with Mustard Greens is a dish I've never seen on a menu before. I take it that is not a misprint?"

She smiled. "It refers to precooked, shredded pork stomach. We have a very faithful Chinese clientele who order it regularly."

"I don't see that perennial Chinese favorite, hot-and-sour soup, on here. Haven't you worked out a Cajun or Creole version of that?"

"No. I thought I could, and I tried hard, but there are no Louisiana equivalents of some of the ingredients."

"Which ingredients are those?"

"Shredded squid — the Chinese squid has a very assertive flavor. Seaweed — it is more chewy here and would contribute nothing after receiving the additional processing it would need. Wood ears — are you familiar with those?"

"I had them once in Singapore. They're not known in America or Europe."

"They are a fungus that grows on trees. They are dried for storage and sale then soaked in boiling water."

"They taste something like a mushroom," I said.

"They do. Then, of course, there is an essential ingredient that hot-and-sour soup needs to make it totally authentic but I am not allowed to use it."

"Which ingredient is that?"

"Chicken blood."

"Pity," I said. "No substitutes for that?"

"None that are satisfactory. Most of the other ingredients are sold here, though — ground hot red peppers, soya beans and bean paste are in all shops selling Asian food."

"I see you have a lot of crab dishes on the menu."

"Crabs are very common in China. They are always cooked live there, you know. A popular way to eat them is to use chopsticks to put the whole soft-shell crab into the mouth — the Chinese crabs are very small." She smiled again. "It might be difficult to get Americans to eat them that way. You will also notice that many crab dishes are deep-fried. This is because crab is very delicate and is easily overcooked. Deep-frying means it cooks evenly all over and seals in the moisture and the flavor."

"Many people are concerned about the fat content in deep-frying."

Leah shook her head firmly. "That need no longer be a concern. Lots of low-fat alternatives are available in both the batter and the cooking oil."

" 'Leah's Chop Suey, Cajun Style,' " I quoted from the menu. "That sounds like a fascinating fusion of cuisines."

She laughed merrily. "As I'm sure you know, chop suey is not a Chinese dish at all.

A Chinese chef in a London restaurant a hundred years ago was called upon to provide a meal for a large party. It was at the end of the day and all that remained in the kitchen were scraps of vegetables, fish, beef, chicken and so on. The chef made a stir fry of them all and added plenty of soy sauce. It was such a huge success that many of them came back and asked for it again. Asked for a name, the chef said on the spur of the moment, 'chop suey,' which is Chinese for 'odds and ends.' "

"A little similar to the way in which 'buffalo wings' became famous," I said.

"Exactly," Leah agreed.

"To come back to your chop suey, though, to what extent have you Cajunized it?"

"Oh, I use a brown roux and some tomatoes."

I was studying the menu all the time we were talking.

"You've made the choice very difficult," I told Leah. "So many dishes I'd like to taste."

"You must be very familiar with spring rolls, won tons, and chicken noodle salad," Leah said. "You want to try something different — am I right?"

"Absolutely."

"Very well, then, if you'd like a soup to start, the Chinese Celery Cabbage and Dried Shrimp Soup is one I would highly recommend. Instead of the traditional rice wine, I use sherry. It is a soup that appeals to lovers of Chinese soups as well as those raised on New Orleans soups. Strangely enough, the small, saltwater shrimp found in New Orleans waters is not only very similar to the shrimp that the Chinese use, but it is even better."

"Celery cabbage is, in fact, what is frequently sold in American markets as 'Chinese cabbage,' isn't it?" I asked Leah.

"It is. There is another Chinese cabbage but it is good only for stewing and cooking and cannot be eaten raw."

So I started with the soup. It was delicate but the ginger taste came through just assertively enough and the celery cabbage enriched the flavor. The Fried Shrimp with Garlic was my next choice, a fairly simple dish but highly flavored with garlic, ginger and hot red peppers — spicy yet not burning — and, Leah told me, given a New Orleans twist with the addition of plenty of paprika.

Carp was sometimes on the menu but, unfortunately, not today. "Instead, for the main course," Leah said, "I would suggest either the Braised Duck with Plums, the

Cantonese Fried Spareribs or the Pork Steaks. The Chinese influence in the pork steaks is soy sauce, rice wine, and hot red peppers."

We discussed the relative merits of the three dishes for a while and I finally decided on the spareribs. Leah had retained the Chinese five-spice powder which is so readily available in the U.S., the garlic and the soy sauce, but added curry powder.

"This makes it like an Indonesian recipe," she said. "They garnish the dish with carrot and parsley and we do the same." The ribs were dipped in a mixture of the spices, then coated in egg yolk and cornstarch and fried to golden brown. They were exquisite.

"The idea of serving dessert at the end of a meal used to seem strange to Chinese people," Leah told me when the table had been cleared. "Still today, dessert is not popular in China. At important banquets, it is sometimes served between courses. Here, of course, customers expect dessert so we offer preserved fruit, lichee nuts and tangerine-and-ginger mousse. Our specialty, though, is orange tapioca."

"How do you prepare that?"

"We use the tapioca pearls, and fresh oranges with the membrane removed."

"I'll have that."

It was delicately flavored, as I'd expected, and with it Leah brought a tray of almond cookies and sat down with me. I congratulated her on an excellent meal.

"Very ingeniously blended cuisines," I told her.

"Thank you," she said with a charming smile. "But now we have talk about more serious matters."

"Very well," I said, "but first I want to say that I was strongly tempted not to tell the police that I saw you leaving Earl's rooms. I didn't believe that you were involved in killing him and I still don't, but, as I mentioned earlier, the carriage driver I was with saw you, too, and he would have told the police if I didn't."

"That's all right. I understand. I wanted to explain something to you also. Earl has always had an eye open for anything shady, any way to make money easily. That's why I had to get him out of the restaurant. He spent little time here, was no help at all, and used it as nothing more than a source of cash.

"He was never there when I needed him, and I got used to running the place single-handed once I found a good chef to take over in the kitchen."

"Do you think he was mixed up with

Richie Mortensen in the scheme to steal the Belvedere book?"

She hesitated. "He may have been. Through me, he knew several of the Witches and — I don't know if you agree with this, but I think one of them wants the book."

"For herself, you mean?"

"Yes."

"Who do you think it is?"

"I don't know." Her eyes were wide. "I really don't."

"Have any of them ever done anything to make you suspect that they could commit a crime — even a crime leading to murder?"

"No. I don't know anything about any of them that would suggest that."

Well, that was turning out to be a very popular idea. "I appreciate your being so frank with me," I told her. "I hope this case is going to be brought to an end very soon."

"Before there are any more murders," she said in a low voice.

I left, in full agreement with that sentiment.

chapter twenty

The Acme Employment Agency didn't get many marks for originality of nomenclature. There seems to be one in every town in the country. The name certainly gets it into the first page of the telephone book although the American Automobile Association and Alcoholics Anonymous are still battling for those next places.

Miss Ellen Lennox was young, bright and ambitious. She wore glasses she probably didn't need and she handled her computer like a female Marine with a rocket launcher. She listened attentively while I told her why I was there.

"Our marketing department sees perhaps five, possibly as many as ten restaurants in New Orleans. You will be receiving our official list of requirements shortly but I am here to get a preliminary idea of the labor situation. I know this is a restaurant town so a large labor pool hopefully exists. However, what I want to examine is the depth of knowledge of New Orleans–style cooking."

"That should not be a problem," Miss Lennox said crisply as her fingers danced over the keyboard. From my angle of view of her screen, all I could see were pretty colors. No matter how much I squirmed, I could not get a better angle, so I would have to adopt more subterfuge.

"And made even easier by the fact that I went through this exercise last week," chirped Miss Lennox, fingers still flying.

"Oh, who was that for?"

She smiled just slightly, not enough to disturb her concentration. "They were concerned about remaining anonymous for the time being, just as you are." She paused. "Now, how many people are you looking for, initially?" she asked.

"Let's say one chef in each restaurant, experienced, reliable."

She nodded confidently.

"Can you give me a few words' description of some of the candidates you may be suggesting?" I asked, and as she flashed me a look that I knew might pack a question, I went on swiftly: "Save you and me both a lot of time. Once you get to know exactly what we want, I'm sure your system will be able to pull up names by the dozen."

"Very well." Miss Lennox could see a lot

of commission payments looming and was ready to be cooperative. "Let's see, now — here's one . . . Four years with Mulate's, three years with Olde Nawlins Cookery, and three years with Holiday Inns." She beamed triumphantly.

I looked dubious. "Before that?"

"Worked in Natchez and Corpus Christi."

"No other New Orleans experience?"

"No, but —"

"Our theme is going to demand chefs who have heavy local experience."

Her fingers flew like wild birds. "Here's another one —"

I interrupted her. "It might save time if you would just give me the names of the restaurants these candidates worked at, their more recent experience —"

"Very well." She was used to clients and their funny ways, and was willing to do whatever. "Dickie Brennan's Palace, Planet Hollywood, Landry's Seafood House, the Redfish Grill. He came from Baltimore so that's all his local experience. Then we have . . . Oh, this one is a woman."

"That's fine. Many of our best chefs are women." I trusted that word of this would never get back to the Witches, who would batter me with wet noodles at such a patronizing statement. It worked with Miss Lennox, though, who beamed again and rattled off a formidable list of names. None of them was the one I wanted, though. But a couple of minutes later, it came.

"Then we have Eli Richter who was six years at the Court of the Two Sisters and eleven years at Restaurant Belvedere . . . but I believe he's on cruise ships now."

I let it go; then, a few minutes later, Miss Lennox was reeling off more names of chef candidates and restaurants when — "he worked at Mike Anderson's, the Hyde Park Grill, Tony Moran's and the Restaurant Belvedere" — she broke off. "Oh, but Chester isn't available any longer. He retired."

"Chester?" I asked. "Chester Jones, by any chance? He was one of our top chefs back in —"

"No, I'm afraid not. This is Chester Garland."

"Oh, what a shame. I'd like to see old Chester again. Well, I hope this Chester is enjoying his retirement. He's local, I suppose?"

"Very much so." She glanced at the screen. "Living out on the river in Algiers."

I spent a little while longer with Miss Lennox. She was eager to fill all our personnel needs but I didn't want to keep her from really remunerative work. I thanked her profusely and left.

A nearby drugstore had a phone with a directory that was not too torn. It was easy to find Chester Garland in Algiers, easier than it would have been to find a Jones.

"No Time Like the Present" continued to be one of the more popular platitudes. Chester lived in a small clapboard house near the banks of the Mississippi River. Fishermen were leaving and arriving, some with strings of fish, some with baskets and boxes. All looked cheerful, whether they had successful catches or not. Most of the fishermen were black and it turned out that Chester Garland was, too. His face was creased and his skin papery but his eyes were bright. He moved painfully as he let me into a room decorated with personal photographs everywhere, on tables, on shelves, on racks on top of the TV. Posed with movie stars, football stars, politicians, basketball players who towered over him, Chester always in his white chef's outfit with a tall chef's hat and a big smile.

He had an expensive TV and the place was well-maintained so I deduced that he had retired under good financial circumstances. He evidently lived in a small house in a modest neighborhood by choice. I deduced that he didn't get many visitors because he was certainly glad to see me. He insisted on brewing coffee and was delighted to learn that I loved it with chicory.

"Seems to be a good fishing spot. Do you do much fishing yourself, Chester?"

"Coupla times a week. Get me enough catfish for two or three meals."

"Let me guess — you mix red and black pepper, mustard, basil and Tabasco, you melt butter and sauté chopped onions and garlic in it, then add the fish and the seasonings. You serve it over rice. Am I right?"

Chester laughed, slapped his thigh. "You're close, man, you're awful close." He had a happy manner, probably got along well with others and must have enjoyed working as a chef in busy kitchens.

"Thing I like to do is add a cupful of oyster soup at the end. I like a nice sauce and that holds the spices and gives a bit extra flavor all its own."

"I'll remember that," I said.

"Now, what can I do for you — seeing as you know how to cook catfish?"

"I worked as a chef for several years, various parts of the world."

He nodded, sipped coffee.

"What I do now is — well, I'm sort of an information gatherer. Anything to do with the food and restaurant business. Sometimes I look for rare spices, other times I recommend substitutes for food items, you know, when they become expensive or hard to get."

"Interesting job."

"It is." I had, in fact, described part of my job accurately but I hadn't given Chester a business card because I didn't want the word *detective* to upset him. It affects some people, mostly those with something to hide, but also others who have exaggerated ideas about their privacy. It intimidates some people but this was not one of those occasions. Chester didn't seem to be in any of these categories. From this point on, though, I had to stray a little from the truth.

"People who write books sometimes have me do a little research for them. Right now, there is interest in a book that describes the families who have built up the great restaurants in this country. I was given your name as a man who could tell me something about the Belvedere family."

Chester cocked his head on one side and regarded me.

"What kind of a book?" he demanded warily.

"Describing the family's achievements, how they built up a restaurant dynasty, why it survived through several generations, the secrets of its success, where it's going in the future."

"The latest in the line, Ambrose, he's going to reopen the restaurant. You know that?"

"That's what I've heard. Another book would be a different angle — a great restaurant closes down then reopens."

I wanted to keep chatting, get him in a cooperative mood. He seemed cautious and I wondered why.

"You were chef there for how long?" I asked.

"Ten years, till they shut down."

"You must have known Eli Richter."

His expression lightened. "You know Eli?"

I shrugged. "Oh, not that well."

That helped. Chester told me a few stories about Eli and we both chuckled. "And now he's leading the cruising life," I said.

"Yeah, guess so. Feeding two thousand people a day, four meals. Must keep him busy." We both laughed at that, silently agreeing that it was a different life from the one inside a restaurant kitchen, but to each his own. "I worked on cruise ships for a while," I told Chester.

"You did?"

I told him a few of the routes and the ports and he raised his eyebrows. "Man, you've been around." We were on the same wavelength now and I was ready to ease him into the information zone.

"So tell me about the Belvederes, just overall, you know, how were they to work for, any little peculiarities, that sort of stuff."

"Well, Ernesto Belvedere was running it when I worked there. His father came in a few times but he was pretty far gone by then."

I feigned ignorance. "Far gone? Drink, you mean?"

"Mind. It had been going for a while. They got fancy names for it today, Alzheimer's, Creutzfeldt-Jacob and whatever. It ran in the family."

"That's too bad."

"Arturo — he's the one started the business — had the same thing. So did his son, Edgardo."

"The whole family? That's terrible. What about Ernesto?"

Chester hesitated. "Him, too. Wasn't too bad when I started there but it got worse fast. See, that's why young Mr. Ambrose, he wanted to get away, have nothing to do with the business. So with Ernesto gone and his son wanting no part of it, the place just faded."

"But now Ambrose wants to reopen it."

"Surprised me," Chester admitted.

"Ernesto's symptoms must have interfered with the smooth running of the place when you were there." I tossed out the comment like bait on the water.

"Ernesto was forgetting. He'd give orders to somebody then forget and tell somebody else to do it. He'd insist he wanted to order supplies himself then he'd forget. He'd insist on answering the phone, take a reservation, then forget to enter it in the book. He'd get mad at us for practically no reason at all. He'd scream and yell. He'd get crazy ideas about new dishes. Got to where the place was like a ship outta control, going too fast, heading for the rocks."

"Terrible," I said, and meant it. "How long did the restaurant continue after Ernesto began behaving that way?"

"Let me get you some more coffee," Chester said, and did so.

"Great coffee," I told him; he grinned.

"A year at least," he said in answer to my question. "The staff all covered up for him. Made it difficult to operate but they managed. They were all loyal. All good people."

"Did you know his father, Alfonse?"

"No, I didn't. Heard a lot about him, of course."

"You said he went the same way."

"Yeah. Guess it's common for it to happen in several generations."

"That's awful. Fortunate that great strides are being made with that kind of disease today," I said. "Pity that progress is too late to save all those great chefs of the Belvedere family, though."

"Right enough," Chester agreed.

"What do you think made Ambrose change his mind and decide to reopen?"

"Lotta people wonder about that. Haven't seen him myself since he decided. Don't know him that well anyhow. When he was in college, he used to come in the restaurant occasionally but he never showed any real interest in it."

"You think the Restaurant Belvedere can get back to the rating that it had before? Back up there with Commander's Palace, Brennan's and Antoine's?"

I threw the last name in, expecting him to comment on it first. He did. "Well, Antoine's ain't quite what it used to be . . . It's a tough business — I don't know."

"Is Ambrose going into it alone? Does he have any partners?"

"Haven't heard of any," said Chester.

"Business or financial?"

"Not that I know of."

His face, somewhat lugubrious to begin with, looked long and sad. Clearly he felt for the family that he had worked for so long and, I had no doubt, industriously.

"I'll bet you put in a lot of hours there."

He gave me a flash of a grin, acknowledging the understanding of someone who had experienced the same kind of life. "Bet I did. Loved it, though — every minute."

We discussed food, especially Creole and Cajun food. Chester had supervised the cooking of all the fish dishes and we talked about Gulf fish, especially the ones not found elsewhere.

When I left, we were chatting like old friends. I walked away, saddened to think of such a great restaurant dynasty felled by such a terrible disease. I wondered what hope Ambrose had of reviving the family tradition and bringing back greatness to the Belvedere name.

Another thought struck me: Did Ambrose face a dark future from the same mental affliction that had ravaged the earlier generations?

★ ★ ★

I had to walk a few blocks through the residential area and away from the river to find a likely place for a taxi. I spotted a shopping mall and one of the shopkeepers showed me where a taxi rank was located. It was a quiet day, the cabbies reading newspapers and making bets on some upcoming sporting event. A smart-looking young fellow was first to be willing to forgo the sporting life and offer me a ride.

We turned in the direction of the nearest bridge to cross the river back toward New Orleans. The cabbie was a good, attentive driver and I was just sitting back, relaxing and looking at all the craft plying the river when he called out, "Got somebody mad at you?"

"Not as far as I know," I said almost automatically.

He looked intently into his rearview mirror. "Car behind us. Think he's following us."

I looked back but the car appeared ordinary to me.

"Make a few turns," I said. "See if he is."

The driver did so. A few minutes later, he said, "Sho'nuff. He's on our tail and no mistake."

I sighed. Not again . . .

"You ain't FBI," the driver said conversationally, "otherwise, you'd be followin' him. Am I right?"

"Sounds logical," I agreed.

"Whaddayou think, then?"

"Keep driving. Go slower. Let's be sure."

A few minutes later, he glanced at me through the mirror. "Still hangin' in there. He must want you real bad."

"I think you're enjoying this," I told him.

He grinned and showed two rows of fine white teeth.

"Makes a change. Bit of excitement. What now?"

I wasn't sure what now. Stop and try to find out who was in the other car and why it was following me was one alternative, but I set that aside for the moment. Try and lose him was another possibility but that way I would learn nothing.

The dilemma was solved almost immediately. Along a quiet street, two large tour buses had pulled up and were discharging lines of passengers. A uniformed woman was holding up the traffic until they were all out.

"Where are they going?" I asked my driver.

"Place where they build the floats for the Mardi Gras. Getta lotta tourists here."

"Big place, is it?"

"Yeah, real big. Interestin', too, every-body says. Never been there myself but lotsa people —"

I thrust a couple of bills at him and climbed out on the curbside. I slipped between the two lines of discharging passengers and headed for the entrance.

chapter twenty-one

I paid my eight dollars and fifty cents and hurried into Mardi Gras World. I used the lines of tourists coming off the buses as cover. They were from Madison, Wisconsin, they told me and were members of a seniors group who made quarterly visits various sights around the country.

"Went to Branson last trip," one lady who declared herself an octogenarian told me. She had snow-white hair and a purple jacket with ski pants. "Ever been there? You should go," she went on, without waiting to find out if I had been there or not, "it's great."

This was the first visit to New Orleans for many of them and they were all agog at the sights and sounds. "Went on the Haunted History Tour yesterday," said another lady of about the same age. "Saw the home of Anne Rice, you know, writes the vampire stories, and the house where Jefferson Davis died." Another elderly member of the group made her contribution: "Lafayette Cemetery — that was the best," she piped up. "That's where Anne Rice's vampires are buried."

As I was sure that Anne Rice wrote fiction, I could only conclude that some clever PR was at work here, but an even older member with a cane that he wielded like a swordstick joined in. "Wouldn't want to be there at night. All those tombs and vaults. They're all aboveground, you know."

During these conversations, I was watching the entrance to see who came in other than the Wisconsin Leisure Tour group. I could see no one suspicious. There were a couple of families with several children each, and a couple speaking Dutch, then a class from a local school. I didn't want to subject any of them to stray bullets but I didn't think it would reach that extreme and they all created such a convenient cover.

Who was following me, though? Larry Mortensen seemed like the only possible culprit. Had he learned something new that had made him suspicious of me all over again? I looked for his easily noticeable figure and his untidy brown hair but could not see him.

I followed the tour. We went first to a

greeting area where we were told about the King Cake, the traditional brioche with a sugary filling, then we were served a slice. A short briefing video was next. I carefully waited until the viewing theater was full then stood near a door where I could spot latecomers.

The efficient guide system kept stragglers away, however, and all looked serene. We embarked on the tour of the huge warehouse complex and, despite my vigilance, I found myself being carried away by the magnificence of the floats and the dedication and skill of the people making them. This was only days after the Mardi Gras and already they were hard at work building the floats for the next one.

From Michael Jordan and General de Gaulle to Elvis and President Reagan, faces bigger than a person grinned or glowered, perfectly captured in acrylic painted Styrofoam. Mermaids, pirates, robots, Revolutionary soldiers, fairies, munchkins were all here. In the really big areas were King Kong and sixty-foot-long floats representing Mississippi River boats and various other concepts from the imagination of Mardi Gras World's own technicians putting into three-dimensional reality the demands of the Krewes.

When I emerged at the end of the tour, I made sure I was in the middle of a number of tourists. I had woven in and out of the friendly folk from Wisconsin and we were chatting as if we shared decades of memories together. "Come to New Orleans for the Mardi Gras?" asked one older man who said he was a dairy farmer.

"I arrived the day after," I told him.

"You should have been here," he said reproachfully. "Over a million people."

"Sounds like quite a party."

I came out of the building slowly, carefully checking every person and looking for any loiterers. All was normal and nothing seemed out of line.

There was no taxi rank, most people were arriving by bus. A normal-sized limo was stationary with a driver standing beside it. The name of Mardi Gras World was painted on the side. FREE TRANSPORT, it said underneath.

The driver looked at me. "Want to go to the ferry?"

"When are you leaving?"

"In a few minutes."

I nodded and waited. The driver asked me if I wanted to sit inside but I preferred not to be trapped. I stood by the vehicle, and in five minutes no one had looked suspicious and only a young couple with a baby wanted the ferry. "Let's go," the driver said.

I watched as we pulled out, but saw no one following. The ferryboat was a competent little operation, nonlabor-intensive. As it was free, too, there was no delay; the crossing of the river took only minutes and then we bumped against the dock, almost next to where the *Delta Duchess* had departed.

I walked quickly past Harrah's Casino and up Canal Street. Taxi ranks were nowhere in sight, in fact the city cab service seemed to operate from cruising cabs only. I watched a few go by, then, at an intersection, one stopped and unloaded. I half turned my back as it was about to pull away from the curb, then took some quick steps and jumped in. "Jackson Square," I said to the driver.

I looked out the back window. Another cab was coming and a couple got out. I was about to settle in my seat, satisfied that I had shaken off any pursuit, when a man hurried into view — I wasn't sure from where.

He was a little under medium height, dark hair, and he had a small black mustache. He was wearing a dark suit. Who the blazes was he? He jumped into the other cab. My driver was looking at me in his mirror.

"Where you want to be on the Square?"

"Just head for it," I told him. "I'll make up my mind when we get there."

We went through a knot of traffic and when we came out, I looked back again. The other cab was still there. My driver was a young–to–middle-aged fellow with a sallow complexion. Some Latin blood in his heritage. He drove competently and without the urgency that many taxi drivers show.

"Worried about that cab that's following us?" he asked.

He must have noticed my anxious looks behind. "Some of your New Orleans ladies seem to have jealous husbands," I told him.

"That what it is?" I wasn't certain but there might be a tinge of skepticism in his voice. Still, I thought it was a good subterfuge and I wasn't going to abandon it too easily.

"You look like a man about town. You know how it is."

"Want to know for sure?" he asked.

"Okay."

He was a good driver. He didn't make it obvious that he was trying to shake off pursuit but he increased and decreased speed in a way that could have been simply using gaps in the traffic and he made a couple of turns and reverted to his original route in a way that any experienced driver would use to avoid possible delays.

When traffic smoothed out, he glanced in his mirror. "He's still there."

"Do you know the driver of that cab?" I asked.

He looked back, shook his head. "No. I know a lot of them but I don't know him."

Who could be following me now? I was baffled. I had been convinced that it had been the unpredictable Larry Mortensen, either intent on avenging his brother's death or following some mysterious path of his own. But someone else? Why was I making so many enemies in New Orleans? It seemed like such a nice city.

We made a few turns to accommodate the one-way system that the city favors so strongly. The other cab stayed back but kept a steady distance.

My driver had a slightly amused smile on his face. He was enjoying this, darn him. I was racking my brain for a solution. Well, two could play at this game.

"When you see a chance, pull into a street parking space," I said. "Let him go by then follow him. See how he likes it."

My driver grinned, showing even white teeth. We continued on an even course for a few blocks then he swung sharply into a parallel parking space and stopped on the proverbial dime.

The cab went on by and though I strained to see inside it, I could not make out anything more in the backseat than a silhouette of a figure that meant nothing.

"Good, now follow him," I said.

We did so for about two blocks then he peeled off violently, inches in front of a vegetable truck that stopped with a screeching of tires, effectively blocking us from following.

My driver uttered a few choice words, accentuating them with angry thumps on the steering wheel. "Don't worry about it," I told him. "Where are we now?"

"Business District. Be in the French Quarter, five minutes."

"All right. Carry on. Let me know if you see him behind us."

It wasn't long. "There he is. Son of a bitch is good."

"Okay. As soon as we get in the French Quarter, find a place where you can squeeze in and let me off. Somewhere busy and packed. Make it difficult for him to get close. By the time the guy gets out, that'll give me time to merge into a crowd."

I counted out three tens. Eric Van Linn's

expense account could stand it. My driver did a good job. He turned into a narrow alley, vehicle-negotiable but only just. I didn't see the name of it but for New Orleans that was par for the course. I scanned the building fronts: It was mostly restaurants, a few looking fairly classy but also quite a few of the others, ethnic and no doubt fun places to eat.

It was an awkward time for restaurants, right in between standard mealtimes. But New Orleans was clearly a go-go kind of town and several of the places were open.

"He's turned in after us," my driver called. He accelerated as much as the cramped street permitted, putting as much distance as possible between us and our pursuer. He stopped in front of a store that boasted over 100,000 VINTAGE LP'S; I crammed the bills into his hand and scrambled out.

"Watch out for those husbands, man!" was his final warning. "They can be murder!" Little did he know.

Some of those vintage LP's were competing for airspace, booming out from stereo speakers. I identified one number as Herman's Hermits, issuing their love for their "Ferry Cross the Mersey" while other blasts from the past tried to sink the ferry.

Smells of spicy food wafted along the alley. They were coming from the adjacent café. The door was open and I peered in. The tables were Formica-covered and the floor needed sweeping. My situation might be desperate but I had limits.

I glanced back; there were too many people to see clearly but I saw a smallish man in a dark suit among them. I hurried on. A man stood in a doorway singing "Amazing Grace." His voice was tired and strained but he obviously loved to sing. A bunch of college students stopped to listen to him. In the next building was the "Doorway to the New Age." The doorway itself was open and the "New Age" consisted of a very large lady in a purple dress sitting at a table shuffling cards. She looked up and saw what must look like an easy mark.

"Come on in, sweetheart!" she invited. "The Tarot tells all. Let me lead you into the future!"

Another time I would have accepted her offer, but if I didn't shake off the man following me, my future might arrive all too soon. A good-sized restaurant was next, a wooden front with mullioned windows. It looked enticing and was surely big enough that I could find a back way out. I turned the doorknob — only to notice a sign saying, CLOSED.

Before my frustration could boil to the surface, I saw another sign near it: CHEF INTERVIEWS TODAY. FIRST DOOR IN ALLEY. The alley referred to was almost invisible, a right turn into a pedestrian thoroughfare narrow enough to touch the wall on both sides without needing much of a reach.

I dived into the alley, found the door and went in.

chapter twenty-two

It was dark and cramped when I closed the door behind me. Bolts were at the top and bottom and I took the liberty of pushing both of them. Maybe that would slow down the pursuit.

Pungent aromas of hot pepper sauces and cooking tomatoes brought with them more than a hint of garlic. I turned in that direction and a voice called out, "In here!" I went that way, passing a door into the kitchen and into a tiny office that had never been sullied with anything remotely resembling order or organization. Papers, files, letters, bills, books were everywhere. Shelves were stacked to overflowing and so was the table where a man sat.

He needed a shave and he had not spent a lot of time combing his hair. He was broad-shouldered and heavy. His face was jowly and he had bushy eyebrows. When he looked up at me, his eyes were bright but hard.

"I'm Jasper," he said. I said nothing though he seemed to expect some word from me. "What d'you expect? You're in Jasper's Restaurant."

"I came in by the side door, down the alley."

"Have to," he grunted, "front door's locked." He motioned to a chair. It was the only other one in the small room. I sat in it, by the door. He pushed some papers away and faced me.

"You're here for the chef interview."

"I am."

He gave me a look that suggested I had lost the job already but he said abruptly, "Suppose a customer, a big man locally, wants a banquet — something special, something really different. What would you offer him?"

"Soft-shell crabs with crawfish sauce —"

"He doesn't want seafood."

"Leg of lamb with okra —"

"Not many people like lamb."

I moved into another gear. "Stewed tripe with pig's feet and —"

His eyes betrayed a flicker of interest but he said, "Offal's not that popular."

"Pork chops smothered in onions with —"

"Guy's got a thing about trichinosis."

"He's hard to please, isn't he?" I said conversationally.

"He's a customer."

"And they are always right. Even when they're wrong. What about beef tongue with brown gravy and —"

"Never been able to persuade people here to eat tongue. Few of 'em think of it as food."

"Venison, roasted, with juniper berries —"

"His wife's favorite movie is *Bambi*."

He was trying to get my goat but I knew better than to suggest that alternate meat, delicious as it may be as long as it is no more than ten weeks old.

"Wild goose with apricot-and-rice dressing," I said.

"Where can you get wild goose here?"

"Go on a wild-goose chase — through the markets, that is." I was getting a little annoyed with him but I didn't want to be tossed into the dangerous world outside just yet. It might still be populated with pursuers. I smiled amiably. "You can get anything in this city."

"What would you serve with it?"

"Roasted potatoes and yams."

He leaned back a little farther. "You talk kinda funny."

"Always have. Think I picked it up from my mother."

"You're not from these parts." It sounded

accusing, the way he said it.

"I've been around."

"Yeah, but folks around here have got their own special likes. Know how to cook N'Awlins red beans and rice?"

"There are more recipes for that than there are Krewes at the Carnival," I said. "What I'd do, I'd soak the beans overnight. I'd cook some country-smoked sausage and a hamhock in olive oil, then toss in garlic, onion, celery and parsley. I'd drain the beans and put them in, cook for a few minutes. I'd add seasonings —"

"What seasonings?" he demanded.

"Bay leaves, thyme, basil and Louisiana Hot Sauce with water and salt. I'd bring it to the boil, simmer about two hours at low temperature. Some people like it thick and creamy — if I knew they did, I'd take out about a quarter of the beans, mash them and put them back."

I couldn't tell from his expression how close my method came to whatever he considered as the ideal but he didn't comment. I took the opportunity of the momentary break to listen for sounds of a door opening or anyone else in the restaurant, but I could hear nothing.

Jasper said, "Lots of folk like the traditional New Orleans way of serving red beans. Know what that is?"

"Opinions vary widely," I said. "How about over fluffy steamed rice with buttered French bread and a tossed green salad? French dressing, of course."

He was a tough interviewer. He gave me no clue from his reactions because he didn't have any. Not a nod or even a grunt. As I wasn't really looking for a job, I thought of tossing a few smart-aleck remarks his way but, in a way, I was enjoying this. He wasn't finished, though, and he came at me again.

"Still get a lot of calls for fried chicken but all this talk about fat and cholesterol and such has made a lot of people leery of deep-frying. What do you say to that?"

"I'd put the chicken pieces in a marinade of eggs, milk, onions and hot sauce, leave it overnight. I'd crush a mixture of potato chips and corn flakes, season them with a blend of garlic, thyme, basil and oregano. I'd drain off the marinade, roll the chicken pieces in the mix and bake. They should be nicely golden brown in thirty to forty minutes."

"What would you serve with it?"

"Creamed potatoes go great — I'd use yogurt in place of cream. A side dish of green peas would go well, too."

I used his temporary silence to see if any

other sounds were intruding on it but all was quiet. I began to feel a little guilty about pretending to be a candidate for the job when I had no intention of taking it but he didn't look that busy anyway.

He solved the problem for me. "Got another guy coming in later. He's had local experience."

I felt better. A local man would know more than I did about Cajun and Creole cooking, white and black beans, bluefish and crawfish and pecan pie.

"Fair enough," I said.

"Got a phone number where I can reach you?"

"I'll call you." I didn't preface it with *Don't call me.*

He nodded. I felt a slight disappointment that he hadn't offered me a fabulous salary and insisted that I start that afternoon but, after all, a minute ago I had felt ashamed of myself for taking up his time. I was grateful for the shelter from my pursuer and made my own way to the door. I opened it cautiously and looked out. No one was near and the tiny alley went in the other direction as well. The street there looked just as busy so I went that way and caught a cruising cab. The ride back to the Hotel Monteleone was uneventful and frequent backward views were reassuring.

My first action upon being back in the room was to call Lieutenant Delancey. I was put through to his cell phone at once.

"What's up?" he wanted to know.

"Somebody's following me."

"Yeah, it's Larry Mortensen."

"You know?"

"Sure."

"How? . . . Oh, are you having me followed?"

"For your own protection. We wouldn't want anything to happen to you while you're in our fair city. Scotland Yard would never forgive us."

"They do tend to be a nonforgiving organization," I agreed. "Are you learning anything?"

"Not much about you. You don't go to many exciting places, do you? As for Mortensen, well, he's getting more attention from me every day. He may have been in with his brother on this all along."

"So he may lead me to the book? And you to the killer? I take it you're assuming he didn't kill his own brother?"

"For the moment. I did have a couple cases in New York with sisters, though . . . So what's new your end?"

"While you're having me watched, are you aware that Mortensen isn't the only one following me?"

That got his attention. There was a brief pause. "You must have spotted one of my men. They'll get hell from me if you have. They're the best."

"Under medium height, dark hair, small mustache, dark suit."

"That's not either of my men." His voice had tightened. "I'll have them watch out for this character you're talking about. Has he made any moves on you?"

"No, just followed me."

"If this book of yours is really that important, he may be following you to try and find out where the book is."

"I hope you're saying I'm not in danger of being assassinated."

"I don't think so." He sounded serious. "The pattern here says that if he was going to knock you off, he would have done it by now. No, it's the whereabouts of that book — that's what they're after."

"Lieutenant, if you want to reassure me, you're doing it — and I appreciate it. But don't kid me, if I'm really in danger — you can tell me."

"I'm telling you the truth, based on experience. New York experience — and when it comes to killing, that's the best."

"Okay, I can breathe again."

"Be my guest. I'll talk to the guys watching you. Keep 'em a bit closer, just in case. And I'll tell 'em to keep an eye out for this other character."

"What did you mean when you said you were getting more interested in Larry Mortensen?"

"Well, when we first checked him out, he looked clean. No convictions. Now we've looked a little deeper. We have files which show only suspicion, involvement, associates and lots of other things I'm not going to tell you about. Mortensen shows up on 'the Yellow List,' as we call it, quite a few times."

"So he's probably been lucky in keeping out of jail so far."

"Could be."

"So he might have been in partnership with his brother and Whelan as far as the book scam was concerned," I said.

"Possible. We're still digging. Incidentally, that forger of yours, Harburg, is no lily-white. He's been investigated — not by us but by private outfits. You didn't tell me how valuable some books are."

"They are. They don't have to be first editions, either. Agatha Christies bring over twenty thousand dollars. So do Graham Greenes —"

"Which ones?" he asked quickly. "I've got a few of his — *A Gun for Sale, Brighton Rock* . . ."

"I think both of those bring that kind of money, yes."

"John LeCarré?"

"His too, definitely. Ian Fleming, Tolkien . . . lots of others."

"Hmm," he said thoughtfully. "Anyway, we've talked to him — Harburg, I mean, not Fleming or Tolkien. Got nothing."

"He's alerted, though —"

"No, he isn't. We started out by asking him about break-ins in the neighborhood; sort of led into other areas."

"All right," I said. "I'll be in touch."

"Yeah, me, too."

His assurances that I was not in mortal danger helped although I wondered about this new light on Larry Mortensen. If he had been involved with his brother in the book theft then he might be more dangerous than I'd thought. This other man following me was still a worry. Who on earth could he be? And what was his interest?

chapter twenty-three

I was thinking about Lieutenant Delancey's words. When I had told him that I was still being followed, he had said that it was Larry Mortensen before I had informed him that I was attracting the attention of another follower. I had assumed that Mortensen's earlier intention of shooting me in revenge for the death of his brother had been diverted. I had also assumed that he was not deadly serious — very appropriate, I thought — in that intention, as he had threatened Elsa Goddard similarly.

But if I had persuaded him of my innocence, why was he still following me? Well, if he no longer believed I had killed his brother, the only answer was that he was after the book and was now hopeful that I would lead him to it. Lieutenant Delancey's further comment engaged my interest, too, when he had said that Mortensen was getting more attention from the police every day. What were they finding out? That

Mortensen had been in with his brother in the plot to steal the Belvedere chef's book? I wished I had asked the lieutenant to be more explicit on that point but perhaps I was expecting too much. I could hardly hope to be fully in his confidence.

I decided to follow up on that lead but in the meantime, I had one more meal to eat at one of the restaurants of the five Witches who comprised the kidnapping squad. It was about that time a restaurant would be seeing action in the kitchen: chopping, blending, cutting, preparing, mixing and doing the dozens of operations that the diner never thinks about when the sees the final creation on the table.

I called Jenny Kirkpatrick at the General's Tavern, reasoning that she was sure to be there supervising and directing — and she was. Not only that but she would be delighted to see me that evening for dinner. After a long and contemplative bath with its serene therapy, I dressed and went to the Carousel Bar where the "experienced" drinkers — like me — were watching the inexperienced newcomers discover that the bar was rotating. By the time I had consumed a Ramos gin fizz, I was ready for Jenny Kirkpatrick, the last of the inner circle of the five Witches.

Jenny looked resplendent in a purple, ankle-length gown with a delicious décolletage and an ample bustline. She was a bigger-than-average woman and certainly came through as a bigger-than-usual hostess. Everything about her was bigger, including her smile and her welcome. We spent the first few minutes discussing the decor as I mentioned the unusual exterior.

"The building was brick originally, I had to re-face it but I have kept to the original appearance as closely as possible," she told me. "The wooden beams inset among the brick are the originals from the late 1700s."

"Was it a tavern then?"

"Yes, but it's had different names. The general it's named after is Andrew Jackson, of course —"

"Later to be president?"

"That's the one. It was renamed for him after he ate here just before the Battle of New Orleans. When we defeated you wicked English," she added with a roguish smile.

"We didn't win them all," I conceded. "Now, my knowledge of the history of the period is only patchy but isn't that the battle that was fought long after the war was over?"

"That's the one," Jenny said as she led me

to a table. The brick-walled interior had low wooden beams and copper lamp fixtures. A few swords and a couple of plowshares on the walls suggested a transition in the right direction while the sparkling white tablecloths gleamed as oases in the pleasantly dimmed room. A tattered flag no longer fluttered bravely but hung alongside a portrait of the general himself.

He was tall and gaunt, almost cadaverous, very erect in carriage. His face was full of decision and energy. He had iron-gray hair and hawklike gray eyes. He wore full dress uniform — a blue frock coat with buff facings, a spotless white waistcoat and skintight yellow buckskin breeches. A blue plumed hat was under one arm.

Jenny saw me looking at the portrait. "Painted from life," she said, "although when he was here, he didn't look like that. For one thing, his left arm dangled uselessly from a bullet fired at him during a duel, which lodged too near his heart to be removed."

"A duel over a woman, no doubt," I commented.

"No," said Jenny. "Over a horse race. Besides that, his eyes were deep in his head and his complexion pale as death."

A waiter brought a complimentary glass full of a sparkling liquid. "Our new house special," said Jenny. "Our version of the gin fizz but with a healthy side to it. We leave out the sugar and the heavy cream and substitute sorbitol and extra egg white. Several customers asked for a cocktail they could feel justified in drinking, avoiding sugar and fat. This is it. What do you think?"

I tasted. "Excellent," I said. "Can't tell the difference . . . So the general had his last meal here before the battle?"

Jenny pursed her lips, her eyes twinkled and she lifted her chin to continue. I wondered why.

"He had that last meal here with Governor William Clayborne; Commodore Daniel Patterson, veteran of the wars against the Barbary pirates; Colonel George Ross, commander of the infantry; and, of course, Jean Laffite."

"Ah, the French pirate. Quite a hero here, isn't he?"

"Actually, he made his reputation as a slave trader and a smuggler. But it sounds better the other way — the man whose pirate fleet saved the day for Jackson."

I took a longer taste of the gin fizz. "You have a strange look on your face, Jenny. Come to think of it, your tone of voice has changed. Is there something you want to tell me?"

She chuckled. "You've sussed me out. I've given you the tourist version but the truth is more likely that there probably was no such meal. Oh, the general may have eaten — or drunk — here on other occasions but maybe not the night before the battle. If he was here then, the assembly probably wasn't as distinguished as the story tells it. For one thing, Jackson distrusted Laffite and called his men 'hellish bandits.' "

"Was the name here always associated with the general?"

"No. It was called the Governor's Tavern at one time because he often came here, but then he had them change it when he ran for reelection. His opponent was making speeches stressing the excessive amount of time he said the governor was spending here."

"Reassuring to know that politicians haven't changed, I suppose."

"There's another intriguing possibility," Jenny said.

"You love this local history, don't you?"

"It's fascinating. Tales are told of the efforts by French factions here to storm St. Helena Island and release Napoleon from captivity then bring him here. The idea being to rally enough French to be sure of winning the Battle of New Orleans which everyone knew was coming."

"No doubt he had enough followers to make a difference," I said. "How much of that is fact and how much fiction?"

"The efforts to release him were probably discussed but it didn't go beyond that."

"Anyway, Andrew Jackson won the day without Napoleon's help."

"He did."

"And how much has the menu changed from those earlier days?" I asked.

"Considerably, in its nutritional value, but I've tried to preserve the original appearance of the dishes and certainly to improve the taste. We know so much more about seasoning and flavoring than we did then."

The waiter had left a menu on the table and Jenny handed it to me. "See what you think."

"Corn chowder," I commented, looking at the first page. "That was a New England preparation originally, wasn't it?"

"That's right, Massachusetts. When it was brought to the South, tomatoes were added. Potatoes and onions are the other main ingredients beside the corn."

"Here's another interesting one. New Orleans pepper pot — is that similar to Philadelphia pepper pot? That's a very old recipe."

"It is. You know the story . . . ?"

"Tell me."

"When morale was low in Jackson's army, the general wanted to lift it by serving a hearty meal. All that was available, however, was tripe, peppercorns and a few scraps. The cook improvised and New Orleans pepper pot has been a popular dish ever since."

"That cook's name should be immortalized."

"It should," she agreed, "but I don't believe anyone knows it. Today we use knuckle of veal with all the meat left on, tripe, onions, potatoes and carrots. We season with parsley, bay leaf, thyme, cloves, marjoram and parsley. We drop dumplings into it just before serving."

"Sounds very authentic." I did a double take as I turned over the menu page. "A whole page of breads? That's unusual."

"One of our historical touches. Breads were very important in those days." Jenny was warming to her theme, obviously fascinated with the challenge of reviving the cooking of the past.

"*Pain perdu.* Now there's a bread you rarely see."

"Do you know it? It's like French toast and a good use for bread which is going stale — they had a lot of that in the past when they didn't know much about food preserving."

"Then you've got pecan bread, walnut bread, buckwheat cakes . . . but enough. I have to make a decision. Tell me, Jenny, which do you consider your specialties?"

"The Poached Stuffed Chicken in Lemon Sauce is extremely popular. The Louisiana Bluefish — now, if you want a dish that's local and historical, there's one."

"Don't see bluefish very often," I said. "It's a real Gulf special, isn't it?"

"It certainly is. We bake it with chopped onion and tomato juice over it. We pour Creole sauce over it, sprinkle breadcrumbs and melted butter, then broil to finish."

"Brunswick stew, I see here. That's a famous old dish for sure."

"Yes. Virginia and North Carolina fight over who cooked it first."

"Originally cooked with squirrel, wasn't it?"

"Yes, and this region had a lot of them. Then squirrels disappeared from the recipe, as people ate so many of them."

"There are plenty to go around today but I don't suppose modern taste would go for them," I said.

"We use chicken now."

"What else do you put in it?"

"Lima beans, corn, tomatoes, celery, ham and potatoes. We season with bay leaf, basil, parsley and red and black pepper."

I pondered. "A tough choice. I'm torn between the Veal in Wine Sauce and the Pheasant in Casserole."

We discussed and I settled for the corn chowder and the veal. The chowder was thick and creamy and Jenny told me that some restaurants serve it with pieces of chicken. The veal came as thick cutlets that were sautéed, then mushrooms, garlic, salt, red and white pepper and tarragon were added along with Worcestershire sauce. In a separate pan, butter was melted, flour added, then white wine. It was simmered until thickened, poured over the cutlets and served on rice.

Jenny had to leave to take care of other customers while I ate. When she returned, she said, "Now you must taste our dessert specialty. It's flummery."

"An old Welsh word meaning 'nonsense, humbug.' "

She laughed. "So I believe. I don't know how it came to be used for this dessert, perhaps because it's light, frothy, not too substantial. But it's delicious, I assure you."

She was right, it was, with a similarity to English trifle — sponge cake immersed in white wine, raisins and chopped almonds sprinkled over it, a layer of fruit jelly, then a smooth and rich custard poured over it. Spoonfuls of red currant jam, slices of orange dipped in sherry and dried, were added before serving.

"Far from flummery," I assured her. "Very real."

"How many of the other girls' restaurants do you have to visit?" she asked.

"As a matter of fact, you're the last of the five."

"Which did you enjoy the most?" she asked, leaning forward in a mock-threatening attitude.

"I plead the Fifth Amendment. They have all been so good, I would have to use the 'eeny-meeny-miny-mo' method."

"Very diplomatic," she smiled. "And now, I have to ask you — the other Witches are very insistent I do this —"

"You want a report."

"Right. In fact, we're having a meeting to-morrow, so a statement on the present situation will be requested and I have to give it."

"Fair enough. Here goes . . ."

chapter twenty-four

"The two dead men, Richie Mortensen and Earl Whelan, were probably working together in the plot to steal the book."

"That's what Leah said," Jenny nodded enthusiastically.

So the members of the Witches were keeping in close touch with each other on progress in the case. I should have expected it, I suppose. They were all clever, ambitious women and each could offer a contribution that must make their organization very effective.

"One thing I don't understand is how they knew the value of the book," Jenny said.

"Richie worked for Gambrinus in his bookshop," I reminded her, "so he must have learned quite a bit about books. And didn't Earl work with Leah in her restaurant?"

"Before she threw him out," Jenny agreed. "The no-good —"

"That's what she told me," I said.

Jenny eyed me thoughtfully. "Leah also told you that she thinks one of us Witches wants the book."

They really were keeping in close communication. "She didn't have any suspicion which of you, though." It was my turn to study her reaction to that. Her full face gave an impression of honesty and her large eyes held mine.

"Several of us are beginning to agree with Leah. Emmy Lou, Marguerite, Harriet — they've all said or hinted very strongly that they think so. I can't believe that any of us would condone murder to get the book, though."

"You're suggesting that one of you may have hired, or conspired with, Earl and/or Richie — but perhaps just to get the book, not commit murder."

Jenny nodded and her blonde hair moved gracefully. "That sums it up pretty well. After all, we've known each other quite a while and I can't accept the idea of one of us committing — or condoning — murder. Especially for a book; not even if it were the greatest cookbook in the world."

"But you realize that Richie Mortensen and Earl Whelan were not squeamish. They might commit murder if it was the only way

313

to get what they wanted."

"I suppose," Jenny said with a sigh.

"You must all have some ideas on what's in the book, don't you?" I asked.

"We've talked about that, as you can imagine. We're all fascinated with the idea of a recipe that's so valuable but none of us can fully accept the notion. The book itself may be worth a lot to a collector but surely not enough to kill for."

"That's a thought I hadn't considered. It implies that collectors who are really fanatical about their own obsession — stamps, coins, autographs, whatever — might see some value in the book that might not be there for anyone else."

"Something like that, yes. But it applies more to somebody who collects — well, as you say, coins. They come in sets, don't they? Like stamps? A collector might have all but one to complete a set. That can't apply here, though — at least, I can't see it."

"I can't either," I admitted. "Unless there's some connection that we're missing. Books like this don't come in sets like stamps or coins. They stand alone."

We both did some conjecturing but it didn't produce any brainstorms. We talked about the restaurant business and about New Orleans and I thanked her for an exceptional meal. The place was filling up by now. "I'll let you get back to your duties," I told her.

"Going on the town tonight?" she asked with a knowing smile.

"I might widen my experience of the Big Easy," I said noncommittally, and she smiled as she took me to the door.

I strolled along the streets of the French Quarter, absorbing the sights and sounds and aromas. I paused to admire the wrought-iron balconies on Royal Street. The city has lots of them but none more impressive than here.

Sounds of considerable merriment were coming from one place I was passing. PADDY O'BANNION'S, the sign said, and I recalled reading about it in one of the brochures at the Monteleone. The bar here was the stuff of legends, it was said. It was the home of the "Typhoon," a fabled concoction of equal parts of thick dark rum, gin and crème de menthe. I went in.

The first bar was very busy and I could see another bar beyond that was just as busy. An inner courtyard was crowded. It was one of those old-time bars you seldom see anymore, though New York has just a few left. A mahogany bar with a brass rail, bottles on shelves behind the bar, and a mirror that showed its age set the style. The floor looked as if the sawdust had just been swept off and a small platform on one side probably would have been occupied by a harpist and a fiddler at some time. Green shamrocks, old photos of Bantry Bay, portraits of Michael Collins, James Joyce and Eamon de Valera and a color picture of the Irish soccer team decorated the walls which were otherwise that dark-yellow color that comes from decades of tobacco smoke.

I edged my way to the bar. "A pint of Guinness," I said to the bartender, a crop-headed fellow wearing a black waistcoat with metal buttons over a shirt that would be white again if more bleach was used next time. Very authentic, I thought.

"A pint of Guinness is it you're after?" he said, reaching for a glass.

"That's right. In a mug, if you don't mind."

His practiced hand found a mug and a beer handle. "You don't sound Irish," he said. The black Guinness surged up in the glass, a thick white foam struggling to the top.

"County Cork," I said.

A man at the bar next to me wore an old black suit and had a careworn face. He turned to me. "Is that right?"

"My father, God rest his soul, sent me to England to school. That's why I talk this way." It wasn't the strict truth but I had found it to be a convenient story to use on previous visits to Irish pubs.

"Ye sound more Galway than Cork," said the man next to me.

"So I've been told," I said, watching the slow progress of the Guinness up the mug. "Never lost my love for the nectar of Finn McCool, though," I added for a touch of color.

A whiskered old man in a heavy jacket was on the other side of me at the bar. "Finn McCool," he said, rolling the name around in his mouth before letting it out. "Now there's a name to conjure with. Hurry up filling that mug, Sean, this man looks like he's in sore need of it."

The bartender, Sean, finally filled the mug and scrapped off the excess foam. He set the mug in front of me. "Five dollars," he said, "and we're taking up a collection for the IRA in a few minutes."

"Are ye now?" I put a five on the bar and put a one alongside it.

"Been in the Ould Country lately?" asked the man in the worn black suit.

"I was in Dublin and Shannon a few

months ago," I said truthfully. "And a great week it was, too. The salmon were biting and the beer was great."

"If ye were in Dublin, ye must have had a drink in the Three Crowns," said the bartender.

"Maybe I did. I don't remember." It might be a trick question. I sipped the Guinness and nodded appreciatively.

"First time here?" asked the whiskered man.

"In New Orleans, yes. Tell me, is there really a Paddy O'Bannion?"

"Used to be. Opened his first bar in 1930 and became one of the best bar-owners in these parts."

"Ye could have taken speech lessons," said Sean. Busy as he was, he had had time to work that out. It took the three of us a few seconds to catch up.

"I suppose I could," I said. I drank some more Guinness. "A fine pint that is," I congratulated him.

"It's no bad thing to sound like I'm from Galway, though," I couldn't resist saying. "People in Cork don't mind me."

"I'm from Tipperary meself," said the whiskered man.

"I'm a Kildare man," the black-suited man wistfully declared.

"Bah! Ye might as well be from Dublin," said the whiskered man scornfully.

"It's fifty miles," the other said defensively.

"Ye're a Dubliner! Can't get away from it!"

The black-suited man pondered over that but couldn't think of a suitable response so instead he ordered another Jameson's.

The crowd was mainly men but there were a few women. A jukebox started up with an electronic clatter that led into what was either a rebel marching song or a number from one of the Irish pop groups that have achieved international renown.

"Ye'll want to follow that with some Irish Punch," said the whiskered man, nodding to my Guinness.

"Or he can mix 'em," added the black-suit.

My puzzlement must have been obvious.

" 'Tis a specialty of the house," explained Whiskers.

"Puts hair on yer chest."

"And fire in yer eyes."

"Sharpens the mind and improves the memory."

"Makes ye irresistible to women, a terror to yer enemies."

The bartender joined in this panoply of

praise. "In some parts of Ireland, they call it a 'Donegal Depth Charge.' But it's smooth as Mother's milk and warm as a colleen's kiss. Are ye sure ye've never run into it?" He made it sound like proof that I had never been near the Emerald Isle.

"Not that I recall. But there was a night in the Rose of Tralee in Limerick when I drank a number of concoctions, all the names of which have slipped my mind."

"Ye couldn't have had Irish Punch," said the bartender darkly.

"Why not? Oh, of course, that's the one that aids the memory. Still, 'twas quite a night."

My reminiscence seemed to satisfy suspicion, though that was only in the mind of the bartender, Sean. The other two were affable enough, and as Sean had to move down the bar to quell desperate thirsts, we had a good discussion going on Ireland's chances in the qualifying rounds of the World Cup, now being played. It was good-natured though controversial and I even had the temerity to say, "Ireland hasn't had a good national team since you let Jackie Charlton, an Englishman, resign as manager." That prompted some lively rebuttals and I was enjoying the repartee when I happened to glance into the mirror behind the bar.

It was not as clean as if it had been wiped with one of the miracle solvents that television offers, and its ability to reflect images was also impaired by its age — whether that was real or manufactured. But it was clear enough where I was looking — and that was at a man in a dark suit involved in a conversation. He was standing by a table with half a dozen seated drinkers. He had dark hair and a small dark mustache.

He was the man I had seen before, and on those occasions I had been sure he was watching me. He had been the one who had driven me to seek refuge in the Mardi Gras World, although I had enjoyed the visit. Lieutenant Delancey had said this was not one of his men. So who was he?

As I studied him in the mirror, he did not seem to be watching me now. If he was, he was not being very clever about it. His conversation with the people at the table was animated and he appeared to know most of them. He did not once glance in my direction.

I was near a curve at the end of the bar and if I moved my stool, I could use the whiskered man to largely block the dark-haired man's view of me. Now I could watch him but he couldn't see me.

After a few minutes, he made his farewells to those at the table. I watched closely to see what he did now. He walked among the tables, stopped once to greet someone then went on to the far end of the bar. He talked briefly with the bartender, who lifted the flap and allowed him through. The man opened a door and disappeared.

It was no way to follow somebody and, relieved, I returned to my conversation with my talkative comrades from the Ould Country. We were on the European Union, it seemed, and a great topic for Irishmen with their natural inclination toward independence.

I kept a sharp eye on the back of the bar at the same time and threw the periodic glance at the mirror in case my pursuer had used another exit and reemerged behind. More customers had come in, and the place was really crowded, which made accurate spotting of a tail difficult. But I kept up my vigil, ordered another Guinness and was rewarded when the familiar figure opened the same door behind the bar and came out.

He did not even flash a look my way. He spoke a few words to the bartender and pushed his way through the crowd. I watched him in the mirror. Again he spoke a word of greeting to someone at a table, then he went out the door.

I hastily finished my Guinness, put down a couple of notes and bade farewell to my chatty comrades who were now moving on to more international matters such as the policy of the World Bank and the prospects in the European Song Contest.

I went out the door, stood in the doorway until I spotted my target, then followed him.

"The pursuer pursued" was the cliché that first came to mind but it was so appropriate that I did not bother thinking about a replacement.

It was late enough in the evening that the streets were well populated but I was able to keep my man in sight. I expected him to seek a taxi but he kept to the sidewalk, walking purposefully. We went only a few blocks when he turned out of my sight. I closed in and saw that it was another bar. It called itself Limping Susan, which I knew was an okra pilaff dish. I peered in.

It was much less crowded than Paddy O'Bannion's, and through the glass door I could see my man heading for the bar. He didn't order a drink, though. Instead, a man came from behind the bar, pulling off his apron. The two of them sat at one of the empty tables and engaged in an earnest conversation.

If I were to go in, the place was too quiet for me to pass unnoticed. That meant I had no chance of overhearing their conversation. I stood, uncertain, then my man rose, shook hands with the other and headed for the door. I quickly moved along the block and stood against a building. When he came out, I followed him again.

I had no idea what he was doing. Was he in the protection racket? No, surely that had gone with the gangster days. The numbers game? That too. He didn't drink anything and I saw nothing change hands so he couldn't even be a bookmaker. I kept following.

This time, he only went two blocks. The establishment he entered here was called Sporting Life, and was packed with customers. The atmosphere was sporty, with banners and posters describing sporting events, NFL team shirts, photos of basketball teams, football teams, baseball teams. Another wall had golf clubs, hockey sticks, tennis rackets, skis and a few other implements that I didn't recognize.

I entered cautiously and promptly blended with a group of seven or eight who were having various conversations among themselves. A waitress was circulating and taking orders. I asked for a Heineken and kept on the edge of the group, looking like I was part of it but watching my man closely.

He went to the bar again. The bartender picked up a phone and a moment later a short fat man came out from the back of the place. He and my quarry leaned on the bar talking for several minutes then they shook hands and he left. I worked my way around the outside of my group to keep out of his field of vision. When he had left, I went to the bar. The short fat man was still there, talking to the bartender.

My beer in my hand, I went up to the fat man. He was several inches shorter than I was and at least fifty pounds heavier. He was not that old, though, and greeted me in friendly style.

I put on an exasperated expression. "Darn it! Did I just miss him? I saw him over here talking to you; I turned away for only a minute and he's gone."

"Who?" he asked.

I was too busy remonstrating with myself to hear his question. "That son of a gun! I should have come over when he was here. He's getting to be a regular will-o'-the-wisp. Now you see him, now you don't."

"Oh, you mean Dom," he nodded. "Yes,

he just left. Off to his next stop."

"He has quite a round, doesn't he?"

"Sure does. Got a nice business going. Not a lot of competition, either. Oh, there's always the big boys but there's plenty of slots in between that he can fill."

"That's right," I agreed, wondering what on earth I was talking about. "Been doing business with him a long time, have you?"

"Seven, eight years, I guess. Know him well?"

"It's, um, recent. Hope to get to know him better, though. You know," I said, sounding confidential, "I'm not even sure how he spells his last name." I held my breath, hoping it wasn't Brown or Jones.

He grinned. "It's Dominic Landers, that's L-A-N-D-E-R-S. I should know how to spell it, writing his name on checks every month."

I nodded agreement. At least, I had his name but still not a clue as to what he did. I knew he filled in slots between the big boys but that gem of information could hardly classify as being helpful. I had to be careful asking because I couldn't figure out whether he had a product or a service or another line that I hadn't even imagined.

I didn't make any move to go but I left my options open in case a chance arose to learn any more. I asked, "Think I can catch him on his next stop?"

"Sure. He's a creature of habit. Always keeps to the same round. You'll find him at Stevie's Bar and Grill."

"Stevie's? Oh, that's over on, er —"

"Claremont Street, yes. Near Burgundy."

"Oh yes," I said confidently.

"They buy a lot of his Violet Dream."

"Do they?" I hardly needed to make it interrogative. I was bursting with curiosity.

"Know it?"

"No," I said honestly.

"It's one of his own concoctions. It caught on over there. Don't see it many other places. It's a bit like a Santa Cruz."

"Santa Cruz." I repeated the name. For the first time in this bizarre conversation, I was hearing a name that made sense. But why? I couldn't pull it out of my memory but my host was most obliging.

"The Santa Cruz is not that popular anymore. Used to be a big seller. But Dom took it and used one of our local rums in place of Santa Cruz rum. Instead of just lemon juice, he uses a blend of lemon and lime, adds a few dashes of Curacao."

"I remember the name, Santa Cruz; quite a while ago, it seems."

"It went out of style like so many liqueurs," he said. "Have you been out to his distillery?"

"No, I haven't."

He grinned. "Not surprised. Dom doesn't exactly encourage visitors. Out on Gallivray, you know, not far from the big hospital."

"Oh, yes." I put a lot into those two words. At last, I had a full picture. My mysterious pursuer was the owner, apparently, of a liqueur distillery. I knew his name and I knew where the distillery was located. I knew that he did his own customer contact and I knew that tonight, he was making the rounds of his customers.

"Well, I'd better get after him before he dashes off to his next stop," I said. "Nice to talk to you." We shook hands and I departed, pondering.

All that remained was to find out why Landers had been following me. A liqueur producer? Was it something to do with the Belvedere book? It didn't seem likely that there was any connection . . . Or one of the two murders? That might be more likely.

The comment about Dominic Landers not encouraging visitors to his distillery was intriguing but might not mean anything. The more I thought about it, it probably didn't. Brewers, vintners, distillers — all had secrets or at least what they considered to be secrets. Many discouraged visitors and some even barred them totally.

I returned to the Hotel Monteleone, watched some mind-numbing television, which had the desired effect. I slept like a baby . . . well, no, they frequently wake up and cry. I slept like a log. Why a log? Deliberating such weighty matters, I fell asleep.

chapter twenty-five

I felt I had some of the answers to the puzzle but a vital segment was missing.

Where would I find it? I was running out of clues. The most perplexing of these was the appearance of Dominic Landers, a distiller, who had been following me. It was a vague trail but I decided I had better follow it. One visit to the distillery might provide the answer.

The mimes, the musicians, the acrobats, the vendors were all there in Jackson Square, and so were a good number of tourists. I wove in and out of them, doubling back occasionally, and circling the square, if that is a mathematical possibility. It might be a waste of time but I was taking no chances.

I passed the mule carriages. My companion of earlier, Benjamin, was not here, probably on some sightseeing mission, and I was not disposed to that form of transport today anyway. Too easy to spot, too easy to follow and too slow.

I walked around the mule ranks, headed for the taxis and jumped into one as it reached the head of the line. I didn't give the driver the name of the distillery but only the street name. We squeezed through the busy streets and as we came on to a major road, I saw the hospital that my chubby friend at Sporting Life had mentioned. I told him to drive along Gallivray, and the distillery was easy to spot.

The street was composed of small- to medium-sized industries. On one side of the distillery was a tile factory and on the other side was an appliance warehouse. It was a modest, industrial neighborhood, by no means rundown but no big names or noticeably major businesses, either. I let the driver go on to the end of the block, and got out.

I didn't want to come face-to-face with Dominic Landers so I had to consider my approach. A small market selling food and drink was on the corner and I went in and found their phone. I had looked up the distillery number while I had been making my phone calls from the hotel, which was just as well, as there seemed to be no directory near the phone.

A female voice answered and I asked for Mr. Landers. "He's out, I'm afraid," came the answer. "Can I take a message?"

"Yes, you can tell him — wait, when do you expect him?"

"It may be much later in the afternoon," she said.

"It doesn't matter, then. I'll call later."

That gave me enough time to reconnoiter. From the market, I walked down the street and all the way around the block back to the front of the distillery. The whole area continued with similar small factories, warehouses and industrial offices.

When I approached the small reception desk in the tiny lobby, I noticed that the receptionist was also the telephone operator. I had put on my best American accent when I had made the call. It was my version of a Midwestern cadence and I didn't think it sounded too different from real ones. I changed it now to my worst American accent. This was what I considered New York and I thought of it as hard and biting. I wouldn't have wanted New Yorkers to hear it but down here in the South, how could they complain about accents? The receptionist didn't appear to recognize my voice when I asked for the owner.

"I'm sorry, he's out. Won't be back 'til later. Can someone else help you?"

A young man with a touch of Creole coloring was brought out. Despite his youth, he was keen and energetic, inclined to be helpful. His name was Poydras, which I assumed was a New Orleans name. I gave him the first name that came into my head — it was Jackson, from the square. I said somberly, "I have to bring a matter of legal importance to your attention, Mr. Poydras."

"Very well," he agreed. "Let's go into Mr. Landers's office."

It was the first room off the reception area, and nicely furnished with the latest in Scandinavia's idea of the business office, all wood and leather. He sat behind the light wooden desk and I sat opposite.

He had a smooth face, very clean shaven. His dark eyes widened slightly. "You're a lawyer?"

"I don't practice much anymore," I said, adhering to the truth as I always try to do. "However, I find myself in New Orleans on a minor business matter right now and in the course of enjoying a few of your social establishments" — Mr. Poydras gave me an encouraging smile to show that he understood the ways of businessmen visiting the fleshpots of New Orleans — "I enjoyed some excellent liqueur. Liqueurs are libations I particularly enjoy and I would like to think of myself as something of a connoisseur."

Mr. Poydras smiled again, showing that the he had no doubts concerning my eminence in that field.

"Frankly, Mr. Poydras, some of these liqueurs I found to be much superior to similar drinks available in Europe. As I also do some consulting work for a chain of liquor distributors there, I wondered what kind of sales representation you have overseas."

I paused, invitingly. He obliged with, "We're — er, not strong in the export market, Mr. Jackson. Not as strong as I personally think we should be."

He meant they didn't export. He was saying, too, that here might be a chance for him to make a name for himself with his boss and boost sales. Mr. Poydras was perfect for my purpose.

"If I recommend that we bring in a trial lot of your liqueurs, we would run a market study and hopefully establish some strong business links. What do you think?"

Mr. Poydras was all for it. I had him primed and ready.

"The reason for my visit therefore is to broach this possibility —"

"I'm sure we could work out some mutually satisfactory arrangement," said Mr. Poydras.

"I think so, too. One question will be

asked of me, I know, when I recommend this to my clients. To answer that question, all I need is a brief tour of your premises."

Mr. Poydras cooled a few degrees. "Mr. Landers doesn't favor plant visits. Not that we have anything to hide, of course, but competition is fierce, as you know, and we all have our — well, not secrets, but special ways of conducting certain processes and —"

"Nothing to worry about there," I told him firmly. "My clients are not in any way competitive."

"I accept your assurance on that point — but, er, Mr. Landers likes to make this kind of decision himself. If you could come back when he —"

I looked anxiously at my watch. "Unfortunately, the flight to Washington, D.C., leaves in two hours." I believed that to be true even though I wasn't going to be on it. I started to get to my feet. "My clients always insist on at least a brief review of the premises and —"

"I can assure you that our all practices are up to code. Labor, equipment, materials — we operate a very tight ship here, Mr. Jackson, and . . ."

"I'm sure you do," I said smoothly, "and all I need to do today is convince myself of that. A brief tour of the premises would suffice."

He leaned back, still a little tight. "Well, I don't know. Mr. Landers usually approves such visits."

"The reason I have this assignment is that I have spent considerable time in the liquor business. It will only take a few moments to convince myself of your efficiency."

"Mr. Landers will be back later. Perhaps you could —"

"Unfortunately, this flight to Washington . . ." I looked anxiously at my watch again.

Mr. Poydras fretted, scratched his chin, looked worried, then said, "Very well. But it will have to be just a quick tour."

"That's all I have time for."

He rose, and as I was rising to accompany him, I noticed a framed photograph on Mr. Landers' desk. It showed a pretty brunette, posed, smiling against the rail of a boat.

Mr. Poydras saw me looking. "Mr. Landers' wife," he said.

"Very attractive lady," I commented, and we went out into the plant.

The distillery was not new but it was maintained in good condition. Most of the stills and condensers were copper, old but showing no signs of verdigris. The piping was the same, no weld or braze repairs. Some places used plastic piping for the sake of economy, but not here. A few automatic controls operated but I saw workers here and there. Some oak barrels were being used; they add flavor.

Instrumentation appeared adequate, nothing elaborate, but minimal. Clipboards showing inspection and calibration were up-to-date and records of temperatures, times and fermentation levels were well kept.

I saw only a few workers but they were in clean uniforms — a telltale sign and, surprisingly, not as common as it should be. I visit vineyards and breweries fairly often and make a personal point of checking that the staff look clean and properly dressed.

We came to an open area on the way to the storage chambers. Mr. Poydras made occasional comments and I replied just enough to make it clear that I was well acquainted with the various operations. A wall on the right had two doors in it. One was old, wooden and had slats nailed across it. The other was steel and had a large padlock.

"We rebuilt this section some time ago," Mr. Poydras said. "The old door should have been bricked-in but wasn't. We'll have to do that one of these days. The steel door was put in as part of the new regulations — that's the alcohol storage chamber."

"Ouch!" I said, hopping on one foot.

"Something wrong?"

"I got a stone in this shoe outside and it must have moved and I forgot about it. Now it's — Ouch!" I leaned against the steel door for support then hopped a pace and stopped near the wooden door. I bent down to untie my shoe. After I had shaken the offending — if invisible — stone, we continued.

I let Mr. Poydras hurry me through the rest of the tour. He was anxious to show me as little as possible and I was anxious to get out before Mr. Landers returned.

One more of the final pieces of the puzzle had slid into place.

chapter twenty-six

When I awoke next morning, I noticed an envelope under the door. It might have been put there yesterday and I hadn't seen it when I came in. It was a large envelope and made of expensive paper. I opened. It was a handwritten letter from Ambrose Belvedere, inviting me to lunch at the Belvedere mansion, and gave an address. It wasn't exactly cold but it was a little stiff and very polite. It apologized for the short notice and I saw that it had yesterday's date and the lunch was today.

I wondered to what extent the fine hand of Eric Van Linn was behind this. He would know that I could respond to such an invitation at short notice and he knew where I was staying. Maybe my attempts to get him to let me talk to Ambrose Belvedere had borne fruit after all. Would Van Linn be at the lunch? I wondered.

I went down to breakfast and when I came back, judged it to be an appropriate time to phone the Belvedere mansion. A young lady with a Southern accent like unstirred molasses accepted my apology for not calling sooner and assured me that there was no problem and that they would be expecting me today.

Did I know where the mansion was? she asked, and I said no and furthermore, I did not have a car or know the city. "We are only just outside the city," she told me.

"That's fine," I said. "I can take a taxi."

"Oh, yes," she said. "All the drivers will know where we are. We will expect you at noon."

I had time to make a few phone calls before taking a taxi to the Belvedere mansion. I stood in the hotel lobby for some time, watching vehicles come and go and keeping an eye open for either Larry Mortensen or Dominic Landers. I could not see either of them and wondered whether they had lost interest in me or some twist had made me unimportant. It was a little deflating, whichever was the truth. An indefinable prestige was attached to being followed.

The mansion was on a plantation just near the banks of the Mississippi River and to the west of the city of New Orleans. We drove in through wide wooden gates and along a well-worn track of hard-packed earth. The vegetation was dense with many trees I didn't recognize.

The house itself was not at all grandiose but it was big. It rose out of the breeze-combed grass and was all wood, which was unusual to me, and after I had paid the taxi, I climbed the steps onto the broad front porch, lined with clusters of chairs and small tables. Its facade was punctured by shuttered windows. The large wooden door had intricate carvings and looked to be made of cypress. A black man, elderly and with white side whiskers that gave him an old-world look, opened the door. He confirmed my name and ushered me into a large hall. Ambrose Belvedere came hurrying across the hall to greet me.

He was in his late twenties, barely medium height and of a light build. His face was lightly tanned and he had one of those smooth complexions that I had seen in this part of the world a number of times. He was pleasant-featured but with a serious air that belonged on an older man. His eyes were brown and his hair black and cut short. He wore a tan suit with metal buttons, rather like an upmarket version of a safari outfit.

"Shall we sit on the porch?" he asked. "We

don't have to worry about mosquitoes or other insects — unlike earlier generations."

We did so and the elderly man approached with a tray. "Robert makes an excellent cocktail — rather like a whiskey sour but with sour mash. Like to try one?"

I agreed and Robert nodded. "Two, Master Ambrose?"

"He still calls me Master Ambrose. Yes, Robert, two." He smiled. "I wonder if he'll ever accept me as an adult," he said as Robert walked away.

"I'm glad you could come," he said to me. "This talk is overdue. I asked Eric to make the arrangement with you and he was perhaps overzealous in not clarifying that he was the family lawyer."

"Someone told me," I said.

"Hard to keep something like that secret in this town. Well, you can understand my interest in getting hold of the chef's book."

"Certainly," I agreed. "After all those generations, it's more than just a family heirloom. Especially as you're intending to reopen the restaurant."

"You mean because of the recipes? Yes, of course."

"Do you intend to change the menu at all?"

"Considerably. We'll keep just a few of

the old classics but the rest will be new versions of the earlier dishes or completely new ones."

"What about oysters Belvedere?" I asked, keeping the question as lightly casual as I could.

He shook his head immediately. That question had already been deliberated. "It's an old classic, I know, but some of the ingredients are no longer available."

"Did you ever see the book?" I asked.

"Not that I recall. Oh, I was in the restaurant from time to time, though I never had any great interest in it — never intended to get involved in the business. Ah, thank you, Robert."

The tall glasses looked inviting, with just a hint of foam on the top as Robert placed them in front of us. The pause gave me an opportunity to reflect that Ambrose was being open and friendly as far as I could determine.

We toasted, drank and I found the drink more full-bodied than the usual whiskey sour but very tasty.

"What made you change your mind about reopening the restaurant?" I asked.

"I studied business at Wharton; then, when I was graduating, I had to decide what kind of business. A classmate said to me,

'Why do you have to look for a business? You already have one.' It should have been obvious to me but it wasn't. I thought about that, then the idea began to grow. Food continues to be a rapidly growing field and the challenge of bringing the Belvedere name back into the top rank of restaurants appealed to me."

"Do you think that locating the chef's book will help you?"

"Not really. Oh, it would be a nice prestigious touch but it's not an important part of reviving Restaurant Belvedere."

"So you don't have to have the original oysters Belvedere recipe to do that?"

He laughed softly. "No. I'd certainly like to have it, but mainly for sentimental family reasons." He twirled the tall glass slowly in his fingers. "Eric Van Linn has kept me informed on your progress. Are you close to recovering the book?"

"I believe so," I told him, and watched carefully for a reaction. He looked a little surprised but no more than that.

"And also close to finding out who killed those two men?"

"That too," I nodded. I must have sounded like Hercule Poirot about to reveal all — I hoped it was an accurate assessment.

"The two are connected, aren't they? The

theft of the book and the two murders?"

"Oh, they're connected," I said, being agreeable but not helpful.

"I understand that you told Eric that forged copies of the chef's book were being offered for sale."

"That's right. I was offered one."

"But you didn't accept?"

"No, I decided it was a forgery."

Ambrose studied me quizzically. "How did you decide that?"

"I was allowed to look through it. Only briefly, but it was enough. It's hard to explain with something like that," I went on, introducing a touch of the mystique. "Difficult to put a finger on the exact difference but I was sure it was a phony."

Ambrose didn't look altogether satisfied with that as an answer. "You could have been wrong," he said.

"I could," I said. "But I know I was right."

Well, you can't argue with someone who gets on his high horse as an expert. That's what I was doing and Ambrose looked about to dispute the point further when Robert entered quietly. "Luncheon is served, Mr. Ambrose."

"Thank you, Robert." To me he said, "Shall we go in?"

★ ★ ★

It was a Cajun meal — I expected no less. The gumbo was thick with okra, tiny shrimp, small peppers, pieces of crabmeat, chunks of white fish, and richly but not strongly spiced. The main course was chicken baked with oysters. It was nicely herbed and served with red beans and rice. I congratulated Ambrose on the meal, a fine example of local cooking, not elaborate but beautifully done.

"I keep the menus modest at home," he explained. "If I am to embark on any flamboyance in cooking, it will be in the restaurant." We had drunk a Château St. Jean from Sonoma, California, a delicious fumé blanc, and as Ambrose poured the last of the bottle, Robert brought in the dessert.

"In the restaurant, it will, of course, be Bananas Foster," Ambrose said, "but this is baked bananas, tropical style."

Simplicity in this case was the key. The bananas had been lightly browned in butter, then, after sugar and lemon juice had been generously sprinkled over them, baked with more butter.

We retired to a relaxing lounge, pleasantly subtropical with coconut matting carpet, cypress-paneled walls dotted with old prints, a fireplace inlaid with marble and even a couple of rocking chairs. Robert poured thick black coffee into thin, china cups with an engraved *B* on them.

We were drinking when Ambrose put down his cup carefully and said, "I had a visit from a Mrs. Pargeter. She's the volunteer lady — one of the committee that runs the book auction. She told me you know her."

I nodded.

"A very sophisticated lady," Ambrose said, sitting back and looking reflectively at his coffee cup. "A lady of great character, a lot of integrity — I mean of the type that is sadly becoming less commonly encountered today."

He rose and walked over to the fireplace. He took down a bronze urn that stood on the dark-rose-colored marble slab. "She left me something, a memento you might call it."

He lifted the ornate cap, tilted it so that he could see inside. I had noticed that Ambrose lapsed now and then into a serious mood that belied his years. He would do well in the restaurant business, I decided. He had uncommon maturity and a balanced attitude that even many successful men do not acquire until they are much older.

I said nothing, just waited for him to go on. He turned the urn so that I could see inside, too. A small pile of black ashes covered the bottom. A few curls indicated burnt paper. He put the cap back and replaced the urn.

"She has not only integrity but, in addition, she has a considerable amount of sympathy for, and understanding of, her fellow human beings."

He smiled apologetically. "I'm sorry. I'll be getting pompous if I say any more."

"I don't know her too well," I said, "but from my brief acquaintance with her, I would say you're right."

He took another sip of his coffee. He didn't have much left and it must have been cold by now so I gathered it was a gesture, a delaying tactic while he contemplated his next statement. When it came, I could see why.

"I believe you will understand me," he said, "when I tell you that Mrs. Pargeter's visit here has led to my decision to thank you for your efforts, and to instruct Eric Van Linn to pay you in full and terminate our arrangement."

He looked me in the eye, awaiting my reply. I was looking him in the eye, too, but I wasn't seeing it. I was seeing a certificate on the wall of Mrs. Pargeter's apartment, I was seeing the photograph on Dominic Landers's desk and I was recalling the wooden door in the distillery. Ambrose Belvedere's words of a few minutes ago came back, too — he had said he wanted the chef's book "for sentimental family reasons."

"I understand completely," I said, "and I am glad this matter has been resolved for you. How are your plans coming along for reopening the restaurant?"

"We should be open for business by early summer," he said. "Maybe you can come over for the opening?"

"If I can, I'd be delighted."

We walked out onto the front porch. A watery sun was squeezing through the clouds and the silvery light dappled the trees. "This porch goes all the way around the house," Ambrose said, and he led the way to the back. We took steps to a brick walkway that led across the grass and to a stand of giant oaks. Beyond it the land had been cleared but nothing was left above knee-height. As we came closer, I could see the ground was blackened.

"I had to burn all this," Ambrose said, and there was a flat tone to his voice. We stood for a long moment and I waited for him to go on but he just stood looking at it then we walked back.

A large, four-door Buick with mock wooden panels and still impeccable chrome plating came rolling slowly toward us.

"I've hired Frederick as maintenance man at the restaurant," Ambrose said, "but meanwhile he's helping us out here. He'll drive you back to your hotel."

My last glimpse of Ambrose was a lonely figure standing on the porch but I had seen his face when I had told him that I understood completely. It was the face of a happy man, one who had finally banished specters that had haunted him for years.

chapter twenty-seven

Frederick obligingly dropped me off at the hotel and, when I checked into the room, a red light was flashing to tell me that I had a message. It was on the hotel answering service and I pressed a button that brought me Emmy Lou Charbonneau's delightful Southern drawl.

"The Witches are having their monthly luncheon tomorrow," she informed me. "It will be at Jenny's place, the General's Tavern. We would like to invite you to join us. Noon for drinks, lunch at one. Hope y'all can be there. No need for a reply — just come!"

I debated, all the way through dressing and shaving and still all the way through grapefruit juice, sausage and bacon, hash browns, whole-wheat toast with strawberry jelly and three cups of coffee. By the time the waitress came with the offer of a fourth cup, I had decided to accept the invitation.

But first, I went back to the room and phoned Lieutenant Delancey.

He listened to the account of all that had happened since I had last talked to him. He listened without interruption then asked, "And your conclusions?"

He listened to those, too, without interruption. "You did good," he said when I had finished. "You did very good."

"Thank you, Lieutenant. That's high praise, coming from you."

"Scotland Yard would be proud of you. So will Hal Gaines when I tell him."

"Give him my regards."

"I'll do that. So you gonna go to this luncheon?"

"Yes. I think I have all the information I'm likely to get but those Witches —"

"What did you call them?"

"Witches — you know, 'Women in the Catering, Hotel —' "

"Those women's-lib broads . . . Yeah, okay."

"Well, I may pick up a few corroborating items there. It's worth a try."

"Hmm," he said. "Yeah, we've been working, too. I alerted the two men tailing you. One of them picked up on Landers, followed him back, ID'ed him. One of our sharp-eyed gals on night duty started a check on his business and that has brought up a few interesting points. She did a rundown on his background and she spotted his wife's name in the file, too."

I was a little deflated. "So you've reached the same conclusions I have, but by a different route."

"It all goes together, all part of the same picture."

"As far as evidence is concerned, I don't know —"

"Don't worry about that; it's our problem. Like I say, you did real good. More I think about it, that lunch may be a good idea. They're not aware how much we know, something might slip out."

"What do you intend to do now, Lieutenant?"

"I'll see you right after the lunch. Where is it?"

"The General's Tavern."

"Oh, yeah, I've heard of it. Never eaten there."

"It's an experience. Certainly will be today."

"That it will. See you after lunch."

The banquet room in the General's Tavern probably dated from the times when it had had large gatherings of the names that mattered in old New Orleans. The old brick had had to be re-faced here and there but that only added to the charm and the atmosphere. The wooden ceiling-beams were even lower here but the copper lanterns gleamed and the tablecloths over the long U-shaped table were excruciatingly white.

Most of the Witches were already there when I arrived, and I renewed acquaintanceships. Leah was among the first to greet me and she looked adorable in a sheathlike garment of distinct Asian origin. It had a silky sheen and blended blues and golds in intertwined patterns. Jenny, the hostess, had on a smart white outfit with neat black trim. Her full figure did justice to it.

Marguerite's features looked even more regular and perfect than I remembered them from that first encounter in the limousine when I had been "kidnapped." Her hair was the same shiny black and her lashes just as long. She wore a black-and-yellow suit and next to her sat Emmy Lou Charbonneau, her soft brown hair, restless brown eyes and wide mouth accented by an autumn-brown pants suit.

Eleanor McCardle, she with the cooking school that I would have loved to visit, was businesslike in pastel colors, and Della

Forlani of the Villa Romana wore an Italian creation — what else? — in swirls of light and dark green that made her look even more like a fashion model. I was still telling her that I was delighted to see her again when a voice behind me said, "Glad you could join us. What are you drinking?"

It was Elsa Goddard — *dressed to kill,* was my first thought but I quickly changed it. She looked as if she had just come from, or was on her way to, a television appearance, and she promptly confirmed it.

"I'll have one of Jenny's specials — the 'light and healthy' gin fizz," I said. "Nice to see you, Elsa. How goes the investigation of crime via TV?"

"On the Belvedere book case, it's slow," she said. "So slow that we haven't aired anything on it for a couple of days. Any new revelations for me?"

"Any minute now," I said airily. I was being sincere but she didn't read it that way. Perhaps the entertainment business blunted the perception.

Twenty minutes later, we were seated and the first course was arriving. I had duly circulated among all the Witches and exchanged pleasantries, traded comments about the attractions of New Orleans and deflected questions about the quest for the book. "Going to keep us in suspense until after the meal?" Jenny asked. "That's right," I told her.

The first course was oyster stew. The plentiful supply of oysters off the Louisiana coast has led to their imaginative use in a number of ways in addition to the conventional raw condition. In this case, the oysters had been poached in a mixture of white wine and their own liquor, Jenny told us. Then they were put in a double boiler with cream, salt, pepper and cayenne.

A portion of Crab Imperial followed. This was served in a coquille shell and I could discern the tang of both Creole mustard and Tabasco sauce. The main course was Veal Detweiler, named, Jenny said, after a customer who came in three times a week and always ordered it. The name was changed in his honor. The small veal tenderloins had been seasoned and dusted with flour, sautéed in butter and set aside. To the hot butter in the pan had been added artichoke hearts, mushrooms, garlic, onions, cayenne pepper and dry white wine. It was a simple dish but exquisite.

The Café au Lait Soufflé was a local institution, said Jenny. Obviously the rich New Orleans café au lait was the basis but preparing it as a soufflé was a touch of inspiration and not easy to serve to that many diners as it needs to come directly from the oven to the table.

Small talk after the meal was at a minimum. I couldn't exactly say that every member of the Witches was agog to hear what I had to say but they were certainly all curious. Jenny, as the hostess of the day, made a few statements about other business of the group, then she turned to me.

"And now, we will hear a report from the Gourmet Detective on his investigations on our behalf."

I thanked them for their invitation to join them and congratulated Jenny on a superb meal. "Now, you want to hear about the Belvedere chef's book . . ." I paused, milking the moment for the maximum effect.

"I'll tell you what happened each step along the series of events that have tragically led to two murders.

"First, during the collection of books for the annual charity book sale, one of the volunteers saw the Belvedere book. Interested in food and cooking, she knew it would have considerable value and she listed it among the items to be put on sale. Then she read through the book. Certain comments by the chefs through the generations — the members of the family — were in the book, among the recipes, and *'aides memoires'*. This volunteer realized that in the wrong hands, the information could be used to blackmail the current Belvedere, Ambrose. She decided not to put the book in the auction."

"What sort of information are we talking about here?" demanded the stern-looking lady with the prematurely gray hair.

"You're asking me to tell you exactly what it was that the volunteer wanted to suppress," I said, and there was a titter or two. I went on.

"The publicity had already gone out and a lot of interest in the book had been generated. The volunteer decided on an unusual solution to the problem — she had a copy of the book made, using only passages that she selected. It was this copy that went to the auction. It was this copy that Richie Mortensen bought, allegedly on Michael Gambrinus' account. Someone else wanted the book, though, and killed Mortensen to get it."

"So where is the book now?" a voice called out.

"The killer realized that the book was a forgery —"

"You mean a copy?" another questioner called out.

"No, a forgery. It reproduced some of the original material but not all of it — and probably not the material that the killer wanted. An acquaintance of Mortensen's tried to take over the book and exploit it but all he did was to attract the killer's attention."

A figure half rose farther down the table. It was Leah.

"That was my husband, Earl," she said in a soft voice. "I don't know how long he had been involved but he apparently wanted to cash in on the book. I used to go to see him periodically and I must have arrived just after someone had killed him for the book."

Murmurs of sympathy went around the table and Leah sat down.

Della raised a hand. "I don't think we would have wanted the book if we'd known it was going to cause all this hurt and anguish," she said, and nods of agreement came around.

"Who would have thought it would come to this?" Marguerite wondered, and Elsa said, "But there was no way we could have predicted all this. We just wanted the book."

"I hate to sound cold-blooded about

this," Jenny said, "and no one feels more sorry for poor Leah than I do, but what did happen to the book? You're telling us that you haven't recovered it, so where is it? And will we never know what was in it?"

There was a rare silence in the room.

"My understanding is that the volunteer returned the book where it rightfully belonged — to the Belvedere family," I said slowly. "I also understand that the family destroyed it."

There was a gasp.

"So we'll never know," said Eleanor.

"Probably not," I agreed. Before the conversation could rise, coming from a dozen parts of the table, I said, "I didn't complete my mission for you. I did not provide you with the book. So we'll call the matter closed. You owe me nothing."

"We did agree on expenses —" Jenny said, but I waved a magnanimous hand.

"Forget it."

They were forgetting about me already. A few faces showed disappointment, probably having expected startling revelations. I nodded to a few of those I had gotten to know and slipped out as surreptitiously as I could so as to avoid questions. It wasn't difficult.

chapter twenty-eight

A man stepped in front of me as I went out on to the sidewalk. "Lieutenant's across the street," he said, and led me across to what looked like a novelty store. It seemed abandoned but the lieutenant and another man were there, involved with some electronic equipment on a bench.

Delancey looked up. "Be with you in a minute." He resumed adjusting the equipment that I realized was of the recording type. Seeming satisfied, he said something to the other man and came to me. "We got it all."

He caught my puzzled look. "We taped your lunch. Got it all, loud and clear."

"You didn't tell me you were going to do that," I said, probably sounding a little peevish.

"Didn't need to."

"Is it evidence?"

"Probably not. But we didn't know till we heard it."

He jerked a thumb toward the door. "There's a station a coupla blocks. Let's go there. Need you to sign some statements."

It was a quiet time, crimewise, in this part of New Orleans, if this station was any barometer. Men and women, some in uniform, some not, moved around, computer screens pulsed with data, phones rang. It was all low-key. Delancey appeared to have visiting rights, though, and we went into a cubicle with a table and a few chairs.

"Tell me the whole story," Delancey invited. "Just the way you see it."

We sat. A tape recorder was already on the table and Delancey pulled it forward. "Any objections if I —"

"None at all," I said, determined to be mature about this. He squeezed down the RECORD button — I noted that the machine was all set anyway — and he leaned back to listen.

It began with Enid Pargeter, a volunteer for the charity organization. Sorting out the donated books, she found one that was a chef's book from the Belvedere restaurant. It must have gotten lost when the restaurant closed down and was found, along with a number of others, when the place was being cleaned out.

"She recognized it for what it was and put it in the catalog as a moderately valuable item. It was evidently a short while before she read it — that's when she found she had a bundle of dynamite in her hands."

"This is where the story gets interesting, right?" asked Delancey.

"It certainly is. The members of the Belvedere family, four of them before the current Ambrose, all kept a record, writing in that same book, recording their favorite dishes and recipes, making notes of tricks and secrets they ran across in the course of their cooking. All of that would have made the book of modest interest but not much more. There was one family secret that should never have gone in the book, though — and it was this that is at the root of this whole affair."

Delancey nodded. "I'm all ears."

"They were all absinthe drinkers —"

"This is where I need some input," Delancey said. "Expand on this for me."

"Absinthe is a liqueur, popular a century or so ago. We all know about Toulouse-Lautrec and the French Impressionist painters who drank it. It's a hundred and sixty proof, that's eighty-percent alcohol — more than twice scotch or bourbon — but that's not its most dangerous feature.

"Absinthe contains wormwood, a plant that is not only habit-forming but causes delirium, hallucinations, memory loss, inability to function normally, permanent brain damage and early death. When its dangers were fully realized, it was banned in France in 1915 and in this country soon after."

"Somebody must have come up with a substitute," Delancey commented. "They always do."

"They did; they came up with several substitutes — anise was the most popular, sometimes mixed with hyssop. Another plant known as 'herbsaint' was used, too, but to an addict, all of these were weak and unsatisfactory. Only absinthe gives the results they want, for drinking purposes as well as cooking. A great many people had become addicted by then and substitutes just didn't do it. The oysters Rockefeller that made Antoine's famous used absinthe but then lost its popularity when absinthe substitutes had to be used. The Belvederes served oysters Belvedere and other dishes, all probably containing absinthe."

Delancey leaned toward me, fascinated by this. "There must have been a lot of addicts in New Orleans in those days."

"A very large number, between the drinks

and the food," I agreed.

"And the Belvederes became addicts, too?"

"Sadly, yes. They managed to conceal it — especially after the banning of absinthe — by spreading the story that mental illness ran in the family, and when Alzheimer's, Creutzfeldt-Jakob and similar diseases were researched, this made a convenient cover. In fact, I made a few phone calls and it was obvious that early confusion was common. One of those calls was to St. Cynthia's, the mental hospital. Some of the symptoms are similar."

"So if the book had fallen into the wrong hands, it could have proved a blackmail weapon against the family?"

"Well, I can think of a journalist or two who would like to make a big story out of it," I agreed. "The point that bothered me, though, was the thought of one of the Witches killing Mortensen to get the book. It seemed out of character and, from a practical aspect, not reasonable."

"You're too soft on women," said Delancey. "Do you know what percentage of them commit . . . well, never mind. Of course, it didn't have to be one of them," he added.

"No, but they themselves thought it was

and I was inclined to think they were more into this whole business than anyone else, so they were more likely right. A quite different motive seemed to be called for, though."

"Before we get to that, I'm a little puzzled about that book. It was a forgery, you said. How did that happen?"

"Mrs. Pargeter," I said. "A woman of uncommon integrity. She realized that exposure of the book would be a terrible blow to the Belvedere family. She probably tried to pull it out of the auction but it had already been publicized. Its disappearance would have been noticed. She wanted to see the charity benefit but not at the expense of the Belvedere family. So she had a copy made."

"That's a point that sticks in my craw," said Delancey. "How did she happen to know a forger? Not many people do."

"On the wall of her apartment is a certificate of achievement awarded to her husband by the National Publishers Association. It refers to his work as setting up the first investigational section of the NPA. I called them and asked about that. It seems that at one time the association found itself encountering a lot of forged books and William Pargeter was chosen to do something about it. It must have been during that time that he uncovered the activities of several forgers. Herman Harburg was one of those interrogated, but no charges were ever brought. There are a few ways this might have gone, the most likely being that Harburg cooperated to a considerable degree with William Pargeter in his investigations —"

"Ratted on some of the other book forgers, you mean? In return for having any charges against him dropped?"

"You might want to put it that way in your report," I said, being urbane but getting in a retaliatory dig at the same time. After all, no one likes to be bugged when they don't know about it . . . "But this is a point you'll have to clear up. Mrs. Pargeter must have learned that her husband included Harburg in his investigations. She could have also known Harburg as a book lover and a bookbinder. He may have always been a supporter of charity auctions and so on — they would be a good cover for him."

"Mrs. Pargeter was taking a risk, wasn't she?" asked Delancey. "She might have been putting a good blackmail lever in his hands —"

"She wouldn't have to take that risk. I would bet that she simply photocopied selected pages and gave them to him to use as a guide to the handwriting. It wouldn't matter if the book looked different overall because no one had seen the original. It would look authentic — well, an authentic copy, anyway — and the recipes and notes and so on would be convincing. All the stuff concerning absinthe would be left out of the material that Mrs. Pargeter gave to Harburg to copy."

"Harburg gave her the book in the first place," Delancey pointed out.

"Yes, but he told me that he never looked at them, especially when there was a large number. Even if he had, it might not have meant anything to him. As the book had come to Mrs. Pargeter from him, his name was uppermost in her mind. The idea of forging a copy might have originated that way."

"That bookseller, Gambrinus," Delancey said. "I don't have a clear fix on him yet. What's your reading?"

"I'm not fully clear on him, either. He's very well-informed on books, including cooking books. He must have suspected that the Belvedere book was valuable but I haven't figured out yet why he thought so. He has lived in New Orleans all his life — he would know about the Belvedere family. He might have known that they used absinthe themselves and put it into their products.

"At any rate, Gambrinus sent Mortensen to buy the book for him. Mortensen was a sharp cookie and could smell an opportunity. He planned to have the book 'stolen' from him and was taken by surprise when someone stole it from him and then killed him.

"Mortensen's buddy, Earl Whelan, tried to take over the book and peddle it. He knew about it from his wife, Leah Rollingson."

"An arrest was made this afternoon, as the ladies left the lunch at the General's Tavern," Delancey said matter-of-factly. "Other arrests were made an hour earlier."

"The other arrests being at the distillery."

"Right. I got hold of a guy called Kilmer — he's with the Louisiana Bureau of Alcohol and Tobacco. We'll probably have to get the FBI in if we find out that the distillery has been selling across state lines, but it's best to nail them here in this state first. Kilmer's known for some time that absinthe is being sold, but he's not been able to put his finger on the source. He's been able to tie in absinthe with several deaths so this case is a high priority with the A and T bureau." He gave me his questioning look.

"How'd you get on to this place?"

"Landers was the character following me — the one I told you about. I turned the tables on him and when I saw him in a bar and followed him to other bars, I learned more about him. I waited till he was absent from the distillery then went there and took a tour."

Delancey raised an eyebrow. "They give tours?"

"They were a bit reluctant but I spun a story —"

Delancey rolled his eyes and put up a hand. "Don't tell me."

"Okay. So I saw this room, heavily padlocked with a steel door. Next to it was an old, beat-up wooden door. I got taken in by that trick once before. I got as close to these doors as I could, first one then the other. I have an extremely keen sense of smell and taste, Lieutenant, it comes with the job. Suspicion would, of course, be aroused by the heavy steel door but at the old wooden one, I detected just a faint aroma of aniseed — characteristic of absinthe."

Delancey rubbed his chin reflectively. "Don't know how to work in that kind of evidence — it's what might be described as 'intangible.' "

"A good description," I agreed. "One

other thing I saw clinched it for me — Landers had a photo of his wife on his desk. The different names fooled me, but when I saw that photograph of Marguerite, I was able to put it together."

"I'm not real clear on the incrimination of the two," Delancey admitted. "But they'll point a finger at each other once we get them talking, whether deliberately or otherwise. She may have committed both murders, he may have, or each could have committed one of them."

"I wouldn't be surprised if she's the dominant one of the pair," I said. I thought back to when I had first seen her, Marguerite Saville, owner of the Bistro Bonaparte. She had been the black-haired, long-lashed number with the nearly perfect features. "She's a very strong-willed woman and the two of them have a lot to lose."

I recalled also that it had been Marguerite who had insisted on hiring me when Della and the others had assumed that I wouldn't be able to act for them, as I was already hired. Marguerite wanted to be sure she knew my movements. It had surprised me when she told me that she had been offered the book, too, but she was close to Leah and, through her, Leah's husband Earl would have known of Marguerite's prominence among the Witches. Marguerite would have been eager to get the book and suppress any possibility of her husband's distillery being exposed.

"The way Kilmer tells me," Delancey said, "there could be murder charges flying in all directions, as well as other charges. A lot of people in these parts might feel that their relatives had their minds destroyed." He waved a hand. "Kilmer would like a few words with you — okay?"

"Certainly."

"He's got a few questions, like where this wormwood comes from."

"I'm sure he does. Wormwood doesn't grow in this part of the world, normally, but it belongs to the sunflower family and is found wild in the Mediterranean so it could be cultivated here. It was probably imported from the Med in earlier times —"

"And since it was banned?" Delancey asked.

I thought back to my visit to the Belvedere mansion and the stroll that Ambrose and I had taken out back, toward the stand of giant oaks. I recalled the large area of blackened soil and remnants of burned vegetation.

"I suppose it would have been possible to cultivate the wormwood plant somewhere around here," I conceded.

"We'll let Kilmer worry about that side of it," Delancey said. "Meanwhile, how about signing these statements?"

chapter twenty-nine

Jack Kilmer was a similar type to Delancey, cautious, thoughtful and an intriguing blend of tough and considerate. I could see the two of them getting along together very well in a field where conflict could arise easily. He looked a lot like Delancey, too, but was taller and skinnier and had a pronounced Louisiana accent. I answered all his questions and tried to skirt away from any theorizing on where the wormwood could have been coming from but it was inevitable that he would press the point.

"Think it was local?" he asked.

"The climate in many of the Southern states is amenable to growing it," I said carefully. "With modern agricultural techniques, soil can be chemically modified if it's not fully suitable. They even grow winemaking grapes in places like Canada today."

He nodded.

"You'll probably make more progress backtracking through the bars that have been selling it clandestinely, though," I said.

"We'll be doing that, too," he agreed. "Of course, if this gets to be a big deal — class-action, maybe, a mini-tobacco case, that kind of thing, we might have to run through some satellite pictures. Infrared, or some variation of it, might show up wormwood crops. Our guys are getting good at that kind of stuff."

I'm sure they are, I thought, *but they won't be able to make anything out of pictures of burnt-out fields.* I didn't say anything, though. I was satisfied to let that alone.

We had been talking in Delancey's home station, and after Kilmer left me, Delancey reappeared. He looked more rumpled than usual but he assured me that he was making excellent progress on wrapping up the case.

"I'll tell Hal Gaines you were a big help. Might be useful, next time you're in the Big Bagel getting into trouble."

"That's never my intention," I told him. "From now on, I'm keeping a lower profile. I've bought a few of your Louisiana hot sauces to take back with me but otherwise, it's going to be milder stuff — tarragon and thyme, basil and bay leaves."

"Think that'll do it?" He didn't sound convinced.

"It's sure to," I said confidently.

"Yeah," he said in that languid way of his that meant he didn't believe it for a second. "Oh, one other thing —"

"Yes, Lieutenant?"

"The book, the original book. You never did tell me what happened to it after it had caused all this mayhem."

I had had time to prepare for this question — and just as well, too, otherwise I would have been running out of hems and haws.

"Neither Mrs. Pargeter nor Ambrose Belvedere want to talk about it, but you can safely work on the premise that Mrs. Pargeter considered destroying it then decided that it was Ambrose Belvedere's responsibility to do that."

"And . . ." Delancey gave me one of his little waves that invited me to be more forthcoming.

"And I would say that Ambrose destroyed it."

He eyed me. "You would, eh? You're saying I can work on it — that premise?"

"Safely, Lieutenant." I couldn't prevent the intrusion of a mental picture of the urn that Ambrose had shown me with ashes in it, paper ashes.

"Tough to put premises in a report," he commented wryly.

I shrugged; a safe ploy under the circumstances, I thought.

"And I wouldn't want to have that book reappear and cause trouble all over again."

"I can understand that," I told him.

"Because if it did, I'd have Scotland Yard put you in a crate and ship you over here within twenty-four hours."

"I prefer business class — but hold on," I added quickly. "I give you every assurance I can that the book has been destroyed. It's hard to prove that something no longer exists."

He digested that for a moment.

"Okay, well, have a good trip back — you are leaving today, aren't you?" His tone was anxious.

"Yes, I am."

"Good. Just one word of advice —"

"Yes, Lieutenant?"

"Try a credit card from the National Bank of New York."

For a moment, I was baffled.

"You mentioned a library card for, er, certain uses," he continued. "I told you it needed to be a credit card. The one that the National Bank of New York issues is the best. We've tried to get them off the streets but can't. Better get one while you still can. Just don't get arrested for using it."

"Thanks for the recommendation, Lieutenant," I said. "I hope I won't need it. How are the law studies proceeding?"

"Okay. Gonna have to make a decision soon on what direction to head in."

"Criminal, civil, real estate — that kind of decision?"

"Something like that."

"Any preferences at this stage?"

"Years on the force incline me toward criminal law but at the same time, I'm thinking of going for something more constructive."

"I'm sure you'll make the right decision. Will you consider going back to New York?"

He shook his head firmly. "No way. I like it here. It's a cockamamy city in a lot of ways but I like it."

We shook hands as a nearby phone rang and a voice called for him.

On the way back to the Hotel Monteleone, I stopped at Eric Van Linn's office. He had my check ready and even offered me a cup of coffee although he expressed regret that they had no chicory-containing product in the building.

"Ambrose Belvedere tells me he is very satisfied with the outcome," he said, regarding me across his shiny-topped desk.

"He told you that he invited me to visit him at the Belvedere mansion?"

"Yes. I am sure you can understand why he wished to remain as our unidentified client earlier —"

"Of course," I said. I could afford to be magnanimous.

He seemed to be hesitating over what to say next. It appeared to be an unusual circumstance for him; he was rarely at a loss. He got it together and went on in his suave manner.

"I must tell you, I suggested to Ambrose that disbursing your check to you should be contingent upon your signing a release form."

"Release?"

"You became privy to a number of matters that are confidential to the Belvedere family. The family's reputation and even possibly Ambrose's intentions of reopening the Belvedere restaurant could be affected if some of these reached the media."

An array of angry responses flashed before my eyes but I didn't have the check yet so I simply said, "Ambrose didn't say anything of this so I presume he is content that he can rely on my discretion."

Van Linn nodded, slid the check across the desk and we parted on remarkably amicable terms, considering that one of us was a lawyer.

The checkout procedure from hotels has long been one of the more infuriating and frustrating activities in the whole travel experience, but at the same time it has been one process that has benefited enormously from computerization. I had completed the necessary details and was heading for a taxi when a voice called to me across the lobby and a blonde in yellow and black approached.

"Hello, Elisa," I greeted her, "you just caught me in time. I'm heading for the airport."

"So it's all over."

"Yes, I suppose you want to do a wrap-up program," I said.

"Not really." Her blonde hair danced as she shook her head. "We have a new revelation in the city council — a big splash. The Belvedere business is old hat — yesterday's news already."

"Ah, how quickly we forget," I sympathized. "It must be hard for you to keep up with the fickle public's appetite for news."

She looked at me, not sure if I was being sarcastic and decided I wasn't. "I'm not happy with it," she confided. "I was hoping to get you and Ambrose Belvedere on the program but he declined and this city council rumpus blew up instead."

"Good luck with it," I said heartily.

"I might pursue the Belvedere story at a later date," she said, but I knew that once it had faded from the forefront of public interest, that was very unlikely.

"Okay, give me a call if I can make any contribution," I said. I was pretty safe making that offer, I thought.

"Just for the record . . ." she said, and I waited.

"A number of loose ends dangle —"

"I've found that's usually the case," I told her. "It's seldom a perfect wrap-up. For instance, you mentioned St. Cynthia's."

She nodded.

"You knew that the chefs of the Belvedere family had all ended their days there."

"Yes. It's a mental home, terminal."

"Was it going to feature in one of your programs?"

As I asked the question, I waited for her to confirm the connection with absinthe. Surely that was an irresistible angle for a journalist?

She shrugged. Had I misjudged her? Did she have some scruples that I hadn't noticed? Did she have some compassion for the family reputation after all?

"Marguerite and her husband are under arrest — did you know that?" she asked, and I supposed I would never know the answer to my mental questions.

"I haven't caught any recent local news —"

"Could that have anything to do with the Belvedere book?"

"The case seems to have slid out of the current frame of interest," I said. "Still, with forged copies floating around, I suppose it would."

"You think there ever was a genuine copy?"

"I strongly doubt that such a thing exists," I said, and waited to see if the switch in tenses slipped past her. It did.

She tried another tack. "You were hired to buy the book, weren't you? That's why you came to New Orleans."

"Yes, I was."

"Your principal must be dissatisfied that you failed."

"You can't win them all," I said, wondering when my supply of clichés would run out.

"I suppose not. Well, I'll let you go; you

must be anxious to get home."

"It's been an enjoyable visit. This is a great town. Next time, I'll have to stay longer."

The bellboy approached. "Your limo to the airport is here, sir."

Elsa looked as if she had more questions, but she probably realized that the flow of answers was drying up.

"Got more cases at home to take care of?" she asked.

"I have a trip on the Danube Express coming up. I have to review their menus."

"Sounds like fun. You can't get into trouble doing that."

We exchanged friendly farewell kisses, and, as I entered the limo, I wondered if they might have developed into more. But then I was winding through the narrow streets — New Orleans was displaying her colorful mishmash of African and European cultures, and I was glimpsing all the restaurants that I would have liked to have tried and picturing all the meals that I had missed. . . .

The employees of Thorndike Press hope you have enjoyed this Large Print book. All our Thorndike and Wheeler Large Print titles are designed for easy reading, and all our books are made to last. Other Thorndike Press Large Print books are available at your library, through selected bookstores, or directly from us.

For information about titles, please call:

(800) 223-1244

or visit our Web site at:

www.gale.com/thorndike
www.gale.com/wheeler

To share your comments, please write:

Publisher
Thorndike Press
295 Kennedy Memorial Drive
Waterville, ME   04901